When SPARKS Fly

ALSO BY HELENA HUNTING

SHACKING UP SERIES

Shacking Up

Hooking Up

I Flipping Love You

Making Up

Handle with Care

STAND-ALONE NOVELS

The Good Luck Charm

Meet Cute

Kiss My Cupcake

The Librarian Principle

Felony Ever After

Little Lies (writing as H. Hunting)

ALL IN SERIES

A Lie for a Lie

A Favor for a Favor

A Secret for a Secret

A Kiss for a Kiss

LAKESIDE SERIES

Love Next Door

PUCKED SERIES

Pucked (Pucked #1)

Pucked Up (Pucked #2)

Pucked Over (Pucked #3)

Forever Pucked (Pucked #4)

Pucked Under (Pucked #5)

Pucked Off (Pucked #6)

Pucked Love (Pucked #7)

CLIPPED WINGS SERIES

Clipped Wings

Inked Armor

Fractures in Ink

When Sparks Fly

HELENA HUNTING

ST. MARTIN'S GRIFFIN
NEW YORK

SARAH,
YOUR KINDNESS AND GRACE
NEVER CEASE TO AMAZE ME.

This is a work of fiction. All of the characters, organizations, and events portrayed in this novel are either products of the author's imagination or are used fictitiously.

First published in the United States by St. Martin's Griffin, an imprint of St. Martin's Publishing Group

For information, address St. Martin's Publishing Group, 120 Broadway, New York, NY 10271.

www.stmartins.com

Designed by Devan Norman

Library of Congress Cataloging-in-Publication Data

Names: Hunting, Helena, author.
Title: When sparks fly / Helena Hunting.
Description: First Edition. | New York : St. Martin's Griffin, 2021. |
Identifiers: LCCN 2021016067 | ISBN 9781250624703
(trade paperback) | ISBN 9781250624710 (ebook)
Classification: LCC PS3608.U594966 W48 2021 | DDC 813/.6—dc23
LC record available at https://lccn.loc.gov/2021016067

Our books may be purchased in bulk for promotional, educational, or business use. Please contact your local bookseller or the Macmillan Corporate and Premium Sales Department at 1-800-221-7945, extension 5442, or by email at MacmillanSpecialMarkets@macmillan.com.

First Edition: 2021

10 9 8 7 6 5 4 3 2 1

1

YAY OR NAY

AVERY

My current state of mind hovers between fascination and disbelief. I adjust my sunglasses and turn slightly, so the warm summer sun doesn't shine directly in my eyes. Across the field, half a dozen adult men lead their "horses" to the "feeding" trough. Two men bump into each other as they approach the trough, which is full of fake feed, for their fake horses.

As a child I wanted a hobbyhorse. As a very young child. It was a fleeting wish, added to my Christmas list when I was about three years old. Probably because I'd seen one in a movie and thought it looked like fun. But the hobbyhorse wish was quickly replaced by soccer equipment, because soccer became my passion as soon as I could kick a ball.

My younger sister London makes a choking sound next to me as we watch a man in his mid to late forties stroke his horse's mane. Like the rest of the men here, he's decked out in full equestrian gear: black riding boots, tan breeches, navy blazer, and red scarf—which matches his hobbyhorse's scarf—black gloves, and a riding helmet. He props his horse against the feeding trough, cooing all the while at the stuffed animal horse head attached to a broomstick.

Apparently, hobbyhorse riding is an actual thing, and a fairly significant one considering we have more than one hundred hobbyhorse enthusiasts from all across the United States currently practicing for their dressage competition.

In planning for this event we're hosting, I've done quite a bit of research on the sport of "hobbyhorsing" and found that it is indeed a very serious sport. After watching YouTube videos on it, I wrongly assumed our guests would be teenage girls. I soon discovered that this sport is certainly not isolated to teens, or girls, as evidenced by the incredible number of men taking up the entire, sprawling, three-acre field behind Spark House. And this group of men is one of the most enthusiastic, energetic, and competitive bunch we've had to date, so who am I to judge?

My sisters and I run an event hotel—Spark House—which we recently took over for our grandmother. She's most definitely earned her retirement and is currently spending the next six months in Italy on a much-deserved extended vacation.

"How are we on the preparations for the bachelorette party next weekend?" Harley asks. She steps up beside me with her camera poised for a candid shot of a group practicing their routine.

"We're pretty much ready to roll." London's eyes light up with glee. "I put the finishing touches on the penis piñata. I think it's going to be a real hit with the bride."

"I saw it this morning. It's almost a shame they're going to wreck it." Harley scrolls through her phone and hands it to me.

I nearly choke on a cough at the photo of London with the glittery masterpiece, giving it a one-armed hug and resting her cheek against the shaft. "You had way too much fun with this one."

"That is absolutely true. And you'll be happy to know I was able to hunt down the environmentally responsible penis straws. Everything should be arriving on Monday, so we have plenty of time for setup." London pulls her tablet out of her bag and flips through the schedule. "And you have that meeting with your alma mater that morning. Declan's supposed to go with you, right?"

"Yup, we're taking his SUV and heading there Sunday morning so we can meet up with some friends. We should be back early Monday afternoon." In my grand plan to expand Spark House's scope, I'm pitching it to the alumni association of my alma mater to host events throughout the year and possibly see if they'd sponsor us. Declan, my roommate and best friend since college, is coming along to see everyone from our old soccer intermural team.

"Perfect. Harley and I will manage takedown, and Tuesday we can start preparing for the bachelorette party. I think this is going to be my favorite event this year. I had so much fun with the centerpieces." London waggles her brows. Everything for the bachelorette party follows the same theme as the piñata. She's had a field day putting together the decorations.

"You should consider selling those on Etsy or something," Harley says. "I posted a picture of one of your centerpieces yesterday in our story, and I must have had fifty people asking where they can get one."

"Maybe that can be my side business."

A ding interrupts us, so we all check our phones.

It turns out to be mine. I make a face when I note it's a message associated with my dating app. It's a new thing. London set all three of us up with accounts last month in an attempt to reactivate our social lives. We spend most of our time working at Spark House and hanging out together. My only other hobby is the recreational soccer league I play on with friends.

London has been out with the same guy at least half a dozen times, even with our busy schedule. Harley is exceptionally picky when it comes to men, so she's turned down more than a dozen prospective dates already.

I try to shove my phone in my pocket before London can see, but she nabs it out of my hand and reads the preview.

"You have a date? You're supposed to share that information!"

"I'm still on the fence as to whether or not I want to go. It's tomorrow night and I should be here for the dinner party. Besides, this guy seems way too enthusiastic about drinks." I'm not a huge fan of being dependent on anyone but myself for my own happiness, so usually any dating I do tends to be casual, and Brock's exclamation point–laden messages seem like a red flag.

"Enthusiasm is usually a good thing, and we can handle the dinner party." London holds the phone in front of my face to unlock it and spins away before I can snatch it back. She clicks on the message and pulls up his profile. "Oh wow! This guy is ridiculously hot!" She fans her face dramatically as she scrolls and reads aloud, "Brock Stone? He sounds like a porn star." Instead of handing my phone back, she tosses it behind me to Harley, who, despite being short and not super athletic, catches it.

"Ooh! Six-two, brown hair, green eyes, loves sports. And he's smokin' hot!" Harley keeps scrolling through his profile. "Played varsity rugby? This one's a winner. London and I will definitely be able to handle the dinner event tomorrow night. This guy is too pretty not to go out with."

"Are you sure? I can reschedule. I don't know what I was thinking planning drinks on a Saturday night. I'll tell him we'll have to do it another time." I try to grab my phone from Harley, but she hides it behind her back.

"You will not! You have been all about Spark House twenty-four seven, and you need to take time for yourself. Even if it's just a couple of hours. You are going for drinks, and if it turns into dinner, you are going to stay and enjoy yourself and not worry. We can totally handle dinner with these guys." She motions to the field.

"I agree you have to go. When was the last time you went on a date?" London asks.

"I dunno, a while." Like several months.

"Exactly. You need to go out for drinks. With a hot rugby player," Harley says.

"It'll probably only be a couple of hours, and I'll stop here before I go home. That way I can help with end of the night cleanup."

"Seriously, we'll be fine, but I know you're going to show up anyway because you can't help yourself." She passes my phone back. "Message him back and tell him you're excited."

"You scheduled some pre-date pampering for tomorrow, right?" London grabs my hands and makes a face at my nails, which are not in the best shape. London is always impeccably put together. She sees her hairstylist every six weeks, goes for bi-monthly manicures, and gets her eyebrows waxed, among other parts. If I remember to shave my legs once a week, it's a miracle. Harley falls somewhere in the middle.

"Uh . . ."

"Oh, come on, Avery, when was the last time you plucked your eyebrows?" She gives the hairs on the right one a little tug, and I bat her hand away. "You've been hanging around with bachelor jocks for way too long. Do you even have a dress picked out?" She slashes a hand through the air. "You know what, don't say a word, I already know the answer."

I figure drinks at a sports bar call for jeans and a T-shirt, but apparently my more refined, hipper younger sister does not agree. Within ten minutes, I have a waxing appointment and a mani-pedi scheduled for this evening. "I'll bring dresses tomorrow. If he's taking you out for dinner, you need to look like you're dessert."

"It's drinks. Not dinner," I protest.

"Drinks are always subject to change." Arguing with London will get me nowhere. Besides, my wardrobe consists mostly of workout gear and exactly five pairs of dress pants, two pairs of heels, and the Spark House shirts we had designed to circumvent my having to actually shop for girly clothes.

London always looks professional, as does Harley in her slightly more casual, funky way. I tend to dress for comfort since I'm the one who plans all the physical and group activities, many of which take place outdoors. Wearing heels, dress pants, and blouses is certainly not conducive to hobbyhorse rail jumping. And yes, I've run one of the courses. Hobbyhorse and all. It's harder than it looks.

"I'll accept the offer for dresses, but I cannot promise I'll wear any of them." She's going to bring them to work tomorrow anyway, so saying no is pointless.

"Come on, Avery. You have this rockin' body, and you're always hiding it under yoga pants and hoodies."

"Because they're comfortable."

"You can forgo comfort for style for a few hours."

"Fine. But it's a pretty casual place, so none of your night-on-the-town attire."

London gives me the side-eye. "I'll be sure to bring only my Sunday finest."

I'm pretty sure the last time London stepped inside a church was when our uncle Mortimer got married—for the fourth time. And that was when she was still in college.

Commotion from across the field catches my eye. Two of the riders seem to be at odds with each other. The hand on hip, head tip, nose-to-nose business gives me reason to believe there's some kind of disagreement happening.

"That doesn't look very friendly." I nod in their direction.

"Maybe the horses need a time-out," Harley mutters.

I give her the side-eye, and she fights a smirk.

"Uh-oh, we have hand and hobbyhorse flailing," London says, pulling my attention back to the field. The argument seems to be heating up, not cooling down.

"You need to deal with that." London gives my shoulder a shove. She's amazing with finances, and she's great at connecting me with the right vendors, but dealing with conflict is not her strong suit.

"Not in the mood to mediate stuffed horses?" I drop my bag on the ground beside Harley's feet and briskly cross the field as the argument escalates to yelling. I'm about twenty feet away when one of the men hauls off and whacks the other one with his hobbyhorse.

"Whoa! Whoa! Gentlemen! Time-out. That's not very sportsmanlike conduct!" I call.

My admonishment goes unheeded, and the two men begin dueling with their hobbyhorses. The bigger of the two jabs the other man in the stomach and snatches his hobbyhorse when he loses his grip on it.

"Gentlemen! Please!" I shout, but it's hard to be heard over their yelling and the newly formed crowd of hobbyhorse enthusiasts who have gathered and are now heckling the fighters.

Two other men toss their hobbyhorses to the hobbyhorse-less man with shouts of "Kick his ass!"

And here I thought this was a chill sport. Apparently I'm very, very wrong.

The hobbyhorsers face off again, each one holding a broom horse between their legs and another like . . . a sword, maybe? It reminds me of medieval jousting. Especially when they start stomping their feet, pawing at the ground, and prancing in place. I know things are about to escalate when they shake their heads back and forth, braying loudly and breathing out through their noses in a hardy snort.

Then they run toward each other, while yelling. Even if they're beating on each other with stuffed horse heads, I'm not interested in anyone ending up with a concussion.

I jump in between them before they collide, which I realize a second too late puts me in a very perilous position. However, the man on my right swerves at the last second and ends up crashing into the trough, toppling it and at least half a dozen of the "feeding" hobbyhorses. The other man skids to a stop mere inches from me, loses his balance, and falls backward onto the ground. It rained yesterday, so while it's sunny and dry now, the ground is still soft and mucky. And he happens to land in a seriously squishy pile of muddy grass.

He also manages to hit himself in the family jewels with the hobbyhorse. He rolls onto his side, clutching the muddy horse head and his junk. It's quite the spectacle. Before it turns into absolute mayhem, I grab the megaphone from the group emcee and shout, "Whoa, Nelly!" like an idiot.

However, it does the trick. Every single one of them freezes. "Riders number seventeen and twenty-three, you are disqualified from this round for roughhousing and inappropriate use of your hobbyhorse!" I'm totally making this up on the fly, but someone needs to get these guys under control, and they don't seem to be able to manage it on their own.

The guy who nut slapped himself—number twenty-three—picks himself up off the ground and hobbles gingerly over to the bench, which is now assigned to disqualified hobbyhorsers. Number seventeen throws himself down on the other end with a huff.

I lower the megaphone and cross my arms. "This is supposed to be about team building and sharing something you're passionate about. If you want to joust, I suggest you either join a club or interview for a position at Medieval Times." I motion between them. "Now apologize to each other."

They look from me to each other and back again.

I cock a brow.

They mutter a half-assed "*Sorry.*"

"You're going to have to do better than that if you want to earn the right to compete again. You're adults, not children, and I expect you to conduct yourself with class and grace." Man, I'm glad I watched all of those YouTube videos in preparation for this.

"I'm sorry I attacked you with your hobbyhorse," number seventeen says.

"And I'm sorry I called yours a cheap knockoff." Number twenty-three seems appropriately chagrined by his juvenile insult.

I force a smile. "There. Doesn't everyone feel better now?"

Honestly, no one would believe the weirdness I deal with on a daily basis.

I hang around for a while to make sure the situation is under control before I head to the mani-pedi-waxing appointment London so graciously set up for me. I have no idea how she managed to get me in with no notice, but I suppose I'm somewhat appreciative.

I feel a little bad about leaving my sisters with all of those apparently high-strung hobbyhorsers tomorrow night, but I'm hopeful I embarrassed them into submission and that they'll behave themselves.

Once I'm at the appointment, I almost instantly regret it. I'm not awesome at stillness at the best of times. Add in the discomfort of someone picking at my nails and my eyebrows and ripping hair out of my lady bits—I'm not sure what the purpose of that is since there is zero chance I'm letting Brock into my pants on date number one—and I'm practically crawling the walls by the time I'm done.

I have to admit, my nails look nice, though. I didn't want anything too vibrant since I usually keep my nails completely naked, so the woman convinced me to go with a French manicure. And once the redness around my eyebrows calms down, I'm sure they'll look good too. Hopefully.

2

CHILLING WITH MY BESTIE

AVERY

It's almost eight by the time I get home. I live in a high-rise, two-bedroom condo complex in a bustling area on the outskirts of Colorado Springs with Declan. We met during our freshman year in college, and he, along with our other two friends Jerome and Mark, made up my primary friend group while there, and we've stayed close over the years. It helps that we all moved to the same city after college, as opposed to a few of our other friends who scattered across the country.

We have weekly hangouts when we order pizza and watch sports. Usually it's soccer, which we all played together in college, but Jerome is a huge football fan and Declan loves hockey, so if there's a game, we'll flip between them. They're my buds and they've always treated me like one of the guys. My sisters make up the rest of my circle, but neither of them enjoy sports, so they don't partake in our sports and pizza nights.

I almost trip over Declan's running shoes when I walk in the door. I kick them off to the side, toe my own onto the mat, and hang up my keys. I glance at the side table, where a Thor action figure greets me. I give mighty Thor a pat on his plastic head, but I still shout, "Honey, I'm home!" before I pad down the hall to the living room.

It's a habit I've gotten into since we moved in together, in order to avoid being exposed to things I can't unsee. Once I didn't announce myself and walked in to find one of Declan's lady friends riding him naked on the couch while he was half paying attention to the soccer game. I entered the room as he shouted a "Fuck yes!" I discovered mere seconds later that it had nothing to do with the woman in his lap, riding his joystick, but because our favorite team had scored a goal.

After that we created our own Bat-Signal. When the Thor action figure is facing the wall, it's a sign that Declan has company. For a while, Thor often faced the wall, but it's been happening a lot less frequently over the past several months.

"Thank God, I need a beer," is the response I get as I round the corner.

I step into the living room, one hand already on my hip and a bitchy retort on the tip of my tongue. I find my roommate on the floor. He's wearing navy basketball shorts, and he's shirtless. Declan is built like an athlete. His abs ripple as he rolls up in a crunch. A bead of sweat trickles down his temple and lands on the area rug.

"What are you doing?"

"What does it look like?"

"Sweating all over the carpet." His dark hair is wet at the temples, turning it almost black. His chest glistens and new beads of perspiration form and travel in slow rivers between his pecs.

This isn't a sight I'm unfamiliar with, but he's usually not shirtless, so mostly I get to look at sweat stains instead of all those cut muscles. My best friend is easy on the eyes. Thankfully, I've had enough exposure over the years to his pretty face and his ridiculously impressive body that I'm immune. Mostly. A bit. Okay, maybe 65 percent of the time.

"I couldn't make it to the gym this morning, so I thought I'd get in a quick workout before you came home. Earn the takeout I'm about to destroy. Ten more and then I'm ready for that beer." His blue eyes glint with humor.

I flip him the bird. "If anyone should be asking for wait service, it's me."

I pass through the living room and make a right down the hall to my bedroom.

"Where are you going?" he calls after me.

"I need to change into something more comfortable."

"You're wearing yoga pants and a T-shirt. How much more comfortable can you get?"

"Let me rephrase. I need to change into something *clean*." I return two minutes later wearing oversized gray jogging pants with holes in them and a loose, baggy shirt.

Declan has finished his workout and is wearing a shirt that probably fit him a lot better in college than it does now. I'm guessing laundry day is coming up. There's a discarded towel on the floor, likely used to mop up his sweat trail.

Declan, being the sometimes-thoughtful roommate he is, has done me a solid and poured me a beer. I drop down on the other end of the couch with a groan, and he passes me the full pint glass.

"I need this more than air right now, so thank you."

He cocks a brow and turns his attention back to the soccer game. "Should I even ask how your day was?"

I grab my phone and pull up my group messages with my sisters and click on the video Harley sent about an hour ago, while I was getting my nails done and the hair ripped out of my sensitive bits. I toss it to Declan and he presses play. "What the hell am I looking at right now?"

"A hobbyhorse fight."

He cringes at the loud thwack, rewinds the video, and bursts into laughter. "Are they jousting with stuffed horses?"

"Yup."

"Jeez, who won?"

I chuckle. "No one, because I took care of the situation."

"Huh, I can't decide if that's disappointing or not." He plays the video over again, much like I did while I was getting my nails done. "Is this a normal thing? Like, I can't imagine that hobbyhorse riding is actually popular."

"You would be surprised at the number of people involved in the sport."

"Seriously? How have I never heard of this? And how many times have you held a hobbyhorse . . . fence jumping event?"

"This would be a first for Spark House. And possibly a last, depending on whether there's more jousting between now and Sunday."

He passes my phone back, and I set it on the side table.

"Looks like a lot of people are into it, though, so maybe it'll be worth the headache. Is it a lucrative sport? Do people bet on it like they do actual horse races and competitions?" His eyes light up.

"I have no idea, but I'm going to say probably not, so whatever scheming is happening up there, you can shut it down right now." I reach over and tap his temple.

Declan works in finance. In fact, he handles the financial portfolio for Spark House and works with London to ensure we're meeting all our financial goals. He's excellent at what he does, and there's no one I trust more than him to keep our finances safe. Any time I need to discuss additions, renovations, or potential expansions I can go to him and talk it through. I try not to hound him about things like that on the weekend, but he loves talking about money and investments.

"It was just a question. I know you've been talking about fixing that fountain in honor of your grandmother this spring, and it's not going to be cheap, or really a value add."

"We'll only do it if we can afford it, but it would be a really cool surprise if we could fix it before she's back from Italy." At eighty-one, Gran is still spry and incredibly active. She ran Spark House with my grandfather, and then after he passed, with the help of my parents. When we lost them in the car accident, Gran took over full-time again. At least until my sisters and I were ready for the responsibility. I've always loved Spark House and knew I wanted to take it over one day. And now that's exactly what we're doing.

Declan flips his pen between his fingers. "If hobbyhorse riding is half as lucrative as actual horse racing, the jousting matches might be worth it. Actually, they might be even better than the riding."

I roll my eyes. "I'm not condoning adult men beating one another with stuffed horses. I'll make sure we have the capital to fix up the fountain before I start throwing money at it."

He reaches across the back of the couch and gives my neck a squeeze. "London still on the fence about it?"

"She doesn't want us to get in over our heads. Which I get. I know it's not a necessary expense, but it would still be a great surprise." Declan knows how important Gran is. She's the one who stepped in and raised me and my sisters after our parents died when we were teenagers. The loss of our parents created a hole in the fabric of our existence, and my sisters and I have mended our hearts as best we can by sticking together. "Anyway, enough about that. How was your day?"

"Not nearly as exciting as yours. Although I did land a pretty kickass client, so that's something."

"Oh yeah? What kind of client?"

"Super into eco stuff, has this massive company that's really making waves, innovative and smart. Guy is only in his early thirties and is making more money than I could in the next three lifetimes, but I'm not going to cry over the management fee."

"Congratulations! That's amazing! Does that mean you're buying the pizza and wings tomorrow? Because if you are, I'd like an extra-large meat lover's with the stuffed crust."

"Don't you have an event?"

"I'll be in and out."

"Right. Cool. Well, I can definitely accommodate the pizza request even though it probably means I'm going to need extra hours at the gym next week." He pats his six-pack. He can eat an entire pizza by himself and never gain an ounce.

I roll my eyes. "You just go to the gym so you can pick up women."

"Untrue. I know better than to date the women who go to my gym. It's the same as dating someone you work with."

"Or someone in your friend group," I mutter. I'm referring to my sophomore year when I stupidly started dating Sam, one of the guys we all used to hang out with, and Declan's former best friend. Sam was a year older and a junior when we first got together. At the time, Declan and I had become good friends. Like most of the female population at our college, I wasn't totally immune to his charm. He oozed charisma and was ridiculously hot. But his parents had been in the middle of a messy divorce, and he had a habit of leaving a trail of broken hearts. I thought Sam was the safe, smart boyfriend choice.

Turns out he was neither.

Declan always jokes that I got full custody of him and the guys in the separation. But the truth is, Declan found out that Sam was cheating on me, and he was the one who told me. The guys sided with me, and their friendship didn't survive the fallout.

"Everyone makes stupid mistakes in college. Also, the only reason I don't date the women who go to my gym is because I did it once and had to switch my membership over to another location."

"Ah yes, Stalker Sue. I remember her. She showed up here once after you broke up. Made me almost consider getting my own place," I tease.

"I had to buy pizza on your night for like six months to make up for that." He grins sheepishly.

Declan and I could definitely afford to live on our own, but I like the company of a roommate. I've never lived alone. Ever. I went from my parents, to living with my grandmother, to college dorms, to off-campus housing with roommates, back to living in my grandmother's house, and then here with Declan. I could have moved in with my sisters, but I felt like it was better for me to have my own space, especially since we all work together. And London and Harley have a special bond. It's not that I don't, but I went off to college not long after we lost our parents, and they stayed in Colorado Springs together.

So I made it easier on all of us and moved in with Declan. Guys are way easier to live with than girls. They're uncomplicated, and they say what they mean when they mean it. We've been living together for two years, and I've never regretted the decision. Apart from Stalker Sue, anyway.

I peek inside the take-out box sitting on the coffee table. "Oh my God! You are literally the best." I grab half of the buffalo chicken wrap and take a massive bite. At the salon, they gave me tea and flavorless biscuits that reminded me of Communion wafers. I haven't eaten since lunch, which was a delicious, but not entirely filling, salmon salad.

"Wow. Vultures look sexier feasting on roadkill than you do scarfing down that wrap." Declan wears a look somewhere between amusement and disgust.

"I haven't eaten since noon."

"I can tell." He returns his attention to the game while I shovel the rest of it into my face. I eat the second half a little slower.

My phone pings with a reminder for my tire appointment next week. "Oh! You're still coming with me to the university on Sunday, right?"

"Huh?" Declan's eyes are glued to the screen. Our team is down by a goal and they're currently in control of the ball.

"Sunday. We're supposed to meet up with the soccer alumni. We're going to see a game, remember?" I extended the invitation to Mark and Jerome, but they're both busy. Jerome has some afternoon date planned with his current girlfriend—he's also not sure if he's planning to break it off or not. Usually that's a sign he's bored and ready to move on, but it's really not my place to say. Mark is going fishing with his dad for the weekend, so it's just me and Declan making the trip.

"Oh, fuck, yeah, of course I'm still in for that." He drops his feet and leans forward, resting his elbows on his knees. "Come on! Get with the program, Donahue! You were right there!

"And we can take your SUV?"

"Yup, for sure. I'll drive," he says.

I pull up the weather app. "Good, it's calling for heavy rain, and I can't get my car in for a tire change until Tuesday."

"I got you covered, Ave." He pats my knee, then jumps off the couch and shouts victory when our team manages to get the ball past the goalie.

I wait until he's seated again before I ask, "Do you need me to put an alert in your calendar?"

"Nah. It's already programmed up here." He taps his temple. "Oh, you're up on the crossword puzzle. I got carried away and did twelve instead of ten. Sorry about that." He looks under take-out boxes until he finds the newspaper crossword. There are a couple of grease stains and possibly some buffalo chicken sauce on it. Declan and I always share the weekly crossword puzzle.

"I was hoping it was my turn." I grab the paper and scan the answers. "Did you have trouble with eighteen?"

He gives me an *as if* look and then smiles when he realizes I'm kidding.

For the vast majority of women, it would be considered a panty-dropping smile. I love him, but he's got more baggage than a packed airplane, and I've already been down that road once before.

3

JUST ONE OF THE BOYS

DECLAN

Mark, these must be for you." I drop the box labeled MILD on the coffee table.

"Don't judge. I've had heartburn lately." Mark scoops them up.

Mark never goes above medium, and even then, he hiccups and sweats buckets. "Do you think that might be attributed to the fact that you've been here for less than an hour and already polished off three beers?" Avery grabs the box of suicide wings out of my hands before I can check to make sure the contents match the label.

There's a place down the street that has the best pizza and wings, but they often mislabel the boxes, so most of the food requires a sniff test prior to consumption. They've labeled the suicide wings MILD on more than one occasion in the past. Once, Mark ate a supposedly mild one without the requisite sniff test, and we thought he was having a heart attack. He sweated all the way through his shirt and his face went beet red. He proceeded to chug half a gallon of milk and instantly regretted that as well.

"It's all about balance," Mark says defensively. He pulls an economy-sized pack of TUMS out of his backpack, pops the cap, and shakes a bunch directly into his mouth.

"How many bottles of those are you going through in a week?" Avery asks.

"Uh, two, maybe three?" He offers them to the rest of us like they're candy, not chalky antacids.

"That's not normal." Jerome reaches for the honey garlic wings.

"Maybe you need to see a doctor?" Avery tosses her first wing bone into the discard bowl in the middle of the table and goes for the nachos. She tucks her hair into the neck of her shirt and leans over the box as she shoves three loaded chips into her mouth, one after the other.

Despite Avery growing up in an insanely tight family who hosted family events in a dining room with a table that's probably as long as this entire condo, she eats like a pig. Unless she's in a restaurant. Then she uses all the right forks and spoons and knives and is extra delicate. It's hilarious to watch because Avery is very much the opposite of delicate.

"Nah, I've been trying to up my hot sauce tolerance for the past month, and I just need to slow my habanero roll."

Avery's phone chimes from somewhere on the coffee table, under the discarded bags and take-out boxes. When she finally finds it, she checks the alert, and mutters, "*Oh shit.*" She grabs two more loaded nachos, shoves them in her mouth, and springs up off the couch, rushing down the hall.

"What's that about?" Jerome asks.

"Dunno." I shrug and dig into my wings. Avery always has a million things going on, so it could literally be anything, but usually it's work or sports related. Work tends to be her primary focus, as it is mine, apart from nights like these, anyway. The four of us always get together for Monday Night Football. Then we play in a rec soccer league on Wednesday nights, and every other weekend me and the guys hang out like we are tonight. Avery works most weekend evenings for whatever event they're hosting, but maybe tonight her sisters are taking control of things. Usually Avery's the one to handle all the people aspects of the events, since she's pretty much the face of Spark House—not that she would agree with that title at all.

I shift into the corner of the couch—which is Avery's spot, but on sports night, if you move, your seat is always fair game.

A while later an odd clicking sound draws my attention away from the game. I can't place it until Avery steps into the living room. She's no longer wearing sweatpants and a ratty, threadbare T-shirt. Instead, she's poured herself into a slinky black dress that hugs every single one of her athletic curves. In all the years I've known Avery, and I've known her for a lot of years, I can probably count on one hand the number of times I've seen her in a dress. And I've never seen her wear anything this . . . sexy.

I'll be honest. It's kind of freaking me out, because ever since college, when she started dating my former best friend Sam, I regarded Avery as a friend—she just happens to have a chest that she usually flattens into a uni-boob with a sports bra. The fact that her ex, Sam, screwed her over and nearly caused our friend group to disband helps keep her in the friend zone.

Except right now it's hard not to see her as the attractive woman she is. "You're a little overdressed for soccer and beer."

"Ha-ha." Avery rolls her eyes. "I'm going out. Obviously."

"You got a Spark House event or something?" I know we've got that alumni thing tomorrow, but I figured her being home tonight meant she didn't have anywhere to go. And I'm not sure I would consider that work-appropriate attire—even if it is a night thing—especially since those hobbyhorse dudes look like they probably don't do much in the way of socializing beyond comparing the size of their stuffed horse heads on sticks.

"Holy shit, Ave, you are smokin'." Mark whistles loudly, drawing Jerome's attention away from the game as well.

"What's the special occasion?" Jerome's eyes flare, signaling he's as shocked as I am by the dress.

We're all used to casual, dressed-down Avery, not this hair and makeup done, dressed-up version.

"I have a date." Her cheeks flush, and she tugs at the hem of the dress.

"Whoa. A date? Dude must be killing it in the sack if you're willing to put on this smoke show." Jerome does the finger spin. "Let's see the back of this number."

"It's a first date, so I have no idea if he's killing it in the sack." She turns, pulling her hair over her shoulder to expose the back of dress. The straps are thin. So thin, in fact, that there is absolutely no way she can be wearing a bra. Not to mention it dips low, exposing a significant amount of skin. The dress is also on the shorter side, hitting her mid-thigh, showing off her athletic legs.

Having lived with Avery for a while, I'm familiar with her underwear preferences. Sometimes our laundry gets mixed up, or I have to move her stuff from the dryer to the basket. She's a boy shorts and full coverage kind of woman most of the time. Always basic colors like black and beige. No frills, nothing risqué. However, I do not detect panty lines. Which means she's either wearing a pair of those seamless, ugly-as-fuck beige ones I've had the misfortune of finding stuck inside the leg of my jeans, or she's wearing a thong.

For whatever reason, I would much prefer it to be the former rather than the latter.

"So? What do you think? Is it too much for a first date?" She props a fist on her hip and bites her bottom lip.

"I think if you want to find out if he's killin' it in the sack, that's definitely the dress you should wear," Jerome says.

Mark nods his agreement.

She makes a face. "Do you think it sends the wrong message?"

"Nah, you look sexy as hell. Own it. He'll be begging for a second date." Jerome fist-bumps Mark.

"And picking up the tab." Mark pretends to make it rain dollar bills.

"I'll pay for my own drink, but it's good to know showing off my legs can cut down on my expenses." Avery smirks.

"Do you have any other options? Maybe you want to show us a couple other ones and we can vote on a fave?" I suggest. "What about that army-green shirtdress?"

"Oh! Yes. Okay. London loaned me a couple other dresses, but I think they might be overkill. I'll try on the shirtdress first."

She disappears down the hall with the clickity-click of her heels, and I go back to watching the game. Except I can feel Jerome and Mark staring at me. "What?"

"Why would you want her to change out of that? And what the hell is a shirtdress?" Jerome asks.

"Just for options, you know? Girls usually like to change five times before a date. She probably threw on the first thing she found." There's a silence, but I purposefully avoid looking at either of them.

"Yeah, whatever, man."

A minute later she reappears, this time wearing the shirtdress.

"Oh yeah, that's perfect." I lick the wing sauce off my finger and give her two thumbs-up.

Jerome's expression screams *what the fuck?* "Don't listen to D, he's high or something. Wear the black one."

"Avery looks great in this dress," I argue. Also, this dress is baggy and virtually shapeless. The hem ends at her knees and it has short sleeves, which means there's a lot less skin on display.

"I agree with Jerome. You should definitely wear the other dress." Mark says. "You look like you're interviewing for an elementary school teaching position." Mark happens to teach elementary school, so he's familiar with teacher wear. "And while there's nothing wrong with that dress in an elementary school, it definitely does not scream hot, sexy, and single like the other dress."

"Okay. Thanks, guys!" And off she flounces down the hall. To change back into the other dress. The one I would like to put through a paper shredder.

Five minutes later, Avery's back in the black dress. She's paired it with a cropped jean jacket—I have to assume it either belongs to London or Harley since I've never seen her wear it before—and the giant bag she takes with her everywhere.

"Have a good night, guys." She heads for the front door.

Jerome and Mark wave her off, too enthralled with the game to care, I guess.

"You're gonna text every couple of hours with updates, right?" I call out.

"Huh?" She has her phone in her hand, her attention fixed there. Possibly messaging this dude she's going out with.

"You're gonna message and let me know if you're planning to come home or whatever."

"Seriously?" She stops texting so she can arch a brow.

I arch one right back. "Uh, yeah, seriously. We don't even know what this guy's name is. Where'd you meet him? How long have you known him?"

She scoffs, "You're being ridiculous, Declan."

"Am I, though? What about that guy who answered a Craigslist ad for a hookup and ended up dismembered and decapitated?"

Avery purses her lips. "First of all, I would never answer a dating ad on Craigslist. Secondly, I'm driving my own car to the restaurant, and I have no plan to go home with this guy. It's drinks and that's it."

"Yeah, but—"

She holds up a finger. "London and Harley already know where I'm going, and we all have that tracking app on our phone so we can locate one another in case of an emergency."

"Oh. Well, maybe we need to get that app too." Avery's taken self-defense and she's athletic, but knowing she's not locked in the trunk of some random lunatic's car is always a bonus. It's not like she hasn't gone on dates before. She has, plenty of times. She's had a few short-term boyfriends even, but they usually don't last very long. I've never seen her put this much effort into a date before, especially not a first freaking date.

"I'll send you a link." I can't tell if she's being sarcastic or not.

"Would you also like me to provide updates on the lines he uses when I go to the bathroom?"

"Ooh, yeah! We can rate them based on how bad they are!" Jerome and Mark fist-bump each other again.

Avery laughs and opens the door. "You guys are the worst."

And then she's out the door.

I shift my focus to the game and chug half my beer, not liking the sudden uneasiness in my gut.

As soon as there's a commercial break, Jerome clears his throat, and I glance over to find both of them staring at me. "What?"

"What's the deal?" Mark cocks a brow.

"The deal with what?"

"That shirtdress was fucking hideous," Jerome says.

"It looks good on her." That's a lie. I'm highly aware that it's hideous, which was the damn point.

They give me a disbelieving look.

I sigh and roll my beer bottle between my palms. "It was the first I've heard of this guy, and I want to make sure she's safe. Don't you?"

"By monitoring her with a locator app?"

"What if the guy is a creep?"

"Then she'll message and bail. She can take care of herself," Jerome says.

"I know that."

But it doesn't mean I don't worry about her.

Even when we moved in together, she was casually dating someone, so there was nothing to be concerned about. And by that time, I'd witnessed all of Avery's moods, from premenstrual to downright surly. We'd been through a lot together, and I never wanted to put our friendship at risk.

But I can't say that I love that she's on a date with some random dude whose name we still don't know, wearing a dress that makes me see her through a totally different lens. I need a distraction.

"Do you guys want to hit the bar?"

4

IT'S A BUST

AVERY

I've had more stimulating conversation with a hobbyhorse."

Both London and Harley make cringey faces. It's Saturday night, and as promised, I came straight from my date to help them clean up after the dinner.

Now that the hobbyhorse awards dinner is over, the three of us are gathered in the office, eating leftovers and engaging in a post-date debrief.

"But he was so hot." London pops an olive into her mouth.

"And that, sadly, is all he has going for him. At least one of us has had success with this app." I pull up Brock's profile on IG since he made sure I followed him within two minutes of sitting down. Then he proceeded to go through every single photo and explain, in painstaking detail, how much time, effort, and energy went into training to become as physically perfect as he proclaimed himself to be. I set my phone on the table facing my sisters, presenting them with the glory of everything Brock Stone.

Shirtless, muscle-popping wonder with the intellectual capacity of a gnat. "If I'd had all the necessary information, I could have done the requisite social media check pre-date and avoided wasting my time."

Even as we were walking out to our respective cars, Brock continued to regale me with his impressive lifting stats. We split the bill, although he didn't seem to think leaving a tip was necessary, so I went ahead and padded mine to make up for it.

Harley and London pore over his profile, scrolling through his pictures, both wearing matching unimpressed expressions. There are a lot of pictures. Of him. Posing in front of the mirrors at the gym. There are also a few pictures of food, but otherwise it's selfie central.

"Yeesh, I've never seen a guy do the duck face before. It's . . ."

"A lot like Blue Steel?" I supply.

"Exactly!" Harley covers her mouth with her palm and snorts a laugh.

"I'm so sorry I encouraged you to go out with him." London slides the phone back to me, and I drop it in my purse.

"Eh, it could've been worse. I have to admit it was fascinating to count the number of times he looked at his own reflection in the window. By the end of the date, he'd checked himself out a hundred and seventy times."

"That's beyond excessive." Harley looks appropriately shocked.

"Do you want to hear the best part?"

"Best as in worst?" London asks.

"He invited me back to his place and seemed legitimately surprised when I said no. Like, he was honestly dumbfounded and asked me three times if I was sure I didn't want to go home with him."

"No!" London and Harley say at the same time.

"Oh yes, and then he told me I'd be missing out on a once-in-a-lifetime opportunity and asked whether I wanted to reconsider."

Harley leans forward in her chair. "What did you say?"

"That I appreciated his offer, but losing out on that once-in-a-lifetime opportunity was a risk I was willing to take."

London arches one perfect eyebrow. "I feel like that wasn't the end of it."

"You would be absolutely correct." I lean back in my chair, remembering how confused he seemed. "He told me I shouldn't send mixed messages and that my dress was a green light for a good time."

"He did not." London slaps the table, rattling the charcuterie board, causing a loose grape and several chocolate-covered almonds to roll off. She covers them with her hand before they can do a swan dive over the edge of the table. "Please tell me you told him off. You had to have told him where to go. There is absolutely no way you would ever let someone say something like that to you and get away with it. And that dress isn't a green light for anything but looking sexy. And since when is it a crime to have great legs and a fabulous, toned body?" She huffs indignantly.

I love London. People who don't know her well sometimes think she's pretentious, or maybe even a bit stuck-up, but in reality, she's full of fire and incredibly protective. She likes to keep things close to the vest, and as a result, she's a bit more reserved than me or even Harley. Being the middle child of three girls puts her in a weird position. She's always been a pleaser and a mediator. If our parents suggested an after-school activity, she would sign up. If I wanted to play soccer after school, she'd come outside and stand in as the goalie, even though she doesn't like playing sports. And if Harley wanted to play babysitter, it was always London who'd play the child. She was always happy to step into whatever role was needed. And she was always there to stand up for us, just like she is now.

"Of course I told him off, not that it made an impact. I honestly think this guy had three brain cells to rub together and all of them were on vacation."

"Are you going to try again?" Harley asks, slathering goat cheese on a cracker and topping it with a sliced fresh fig. "Obviously not with Brock the Rock, but someone else? Maybe London and I can help vet someone new and not base it solely on the fact that he's hot and plays sports."

"I don't know. It was such a waste of my night, and I missed a really good game." I checked the score in the bathroom twice and spent a good part of my date watching it in the reflection of the window while Brock watched his own reflection. "There has to be a better way to meet guys outside of freaking dating apps."

"Are there any non-friend-zoned options on your rec soccer team?" Harley asks.

I shrug. "I don't know. Maybe? I haven't ever really checked them out."

"Might be a thought," London says. "At least you know you have something in common, and you can better assess their intellectual competency before you agree to a date." I love that this is the way her mind works. If there were ever a person who could create a math formula to help find the right date, it would be her. Or Declan.

"It's a possibility." And one I honestly hadn't considered before now, likely because my friend group makes it tough to flirt. I'm also super competitive when it comes to sports and very much focused on the game, not the players.

The condo is quiet and empty when I get home. It's not unusual for Declan to be out on a Saturday night, but I figured he'd stay in tonight since the guys were over and we have an early morning. Maybe they hit up the club and decided to pretend they're still twenty-one-year-old frat boys.

I get ready for bed, pull my trusty vibe out of my nightstand—my only sure thing—and get myself off. It's the best action I've had in a long time, which isn't saying much considering how little action I get. It's too bad I can't absorb some of Declan's prolific sex life through osmosis. I try to wipe that thought from my brain because the last thing I need is the image of Declan doing his thing with some random as I'm drifting off to dreamland.

My alarm goes off at seven thirty. I hop out of bed and peek through the blinds. The forecast was right; it's pouring rain, and based on my weather app, it's not going to let up anytime soon. At least we're taking Declan's SUV, which is built for this kind of weather—and off-roading.

I head to the kitchen to set a pot of coffee to brew before I take a shower. As I open the cupboard door, I nearly step on a black lace thong. I frown at the underwear, aware they mean one thing: Declan brought someone home last night. He's been doing that a lot less lately, so this takes me by surprise.

His parents divorced when we were sophomores in college, and they didn't end on the best terms. Their tumultuous relationship and his being constantly in the middle of their fights means he's relationship averse and unlikely to settle down anytime soon, if ever. I don't blame him; if I'd been involved in their screwed-up relationship, I'd probably never want to settle down either.

I get the coffee going before I grab a pair of tongs and pick up the discarded panties his fun time must have left as a parting gift. As I pass through the living room, I notice a woman's jacket and a pair of sky-high black patent stilettos. Which means whoever he brought home last night is still here.

I hang the panties on his doorknob and leave the tongs on the floor for him to deal with later.

I knock on his door. "Hey, Declan, you still coming with me today?"

All I get is a muffled grunt and a feminine groan, followed by a giggle.

"For fuck's sake." I head back to my room to shower and get ready.

Half an hour later, I'm dressed in a pair of black pants and a London-approved shirt, and have my bag packed for the overnight trip. I check to make sure I have my laptop and everything else I'll need for the pitch meeting tomorrow. It's clear I'm making this trip on my own based on Declan's lack of response, and the fact that he hasn't made an appearance since I knocked on his door. I pour myself a travel mug of coffee, stirring in the sugar and cream with more vigor than necessary. Coffee sloshes over the side, spilling on the counter. I don't bother to wipe it up.

I slip my shoes on, double-check my overnight bag and purse one last time, and reach for Declan's keys, but they're missing from the hook. "Dammit."

I have no interest in meeting one of his random one-night stands this morning, or interrupting something I won't be able to unsee, but I also don't want to drive my car on the freeway in the rain. I sigh, resigned, stomp back down the hall, and pound on Declan's door. "I need the keys to your SUV. Where are they?" Yes, I'm bitchy. Yes, I believe I have a right to be.

There's a lot of groaning and grunting, followed by profanity.

"Deck, I gotta go or I'm gonna be late. Where the heck are your keys?" Low-level panic sets in. I don't want to be late this morning, especially since the game starts at noon and our friends secured really great seats. I also hate driving in the rain, and there's a good chance it's going to impact traffic.

The door to his bedroom swings open. His face is flushed, his hair a wreck, and all he's wearing is a pair of boxers. I keep my eyes fixed above the neck. Based on my current view, I've interrupted some morning nookie. It's another reason to be pissed, since he obviously put more value on getting laid than he did on getting his ass in gear so he could honor his commitment and come with me to Boulder.

I poke at my cheek with my tongue, so damn annoyed and ready to go off on him. I was counting on having his SUV today and some company on this freaking trip.

He drags a hand through his hair, biceps flexing. His lips are puffy and his eyes are glassy. I make the mistake of glancing to the right, which means I'm looking at the bare ass of the woman currently sprawled across his dark sheets.

I hold out my hand. "I just need the keys and then you can get back to your friend."

He makes a face. One I don't like. "My SUV isn't here."

"What do you mean it's not here?" I really don't have time for this.

"I left it downtown last night."

"Are you fucking serious?"

"I wasn't gonna drink and drive," he mutters gruffly and motions to the pile of clothes on the floor behind him. "I can find the keys if you wanna Uber to it."

Downtown is in the opposite direction of where I'm headed, and stopping to get his SUV will take time I can't afford to waste. "Never mind, I don't have time to fuck around this morning, unlike you apparently. Thanks for being reliable. Super glad I can count on you when I need you, Deck." I'm annoyed and frustrated, not because he doesn't have the right to bring someone home, but because he put some random woman ahead of our friendship. It isn't like him to bail on me. And I hate even more that I'm worried about making the trip on my own because of the weather. It makes me feel weak and incompetent.

I turn away, and he grabs for my arm. "Ave, come on."

I twist out of his grip and stalk down the hall, calling out, "Dude, you smell like stale beer and used condoms. I hope she was worth it."

5

SO UNRELIABLE

AVERY

"I don't know why I'm so damn surprised!" I turn my windshield wipers up to full speed as a transport truck passes. The weather is crap, the rain makes visibility bad, and my tires are not in great shape. I needed to have them changed a month ago, but my schedule has been hectic, so this coming Tuesday was the soonest I could make it work.

Now I'm stuck in the slow lane, behind what I'm presuming is an old guy based on the fact that it's a gold Buick beast in front of me. Whoever is behind the wheel is going at least ten miles under the speed limit, and I can't pass him until there's a substantial break in the traffic.

Not that I actually want to pass him at all. I have a very good reason for my dislike of driving in the rain. My parents were killed in a car accident during a horrible rainstorm when I was sixteen years old. My sisters and I had been staying overnight with our grandmother—as was typical—and we woke up the next morning to our grandmother's tears and her promise that she would take care of us.

Nothing prepares you for that kind of loss. And although it's been more than a decade, I still avoid driving in the rain whenever I can. But today, that's not an option, so all I can do is white-knuckle it all the way to Boulder and try not to have a panic attack along the way.

"Do you think he forgot?" Harley asks.

I'm on a conference call with my sisters—hands-free, obviously.

"I don't know how he could. We talked about it twice in as many days! I'm so freaking annoyed that he pulled this shit!"

"I'm sorry, Avery. I would've come with you," London says, voice full of empathy.

"It's so frustrating. We've been talking about this trip for a damn month. He was so stoked about seeing all the guys from college, and then he goes and puts some random vagina ahead of me and his friends."

"He's a guy, though. They think with their dicks," London replies matter-of-factly.

She's right, but it still irks me that my best friend couldn't even put me before someone he doesn't know or care about. "It pisses me off that he had to pick last night of all nights to scratch his freaking itch. And you know what else pisses me off?" I don't wait for them to respond. "That I had a date last night who I could have gone home with if I'd wanted to."

"Yeah, but he had the personality of a bag of hair," London reminds me.

"Why can't I look at the surface and not care about what's inside?"

"Is that a serious question or just you rambling because you're frustrated?" Harley asks.

"I don't know. Both, maybe? It would be a heck of a lot easier if conversation skills weren't important. I wish I could be one of those people who doesn't need to connect emotionally with someone to sleep with them."

"I'm sure it would be a lot more convenient for the sake of meaningless sex, but I don't think it would make you very happy to sleep with randoms. I'm also not sure it makes Declan happy either," Harley says.

"He didn't sound very unhappy this morning when he was boning his sleepover friend," I snap. I haven't had sex in like . . . I don't even know how long. The reality is I don't do casual relationships. I need to be comfortable with my partners and that takes time and connection. Which is another thing I have a hard time with. The rain slows a little, so I adjust my wiper speed from hyperdrive to moderately frantic.

"Maybe you need to be a little less discerning if you want the pleasure of a random hookup," London says. "Although, I'm not sure Brock would've been the right choice for that, no matter what. He seemed like the kind of guy who would kiss his own bicep while pose-thrusting and then tell you there's something wrong with you if you weren't able to have an orgasm from looking at his awesome body."

I laugh, because that's honestly what I pictured in my head when he invited me back to his place. I also felt like I would walk into a frat-style house, complete with a home gym set up in his living room and a lot of mirrors in his bedroom. "Going home with him would've definitely been a bad and very regrettable choice."

"Can I ask you something?" Harley's voice takes on her quiet pensiveness that sometimes makes me nervous.

"Sure."

She chuckles, probably because my tone belies my uncertainty. "Apart from Brock the Rock being athletic and hot, what made you want to go out with him?"

"Uh . . ." I tap the steering wheel. "I don't know. The attractiveness and sports were the selling feature, I guess."

"So you based it solely on athleticism and attractiveness?"

"That makes me sound vain and shallow."

"That's not what I'm trying to say; we know you're neither of those things. But don't you have to put your interests in your profile? Didn't you chat online before you went out?" Harley presses.

"Well, yeah, of course we chatted, but it was mostly about the things we have in common." Which was sports. I can see where she's going with this. "Maybe I am shallow, because obviously I was blinded by the pretty."

"Or maybe you're intentionally choosing people who you aren't going to get attached to," Harley says softly.

"You haven't really been in a serious relationship since things ended with Sam," London adds.

"One bad date doesn't mean I'm still hung up on Sam." Awesome, and now I'm defensive about it. Sam and I were together from the middle of my sophomore year all the way through to the start of my senior year. It was the longest relationship I've ever had.

"That's not what either of us is saying, Avery. But you two were together for a long time, and since then, any relationship you have been in hasn't had much depth or lasted more than a few months."

"I haven't found anyone I click with." It's partly true. But I know what she isn't saying: that I'm purposely avoiding getting attached to someone else because I'm too afraid to put my heart on the line.

"We know how tough that breakup was for you," Harley replies. "I'm sorry, now probably isn't the best time to bring that up with you heading to Boulder."

"It's okay. Maybe I'm not in the right headspace to date."

To say I was devastated when Sam and I broke up would be an understatement. I was so in love with Sam. I thought he was going to be my forever. After college, he moved to Aspen to work for the parks and recreation program. Things fell apart after that. He had a career, I was still in college. I wanted it to work, and we'd tried the long-distance thing for a while. The whole thing imploded during midterms my senior year when I found out he'd been cheating on me for months. And he would have kept doing it if Declan hadn't told me.

It was not pretty. I threw myself into sports and studying, hung out with the guys, and didn't date for the rest of my senior year. He'd been Declan's best friend since high school, but after the breakup, Declan cut him off. I needed his loyalty more than I wanted to admit. And I took Sam's place as Declan's best friend.

But Harley might be right that I'm not quite over how bad the breakup was, and I may very well be avoiding a serious relationship because I don't want to get hurt like that again.

Beyond that, I'd been heavily dependent on Sam, something I didn't realize until he moved to Aspen. I'd always lived with someone, whether in dorms or with family. I'd never been on my own before, and I hadn't known how to handle it.

Declan, Jerome, and Mark had all been there for me, solid

friends I could count on, but that dependency weighed on me, and I never wanted to feel that kind of loss again. It felt like an echo of my parents' deaths, and the holes in my heart were too big, too raw, and too painful to deal with.

It had been a dark time in my life. I worked myself into the ground, avoided being at home where all I felt was the vast emptiness that threatened to swallow me whole. My entire senior year was a struggle, one I don't ever want to repeat.

"One of the hobbyhorse guys was asking about you this morning," London says, breaking my train of thought.

I bark out a laugh. "Was it one of the jousters?" I'm glad for the topic shift. I don't want to get sucked back into the sadness of the past, especially since I'm heading back to the scene of that particular crime. Boulder holds almost as many great memories as it does sad ones. Which was another reason having Declan with me mattered so much.

"Why yes! It was! He called you feisty and wondered if you'd be around today. Unfortunately, I had to tell him you weren't going to be in, but his name is Darby and he passed along his IG handle if you're interested in checking out his feed." London snickers.

"I think I'll pass, but thanks." The rain has picked up again, and it's accompanied by the red glow of brake lights up ahead. "I'm gonna let you girls go, but I'll message once I get there."

"Okay. Sounds good. Drive safe. It looks messy out there today."

"Will do, love you!"

"Love you back!"

They end the call, which is great, because I really don't want to take my hands off the wheel. Staying in the slow lane is smart, even if it means it's going to take me half an hour longer than usual to make the drive. I'd prefer to be early, but with traffic, I'll barely make it on time.

We slow right down, crawling along at fifteen miles an hour. I have to assume there must be some kind of fender bender up ahead. It makes my palms damp and my mouth dry, but I'm too nervous to take my hands off the wheel for even a second. Ten minutes and two miles later, the source of the slowdown appears. A sports car is nose-down in the ditch, two tow trucks already at the scene.

The traffic picks back up, but people are being cautious. Well, most people. There's a jerk in a white pickup who's clearly impatient because he or she is weaving their way through traffic behind me. I keep my eyes on the car in front of me, leaving space because of my tires.

I'm in the middle of mentally chewing out Declan for screwing me over this morning because he was screwing a random when my phone rings. "Speak of the manwhore." I'm pretty salty about the turn of events this morning and I'm not inclined to let it go right away, but I also don't love the way I walked out.

I give the voice command to answer the call as the white pickup slides between me and the car behind me. I lift my foot off the gas, slowing down to create extra space in front of me, and to hopefully inspire him to switch lanes.

Seems like dicks are everywhere this morning.

6

IT'S ALL MY FAULT

DECLAN

I feel like a giant bag of shit, and not just because I drank way too much last night.

Although that is definitely *one* reason. Of many. The second reason just left the condo. Mindy was a fun time, until she wasn't anymore. She didn't seem to understand that once Avery left—angrily—that we weren't going to finish what we started.

Once she realized the fun was over, she took her sweet-ass time getting her shit together. She also gave me a lecture on morning etiquette and seemed to think I should've made her breakfast, or offered her coffee and called her an Uber.

Normally I might have done any or all of those things, but I felt particularly crappy about flaking out on Avery. Especially since it's raining and she hates driving in anything but ideal weather conditions.

I don't know what I was thinking last night, other than shots seemed like a good idea and so did hooking up. Part of it may have been a result of Avery's date. It's not that she shouldn't date, or that I don't want her to. I do. But seeing her in that dress messed with my head, and I started thinking about her in ways I don't like. So I figured a distraction was a good idea. And it was, until I completely forgot that we had to leave early in the morning, and screwed Avery over in the process.

Now that the Tylenol has kicked in, I recognize how badly I messed up. I glance out the window, taking in the dreary Sunday morning sky, heavy with dark clouds. Rain patters against the glass and makes me feel even worse.

For the past few weeks, she's been going on and on about getting new tires because her mechanic mentioned the tread is worn. In my opinion, the guy was trying to cash in on Avery's anxiety, especially seeing as we're only a few months out from snow tire season. But Avery wasn't willing to chance it for the drive to the University of Colorado. She's chill about most things, but definitely not about anything car-related since she lost her parents in an accident.

I cross the room, drop down on the couch, and take a deep breath. Avery is one of the most amazing people I know, but it's never good to be on her shit list, and currently I'm sitting right at the top.

I dial her number, expecting to be sent to voicemail, particularly since she's driving and inclined to give me the cold shoulder.

I'm surprised when she answers on the third ring, so I fumble a bit. "Uh, hey, Ave, you on the road?"

"Yup." Her tone tells me she's pretty displeased by my thoughtlessness.

I don't bother to beat around the bush. It's not really how Avery and I operate anyway. If there's an issue, we deal with it and move on, so I'm hoping it won't take too long for her to forgive me. "I'm sorry. I wasn't thinking last night when I brought someone home." It would be a lot easier if we were on a video call, and I could use what she calls my puppy-dog eyes in conjunction with my *I'm so sorry* voice.

"Well, I hope the two of you had lots of fun." I can practically feel her eye roll. "And please make sure you Lysol the kitchen counter since I found your *friend's* panties on the floor in there, and I'm assuming they didn't just happen to fall off."

She is definitely pissed and not reining it in at all.

I cringe as some of the memories come back. Mindy pretty much attacked me as soon as we walked in the door. Somehow we'd ended up in the kitchen—I think maybe I wanted water. I'd had the wherewithal to move it to my bedroom before she got full-on naked, though. "I'm sorry about that too. I feel like shit for letting you down. I can see if there's a train or something and come up there this afternoon, then we can drive back together tomorrow."

"There's only one train on Sunday and it's left already."

"Are you sure? I can check."

"I used to take it all the time when I visited my grandmother. It leaves at nine ten, and the next train out isn't until six tomorrow morning."

"Shit, that's right." Sometimes we'd come back to Colorado Springs together when we were in college. "I could Uber."

She sighs. I can't tell if she's annoyed or what. "Honestly, it's fine. I'll tell the guys you were feeling under the weather or whatever. Geez, I wish this guy would back off."

"What guy? The one you went out with last night?"

"No, not Brock. He had the personality of a wet blanket. I would rather hug a porcupine than go out with him again.

There's a guy riding my ass in a white pickup. He's been driving like a douchecanoe for a while now. Traffic is slow and shitty, and he's clearly impatient and getting on my nerves."

"Can you see his plate? I can call it in for you." Avery gets extra nervous when trucks end up behind her, and I can totally understand why when she's driving her clown car. They could basically use her as a speed bump and keep going.

Avery is confident about most things, but she'll avoid the freeway any chance she gets. If there are back roads she can take, she'll most definitely use them, even if it means the trip will take longer.

"Nah, I can't make it out; it's raining too hard." Her voice has a waver to it, alerting me to the fact that she is most definitely on edge.

I want to take her mind off of the guy tailing her and the bad driving conditions. "What time will you be back tomorrow? I can cook."

She snorts. "Gonna make me one of your famous grilled cheese sandwiches?"

"I'll do way better than that. I'll grill steak and get those double-stuffed potatoes you really like from that place down the street. I'll do asparagus, even though the stinky pee grosses me out."

That earns me a chuckle, which means she's defrosting. There are a few dishes I've mastered over the years, and I've developed a real knack for grilling. "Can you pick up some of those jumbo garlic shrimp too?"

"For sure. I'll even get the bacon-wrapped tenderloin."

"Wow. You must feel pretty damn bad if you're willing to splurge on the expensive stuff."

I run a hand through my hair. I need to shower away last night's bad decisions. "I really am sorry, Ave. I don't know what I was thinking."

"I'm hazarding a guess your dick was doing the thinking for you." And the bite is back.

"Yeah, well, this morning when the head on my shoulders cleared, I realized I'd really screwed up."

"The beer goggles were that thick?" Now she sounds amused.

"Eh, more like I should've prioritized my responsibilities better."

"At least one of us is getting lucky," she mutters. "Shit. This guy is such an asshole."

"The one in the white truck?"

"Yeah. What the hell is he doing? Fuck!"

Horns blare and tires screech, followed by the sound of metal hitting metal. There's a loud bang, and Avery's shriek makes my entire body break out in a wave of goose bumps.

I shout her name, but there's so much noise in the background, none of it good, and it scares the living hell out of me. It's even worse when the metal scraping metal stops and is followed by a painful, terrifying stillness.

"Avery? Babe? You there?" My voice shakes.

I listen carefully and pick up static, horns still blaring, but they seem distant now. And then the softest whimper.

"Ave? You okay? Can you answer me?" I need to call 911, but realize she's on a freeway, and that means someone else has probably already done that. Besides, I have no idea where exactly she is, and telling emergency services that she's somewhere between here and Boulder isn't at all helpful. "I need to call London!" I practically shout into the phone as I jump up off the couch.

I won't end the call with Avery, not when she's unresponsive and I have no idea if she's okay or not. I throw open my door, shove one of my shoes between it and the jamb to keep it from closing, and pound on the one across the hall.

A woman lives there. I wrack my brain for her name. I think she might work in the healthcare field. I always smile and say hi, but she's in her fifties so I haven't really spent a whole lot of time chatting her up, since she's outside of my dating range by about twenty years.

She throws the door open, brows pulled together, frown in place, hair wrapped in a towel, the rest of her covered in a cheetah-print housecoat. Based on her fresh face and lack of makeup, she just got out of the shower.

"Declan?" I had no idea she even knew my name.

"Hey. Hi. Can I borrow your phone? Please."

She glances at the one I'm holding to my ear.

"It's an emergency. Avery's been in an accident and I can't hang up because I'm on the line with her, with Avery, but I need to call her sister. They track each other on their phones. She's on the freeway and I need to know where. Please." The words are stilted and difficult to get out, full of gravel and guilt.

"Oh my God. Of course." She rushes inside, leaving me standing at the door, unsure if I should follow her in or not.

"Ave, I'm calling London," I say, even though she hasn't responded with more than a whimper or a groan so far.

My hands shake, making it tough to pull up London's contact. I've called her a few times over the years, mostly on those rare occasions when Avery accidentally forgets her phone at home and I need to ask her something—like where she put the tongs or if she ate all the bacon again. Fear curls in my stomach like a snake at the possibility that I may never be able to do that again. That the steak I was planning to make for her tomorrow night may never happen. That this phone call could be the very last one I'll ever have with her. It's scaring the living hell out of me.

Avery has been my constant for years. We've been friends for a long time. And that bond has only gotten stronger since we decided to pool our resources, buy a condo, and move in together. She's been the one person I can count on before all others, and I've let her down in an unforgiveable way.

I have to crouch down in the hallway, suddenly light-headed. My throat is tight and it's hard to breathe, like there's a weight on my chest that won't lift. My neighbor's slippered feet appear and she crouches down with me.

I hold up my device. "Do you think you can dial the number for me, please?"

"Of course. You must be so worried about your girlfriend." She punches in the numbers, hits call, and puts it on speaker. I don't care that I'm currently sitting in the middle of the hallway on the less-than-clean floor. I need to know where she is and how soon I can get to her. And that an ambulance is on the way.

"Hello?" London's uncertain voice filters into the hall.

"London, it's Declan."

"You better not be calling me from your one-night stand's phone," she says with a bite in her tone.

Obviously Avery has talked to her already today. I imagine as soon as she got in the car she called her sisters and bitched about the way I'd let her down.

"It's my neighbor's phone." I glance up and give her an apologetic smile and click off speakerphone.

"Your one-night stand was your neighbor? Good lord, you are the literal worst."

"No. That's not . . . I'm borrowing her phone." I close my eyes and clear my throat to get the next part out. "Avery's been in an accident."

Silence follows, tense and thick like tar. When London speaks, all of the fire is gone and in its place is panicked disbelief. "N-no she hasn't, I was just talking to her. Like ten minutes ago. She's fine."

"I called her a few minutes ago. I'm still on the line with her; it's why I'm calling you on my neighbor's phone." Guilt makes the words feel heavy and impossible.

Real panic sets in and she rapid-fires questions at me. "Is she okay? Oh my God, she has to be okay. I should've insisted on going with her. What happened? Please tell me she's okay. Where was the accident?"

"A white pickup was tailing her. I don't know what happened exactly, and I don't know if she's okay right now, and I need you to use that location app so you can tell me where she is. Then we can call 911 and give them a location. I'm sure the ambulance is on the way, but I want to know where they're taking her."

"Oh my God. Oh God." She calls for Harley, and they have a muffled conversation while her youngest sister pulls up the app and finds out where exactly the accident is. Once they pinpoint the location, I pull it up on a map. It's an hour away. And I still need to get my car.

"You were supposed to be with her!" London says. "And now she's alone in her car and we have no idea if she's even okay!"

"I know. I'm sorry. I made a mistake."

"Harley and I are going to head toward the accident site." She practically chokes on the words.

"If I find out where they're taking her, I'll let you know."

"If she's not okay, I will never speak to you again." And with that, London ends the call.

I rush to put on my shoes, grab my wallet and my keys, and order an Uber. I talk to Avery the entire time, telling her I'm on my way and that London and Harley are too. I promise her she's going to be okay, even though I'm not sure she is. Why isn't she responding? I hate that this happened. I hate that I should've been with her, and now I'm not. I'm worried about London and Harley making the trip to the hospital on their own and how scared they must be.

The trip to get my SUV feels like it takes an eternity. By the time the faint sound of sirens can finally be heard in the background, I've been on the call with Avery for more than twenty minutes. Just as I slide behind the driver's seat of my SUV, I hear the voice of an EMT.

"Ma'am? Can you hear me? Ma'am?"

I listen for Avery's voice, but I can't hear anything beyond the wind and faint voices that don't match hers.

"We have another victim here. Weak pulse. She's pinned and bleeding. We gotta get her out and we need to move fast."

My stomach churns as images I don't like flash through my mind. I start shouting, hoping that if I can hear him, he can hear me too.

"Hello? Is there someone else in the car?" Alarm fills his voice.

"I'm on the phone. Hands-free, should be on the dash." It's

always where Avery keeps her phone when she's driving. "Her name is Avery Spark. She keeps her ID in the back of her phone. She's twenty-eight years old and she has a medical plan. She has pins in her ankle from a break when she was in her teens, but no other medical issues."

"Are you her boyfriend or husband, sir?"

"She's my best friend. Is she gonna be okay? Do you know what hospital you're taking her to?"

"We'll be taking her to Mountain General, outside of Golden. Do you know where that is?"

She was on the last leg of the trip, which makes me feel even worse. "I can find it. I'm on my way now. Is she okay?"

"She's breathing, and we're going to do our best. I need to end the call now. Drive safe, sir."

The phone goes silent, severing my lifeline to Avery. I immediately tell my GPS to take me to Mountain General and call London to tell her to head there too. It's the longest hour and thirteen minutes of my life. I think about the way Avery is whenever she's in the passenger seat and I'm driving in the rain. How she bites her fingernails and pulls her knees up to her chest. She rests her forehead on her knees, so she doesn't have to look at what's happening outside of the car. She'll turn the music up and put on a chill playlist, one she knows by heart so she can sing all the songs.

I always make fun of her and tell her she should've tried out for *American Idol* or something. She has a decent voice though, the kind that's perfect for singing lullabies. I would give anything to hear that again.

When I get to the hospital, I find Harley and London in the waiting room, both in tears.

London rushes me. "This is your fault!" Her fists connect

with my chest. Harley's face is etched through with fear and sadness. She pushes unsteadily out of her chair, eyes red, but so stoic as she grabs for London's swinging fist.

I shake my head. I deserve London's anger and her wrath because she's right: I'm the reason Avery is here, in this hospital. I'm the reason she was driving her car and not my SUV, and I'm the reason she was alone.

And I'm the reason they're reliving one of the worst times of their lives again, except it's not their parents who have been in the accident this time, it's their older sister. The one who has been there for them through every single heartbreak and tear.

Despite their grandmother taking the three of them in, Avery still took on the role of head of the family after her parents died. She's integral to the foundation of their family, and I'd knocked the footing out from under them.

I let London pummel me until the fight drains out of her and she wilts against me, sobbing uncontrollably. I've been to plenty of family functions over the years. I've been Avery's backup wedding date on multiple occasions, particularly when she doesn't want to be asked when she's going to settle down. I've attended family birthdays; I got Avery shitfaced on her twenty-first and then dealt with the aftermath—which wasn't pretty. I've even been to family Christmas and Thanksgiving.

I've been there through a lot of ups and downs, seen Avery through the bad times and the good. But I have never, ever felt so devastatingly responsible than I do for what's brought us all here.

I wrap my arms around London, soaking in her pain. I thought I disliked myself this morning when the fog cleared, but it has nothing on how much I loathe myself right now.

"I'm sorry. I'm so sorry."

"I hate you so much right now," London sobs into my chest. She's tall, taller than Avery, but willowy instead of strong. I hold her up, taking most of her weight.

"Not as much as I hate myself," I promise her.

She pulls herself together and pushes away from me. Turning to face the windows, she wipes at her eyes with the sleeve of her sweater.

"Do we know anything yet?" I ask Harley, who is the less emotionally reactive of Avery's sisters, and also the least likely to hold this against me for the rest of my life, even if she should.

"She's in surgery right now. They said there are multiple breaks, but most of them look pretty clean. She's going to need more pins in her leg and possibly a couple in her arm, but they're not sure yet. She also suffered a few cracked ribs. They told us she's lucky to be alive, and they're doing their best."

"Doing their best?" I echo, my brain trying to absorb and reject the myriad injuries Avery has sustained. *Multiple breaks, cracked ribs, lucky to be alive* pings around in my head, making my stomach roil.

"They're worried about her leg. It's the same one that was injured before. It was pinned. They're hopeful." Harley's eyes are haunted, her chin trembling. She was only twelve when her parents died in that car accident. Young enough to still need her mom and old enough to understand what she didn't have anymore, and never would.

"Hopeful." I sit in one of the chairs and run my hands through my hair, gripping it at the crown. My vision goes blurry. "She has to be okay. She has to be *whole*." I can't even begin to consider what it would be like for Avery to lose a limb. She's forever seeking adventure. She's the first to say yes to the riskiest things, like mountain climbing, or biking down the side of an actual mountain. The things we do for fun are things people would do maybe once in their lifetime. She's fierce and effervescent and full of life.

Except right now, she's in surgery and we don't know what the extent of the damage is going to be.

"What about head injuries?" My voice is rough like a freshly paved gravel road.

"Other than bruising and swelling from the airbag deploying, they don't think there's any damage there."

"Thank God." I can handle Avery and physical injuries, but I need to know that her beautiful, amazing mind isn't going to be altered after this.

While we wait, I text our college friends that we were supposed to meet up with for the game and give them an abbreviated version of what happened and tell them I'll update them when I know more. I call Jerome and Mark to tell them what happened. I feel numb as I repeat the same information twice. And twice I get the question: Wasn't I supposed to be with her? Because the guys didn't want to go out, they left before I went to the bar. I messaged a friend from work and met him there, figuring it wouldn't hurt to go for one drink. Which turned into several drinks and some very bad decision-making.

Twice I'm met with silence after I explain what happened. The heavy kind that's filled with unanswered questions. And I realize that if something really bad does happen to Avery, I might stand to lose a lot more than her friendship. I might lose everything that's important to me. Her being at the top of that list.

7

I NEED A VACATION FROM MY LIFE

AVERY

I hurt in ways that don't make sense. It feels like I ran a marathon and then got into a boxing ring. And lost. Every part of me aches, and at the same time I feel heavy, like I'm pinned underwater, but still able to breathe.

I open my eyes, the smells and sounds unfamiliar. I blink a few times, adjusting to the dimly lit room that is most definitely not mine. I try to move, but it makes white and black spots appear in my vision. I suck in a gasping breath as pain radiates through my entire body, making it impossible to do anything but fight to breathe through it.

Once the agony settles back into a nearly unbearable ache, I slowly, carefully take a look around the room. One crucial thing becomes clear as I process the visual information accompanied by the repetitive, rhythmic beeping: I'm in the hospital and I'm very badly hurt.

Panic sets in, the kind I haven't experienced in a decade. The same kind of panic I felt when I came downstairs after a fitful night's sleep and found Gran sitting in the middle of the formal living room on the couch that only adults used when there was a big event of some kind. Her hands were folded in her lap, white fabric peeking out, my grandpa's initials embroidered in one corner.

Despite the fact that he'd been gone for years, she'd kept his handkerchiefs. As I got older I recognized that she only brought them out on special days: her birthday, his, their anniversary, the anniversary of his death.

That morning the hairs on the back of my neck stood up, and I'd wanted desperately to turn around and run. I didn't know where, but I did know that I wanted to disappear. To go anywhere else. To escape something I couldn't see, but could feel.

She'd patted the spot beside her, and her expression told me that this gesture, this allowing me to sit on the sofa reserved for adults wasn't something I wanted. But I sat beside her anyway.

She'd put her arm around me and hugged me. An apology fell from her lips, she murmured it like a mantra until she finally pulled away.

And told me my parents had been in an accident.

That they were gone.

I remembered the way I'd carelessly hugged them before they'd headed out for the night. I remembered the smell of my mom's perfume, the scent of my dad's cologne. His rough cheek against mine when he'd told me to watch Harley and make sure she didn't eat an entire bag of cookies before dinner. I remembered his wink and his smile.

And how I would never hear their voices, feel their arms around me again, get to tell them I loved them one last time.

My sisters were still asleep, blissfully unaware of the tragedy that had befallen us.

But I'd sat there with Gran that morning and watched her shine dim. And that had been the moment I'd realized that even though we'd all lost something that day, one of us had to make sure all of us could still shine, at least a little.

I blink several times and find myself back in reality, a personal hell of my own, and glance to the right. Declan is passed out awkwardly in a chair pulled up beside my bed. Based on the shadow of beard growth decorating his chin and cheeks, he's been here for a while. His hair is all over the place, flattened in some spots and sticking up in others. The baseball cap in his lap accounts for that.

I open my mouth to speak, but it's more of a rasp. My mouth is dry, and all I want is to drink a gallon of water. My stomach is roiling though, so I'm not sure it would be a great idea even though I'm horribly parched.

I clear my throat and try to wet my mouth so my tongue doesn't feel so much like sandpaper. It helps, and this time I'm able to say Declan's name. It's barely more than a whisper, but he jolts as though he's been Tasered. His ball cap falls to the floor and his wild eyes land on me.

"Ave? Oh, thank fucking God." He clasps my hand between his, bows his head, and presses his lips to my knuckle. "I'm so glad you're awake. I wasn't sure . . . I didn't think . . . I'm so sorry. So, so sorry. I'm so sorry."

I don't understand what he's talking about. Or why he'd be sorry. I don't have much in the way of memories. Just sounds I want to block out and pain that makes it hard to think. I note the needle in the back of my hand hooked up to an IV beside my bed. My right arm—the dominant one—is encased in a cast all the way past my elbow and is set in traction, keeping it raised and immobile. My left leg is also in a cast, all the way from my foot to the top of my thigh.

Real panic hits and the words are pitchy with fear. "What happened to me?"

"You were in a car accident. Thank God you're awake. It's been almost two days." His voice cracks with emotion. "How do you feel? What hurts? What can I get you?"

"Thirsty." Everything is too overwhelming to be able to get more than a single word out.

Declan clambers to his feet and almost face-plants into the nightstand beside the bed. He picks up a plastic glass of water with a bendy straw and brings it to my lips. I want to be able to do it myself, but I don't feel strong enough to manage. As it is, I can barely muster the strength to suck the water through the straw.

Even tipping my head forward a fraction of an inch to meet the straw takes an incredible amount of energy. I rest back against the pillow, processing the various aches and pains. I'm foggy, and I don't feel as if I'm quite connected to my body.

"How bad?" I don't need to elaborate, considering my current state.

He sets the glass on the nightstand and takes my left hand in his, eyes flitting from my face back to the IV taped to my hand. "You have a broken ulna and radius in your right arm, and a fractured elbow. Your left tibia is broken and needed pins to keep everything in place while it heals. There's a fracture in your fibula and femur. You also have a dislocated kneecap, bruised ribs, and some bruising and swelling in your face because the airbag deployed."

"So really bad." At least my sarcasm is still intact. It's a deflection from the dread taking hold. Tiny fragments of memory filter in. The sound of metal scraping against metal. Starbursts of pain. Fear. Declan's muffled voice. I can't fit any of the pieces together, but I know it must be the accident that I'm remembering.

"I should've been with you. I don't know what I was thinking. If we'd had my SUV, the rain wouldn't have been a problem. I'm so sorry, Ave." He chokes on the words and bows his head, fingers still wrapped around mine.

I want to be able to tell him it's okay, but I'm in pretty rough shape by the look and feel of things. He's not wrong. There's a chance I wouldn't be here if he hadn't flaked out on me. But at the same time, who knows if being in his car would've even made a difference.

I lie there, breathing through the pain, trying to piece together what happened to put me here. "The white truck."

"Do you remember the accident?" His eyes are wide with horror, and I have to wonder what he's seen and whether there was news footage.

Declan is very good at beating himself up over his mistakes. Usually it's work- or sports-related—missing a goal or pass, losing money on an investment or not securing the client he wanted, but it's not often extended to the people in his life, mostly because he's not a relationship kind of guy.

He's an extra loyal friend and he rarely lets anyone down. He's the first to help someone move, or fix something, or paint a room. Need a date to a wedding? He's a great wingman. Need a friend to go on a road trip? He's always up for the adventure. So the fact that he ditched me for a random hookup hurts more than I expected. And now he's going to beat himself up about it because the hurt isn't just emotional—I'm in a bad physical state. The kind that tells me I'm lucky to be here at all.

I remember the guy in the white truck who couldn't handle being stuck behind anyone, weaving through traffic, and using the merge lane to get ahead when he was tired of my cautious driving. He'd cut off a small car ahead of me, and it had been a flurry of hard braking. I'd followed suit, but with my tires and the slick conditions, I knew I wasn't going to be able to stop in time, so I swerved toward the shoulder, hoping to avoid the car in front of me. Unfortunately, I must not have been the only person with that idea, because someone slammed into the back of my car, causing me to lurch forward.

After that, it was a lot of spinning and screeching and my own screaming. The memories are spotty. I recall bursts of pain I couldn't escape and Declan's voice, telling me he was getting help.

And now here I am. Helpless. And still in a lot of pain.

Declan calls in a nurse, and she checks my vitals, asking all kinds of questions that should be simple, but I can't seem to communicate around the agony, which is worsening by the second. I try to tell her this, but my words are garbled and don't make a lot of sense.

She hits a button, and Declan takes his seat beside me again. I hear his apology and feel the warmth of his hand on mine before the world goes dark again.

The next time I wake, Declan isn't sitting beside my bed, but my sisters are. Light pours in from the window and the sunshine cuts a line across the end of my bed, highlighting my painted toenails. They're probably the only part of me that looks halfway decent. I noticed a chip out of the nail on my big toe as well as purple and blue bruising.

"Hey." Harley pushes up out of her chair and brushes stray hairs away from my face. She may be the youngest, but she's also the most maternal. If someone needs to be taken care of, she's the one who always steps up to the plate.

London drops the piece of paper she's holding on the floor and stands, but hangs back while Harley fusses over me. "You gave us a real scare, Ave." She turns her head away and takes a deep breath, as though she's trying to keep her emotions in check.

I lick my lips. Like the last time I woke, I'm parched. Harley, being Harley, seems to pick up on that immediately and reaches for the water beside my bed. I let her lift it to my mouth, aware I don't have the strength or coordination to do it myself. I have no idea how long I've been asleep this time.

"Declan?" My voice is a raspy whisper.

London purses her lips, her expression shuttering. "We sent him home to shower about an hour ago. I expect he'll be back soon."

"He hasn't left your side since you came out of surgery," Harley adds.

"How long have I been here?" My voice gains strength with use.

"This is day three. They kept you sedated for the first twenty-four hours because they wanted to be able to manage your pain levels and keep you still," Harley explains.

"How long will I have to stay here?" I don't have *time* for long hospital stays. "Oh God, I missed the alumni meeting."

Harley pats my hand reassuringly. "It's okay. We're taking care of everything." She motions to a bouquet of flowers on the table next to my bed. In fact, there are several bouquets. "They want you to heal and so do we, so no worrying about work. Your new job is to rest and let your bones knit and your bruises heal." Her smile is tremulous, her own fears bleeding through in her words and her expression. If this is bringing up memories I'd rather not face, I'm sure it's the same for her.

A few minutes later the doctor comes in, and London and Harley are asked to step out while I'm checked over. Neither of them wants to leave, but they assure me they'll be right outside the room. By the time I've been assessed, prodded, and monitored for sensation in my toes and my ability to follow her finger with my eyes without moving my head, Declan has returned.

He looks clean but exhausted as the three of them step back into the room to discuss my extensive healing and treatment plan with the doctor. "Once you're able to sit up and move from the bed to a wheelchair, we'll be able to release you. However, you're going to need a lot of support, particularly during the first few weeks."

"So I can go home soon?" I ask hopefully.

"Depending on how you progress, it's a possibility, but we don't want to rush anything."

"How soon is soon?" I want to be at home, not in a hospital bed with all the unfamiliar smells and sounds.

"It's one step at a time, Avery. The breaks in your arm are clean, and we're hoping for a six-week healing time, but your leg has multiple breaks, and because of the femur fracture, we're looking at closer to eight weeks' recovery time. The bruised ribs and hairline fractures mean you're going to need to take it easy for quite a while, and you won't be able to use crutches until your ribs have healed. We'll be able to assess your recovery time and what the next steps will be in a couple of weeks."

Harley steps up and slips her hand into mine as dismay starts to take over. Weeks of rest and relaxation might sound like a dream to some people, but to me it's a nightmare. I *need* to stay busy, and being physically active is part of that.

I remember what it was like when I had to have pins put in my ankle as a teen, before my parents passed. Two months of sitting around watching TV, not being able to do the things I loved was torture back then. I can't even begin to imagine what it'll be like now.

It feels a lot like I can't breathe. "What does all of this mean?"

"You'll need someone to be with you around the clock to help you with your basic needs and moving around for the first couple of weeks in order to avoid any potential setbacks. Your injuries could have been far worse, and we're very lucky that we were able to treat you as quickly as we did; otherwise, the prognosis might not be as positive. But you'll be able to walk again and have full use of your arm."

"I'll be able to walk again?" The alarm is clear in my tone. "What about sports? Will I be able to play again?"

"It's possible that no-contact sports could be acceptable, but we'll need to assess that as you heal."

"Right. Okay." My mind feels like it's spinning out of control. How will I bathe? Use the bathroom? How am I going to sleep? Get into my bed?

The doctor says she'll be back later today, giving us time to discuss the bomb that has been dropped on me.

"Hey, hey, it's okay, just take a breath." Harley brushes my hair away from my face, and I realize I'm in full-on panic mode, breath coming in short, quick bursts, nausea making my stomach ache and twist.

"Obviously you'll come stay with us while you're healing," London says, all authority, her hard eyes on Declan.

They usually get along, but right now I can feel the animosity brewing, and I'm not sure what's happened in the past few days, apart from me ending up in my current state.

"She'll come home with me. I'll take care of Avery," Declan, who has been hanging back so far, says with quiet certainty, as if any other option is ridiculous.

"Like hell she will," London snaps. "You were supposed to be with her when this happened." She jabs a finger in my direction, her expression fierce, but her chin trembling.

Declan runs a hand through his hair, and his jaw clenches and releases several times, as if he's trying to compose himself and struggling to do so. "I know. And I wish I could go back in time and fix it, but I can't. I've already cleared time off with my boss, and she's agreed to let me work from home." His gaze shifts to me, imploring. "I let you down and I'm so sorry about that. If you want to stay with London and Harley, I completely understand, but I've already made arrangements with work and I've talked to the doctors, so I know exactly what I need to make you comfortable while you're recovering."

His guilt feels like another body in the room.

"Harley and I can help you recover. You can stay with us," London assures me.

"How can you do that when you both have to run Spark House? Someone needs to handle Avery's responsibilities. You can't do that and take care of her at the same time."

"We'll make it work. We'll hire a nurse's aide if we need to," London argues.

Declan's lips thin. "Are you going to interview for that? When will you have time? And how is it better to have a stranger helping Avery recover?"

"How reliable have you proven yourself to be?" London grabs the bedrail, knuckles going white. "What happens when you decide you want to go out? Are you going to drag Avery along with you? Will you leave her at home alone? There are two of us and one of you. I think we're the better option here. Besides, we're her family. At least with us, she knows she's our first priority."

I hold up the hand that isn't in a cast. "Can we call a time-out for a second?"

Both of them snap their jaws shut and turn their heated gazes my way.

Logically, staying with my sisters doesn't make a lot of sense. They're going to have to pick up the slack for me, and that means they'll need to be at Spark House, even more than they already are, and I'll have to work remotely—with one hand and one working leg—and that's when I'll actually be able to keep my eyes open for more than an hour at a time.

My head feels like a jumbled mess of information and worries, and we haven't even made an actual decision yet. All my stuff is at my place. Moving it all into Harley and London's would be a huge pain in the ass.

"Considering the demands that are going to be on you and Harley while I'm recovering, and Declan being able to get flex hours, it makes the most sense for me to stay in my condo."

"You don't need to do that. Harley and I can make it work," London repeats, worry in her voice.

"But how? You don't even have a spare bedroom."

"We'll convert the office, or Harley and I can share a room." London wrings her hands.

I cock a brow. "Really? You two are going to bunk together? I know how much fun it was when we were kids and you and I had to share a room during family vacations." I motion between London and me. "I can't imagine any of us have gotten more flexible about our personal habits. Besides, you can't relegate one person to come and take care of me because you'll both be needed at Spark House. If Declan already has the time off to help me manage while I'm healing, then staying at my own place where I'm most comfortable makes the most sense."

"I've ordered all the stuff the nursing staff said you would need, and most of it has been delivered already. I'm reorganizing the living room, so you'll be able to get around a lot easier when you're ready to come home," Declan says to me and then turns to London. "I know you're angry with me and I understand why. I get it, and I know you don't have a lot of faith in my abilities considering where we are, but I can be there, and Avery's right. You're going to need to be free to manage events since you're down a person."

London finally backs down, but she sure doesn't seem happy about conceding. "Fine. But Harley and I will be checking in daily." She takes my hand. "And if you change your mind, you can come stay with us. Or we could figure something out at Spark House if we really need to."

The last thing I want is to be at Spark House, bedridden and watching my sisters pull double time while I can do absolutely nothing to help. But I don't want to hurt London's feelings or incite more anger, so I nod my agreement.

8

LET THAT REALITY SINK IN

AVERY

I spend a week in the hospital. Seven days has never felt so long, and all I want is my bed and my bathroom and the use of my arm and my leg.

The first time I saw my face post-accident, I cried. I'm not really a vain person. I don't wear much makeup or put a lot of effort into dressing up and getting fancy like London sometimes does. At best, I'm a lip gloss and coat of mascara kind of woman. But seeing the bruises under my eyes and across the bridge of my nose, the healing split lip, and the scratches across my cheek from the shattered driver's side window was a huge wake-up call.

Because apart from broken bones and a banged-up face, it could've been a lot worse.

I could've been one of the four friends who were in the car behind the white pickup. They were in a sedan, and when the pickup cut them off, they braked, but not fast enough, and ended up crashing into the back of the truck. The driver and passenger in front died on impact, and the two friends in the back were rushed to the hospital. Only one of the four survived.

So I have to remind myself that bruises fade and broken bones heal. I'm lucky to be alive, even if the time between being broken and feeling normal again is going to seem like an eternity.

The day I'm discharged from the hospital my sisters are there, along with Declan. God forbid London would allow him to take me home on his own. She's become a hovering mother bird. I send him to the SUV with my bag so I can get a minute alone with my sisters.

I take London's hand in mine and give it a squeeze. "Hey, I know you're still mad at Declan, and I get it, but if you can pretend to be civil this morning, I would really appreciate it. Going home is really stressful, and Harley mediating while you glare daggers at Declan and argue about what's best for me, while somewhat entertaining, isn't all that helpful. Besides, he already feels bad enough."

London drops her head and sighs. "I want to make sure you're okay and taken care of, but I can't do that when you're living at your place and not ours."

"I know, and I appreciate that, but this makes the most sense. Declan has the ability to take the time off, and he's better equipped to help me physically. Besides, he owes me, so let him do this, and if it's not working, you'll be the first to know."

"I'm sorry if I've been overbearing. Just . . . seeing you like this is hard." Her eyes are watery and she clasps her hands tightly in front of her, as if she's struggling to keep them still.

"You're not being overbearing at all. I know you're worried, and I completely understand. I think we're all feeling the same thing, thinking a lot about Mom and Dad, and how this could have gone a very different way. But I need you and Harley to focus on Spark House and let Declan focus on me."

She blows out a breath. "Okay. But please promise if things aren't going well, you'll tell us. We will make it work, no matter what. You come first."

I give her hand another reassuring squeeze. "Promise."

Declan returns a few minutes later, and they wheel me to the front doors of the hospital. Getting out of a bed and into a wheelchair is one thing, getting my ass into the back of an SUV is totally another. I need help, a lot of it.

Declan wraps one arm around my waist and loops my working arm over his shoulder as we hop-hobble to the open door. I can't even pull myself up into the vehicle because my ribs are still tender and I'm annoyingly weak.

It takes some planning and maneuvering, but I eventually manage to get into the back seat while London stands behind Declan with her arms crossed and her lips pursed. This is going to be a long recovery if she can't forgive him.

Harley gets in on the other side and helps me adjust my position so I'm semi-comfortable. Once Harley secures my seat belt, she and London give me awkward hugs and insist I call them as soon as I'm settled. London wanted to follow us home, but they have a meeting in an hour and need to get back to Spark House—yet another reason why Declan taking care of me is logical.

I close my eyes when Declan shifts the SUV into gear and leaves the parking lot. It's the first time I've been in a vehicle since the accident and the anxiety is overwhelming.

"You doing okay back there?" Declan asks, eyes flitting between the rearview mirror and the road every time we stop at a light.

I crack a lid. "So far so good. I'm sorry about London. I know she hasn't been easy to deal with."

His knuckles go white as his hands tighten on the steering wheel. "You don't need to apologize. She's being a sister and she has every right to be angry with me, considering I'm the reason you're in this state."

"The guy in the white truck is the reason I'm in this state." According to the news, he was twenty-one years old. He slammed into a transport truck and did not survive the crash he caused. I don't know whether it's better that he doesn't have to live with the consequences of his actions and all the people he hurt as a result or not. Regardless, it's sad that he had to die due to carelessness, and a reminder that life is fragile.

The difficult part of being in an accident that is well-documented by the news is that I can review the footage on a regular basis should I so desire. It's become a bit of an unhealthy obsession, a constant reminder that it could have been so much worse. And likely would have been if I hadn't swerved when I did.

It's hard to breathe properly on the drive home, fear needling its way under my skin. The sound of metal on metal feels like so much more than a memory. "Can you talk, please?" I ask Declan.

"Sure. Yeah. You okay?" His jaw flexes along with his hands on the wheel.

"Yeah. No. Just memories of the accident. I need a distraction."

"Right. Okay." He taps the wheel like he's searching for something to talk about that isn't going to make my anxiety worse. "Mark went out with a woman he met through a dating app last weekend."

Mark is pretty old-fashioned about the whole dating thing. He prefers to meet people organically, but he's not big on anything but sports bars and sports. And while he's one of very few male elementary school teachers, he won't date anyone he works with, so that's another obstacle for him. "Oh wow! How'd that go?"

"Eh, well, it started out great, but it went south pretty fast."

"Why? What happened? Did she catfish him or use a picture from a decade ago?"

"Nope and nope. So they have an amazing amount in common, grew up a couple of counties over from each other, and even had common friends from the neighboring high schools. He was pretty sure he recognized her, because he grew up in a small town and all."

"Uh-oh, did he date her sister when he was in high school or something?"

Declan shakes his head with a smile. "Nope, it's even better, or worse, depending on how you look at it, anyway. So, you know how Mark always has a family reunion every five years?"

"Yeah, big huge thing, right? Couple hundred people? Like the whole extended family get together and they basically rent the majority of a park for a weekend and do the camping thing."

"You got it. Well, they start talking about camping and their families, and he mentions how he looks forward to his summer camping trip he's going on, and she says her family does exactly the same thing."

"That seems entirely too coincidental." I can 100 percent see where this is going, and it's not good.

"Oh yeah, it's definitely not a coincidence. It turns out he's right and he does recognize her because they're second cousins, and they've been attending these freaking things since they were kids."

"Oh man. Only freaking Mark."

"Ah, but that's not all. The girl didn't see the issue with them dating even though they're related. She figured second cousins was removed enough for it to be cool."

"No! How did Mark handle that?"

"Well, next year happens to be the reunion, and he told her he didn't really think it was a great idea to get involved with family because biologically it meant having kids was a no-go and he definitely wants a family."

I have to choke back a laugh because it makes my ribs ache. "Leave it to Mark to drop the *I want a family* bomb on his first date with his second cousin. There are going to be jokes for the next decade."

"I know. And she was all, 'But we could adopt.'"

"You're kidding!"

"I shit you not. Mark thought bringing up kids on the first date would send her packing, but apparently he was wrong. The best part was that she thought it would be easier since they already knew and liked each other's families."

"Good lord. How is he going to manage next year's reunion?"

"I don't know, but he may need to bring a fake girlfriend if he doesn't have one by then." Declan pulls into the underground parking, and my shoulders finally come down from my ears.

Getting me out of the SUV and into my wheelchair is a feat all on its own. It's a lot of awkwardness and trying to figure out how to hang on to Declan without my casts getting in the way.

He shoulders the bag my sisters packed for me and wheels me

to the elevator. "How you feeling?" he asks once we're on the way up to the twelfth floor.

"Glad to be home, but nervous," I say truthfully. Being in a hospital sucks, but the staff is trained, and the environment is designed for people with limited mobility. Now I'll be back in our condo, and I'll basically need help doing everything. All I'll have is a nurse popping by in a few days to check on me, and weekly doctor appointments to monitor healing.

"It's gonna be okay, Ave. I've got everything set up to make things as easy as possible for you."

I nod but don't say anything as the elevator comes to a stop at our floor. It's more awkward maneuvering to get me down the hall and into the condo, which has been totally reorganized.

The dining room table, which we never really use apart from when we have the guys over and serve food buffet style, has been removed. The couch and chairs have been shifted around to make a straight path from the front door to the hospital-style bed in the center of the living room. There's one of those wheelie hospital tables right beside it, and it's positioned so I have a great view of the giant flat-screen TV.

"We couldn't get the bed down the hall unless I rented the smaller one, and I didn't think you'd want to be crammed into something tiny, so I figured this was a better option. Once you have a bit more mobility, we can work on getting you into your bedroom, but for now, the doctors suggested this would be best."

"When did you have time to do this?" Almost every piece of furniture has been moved.

"It took me and the guys an afternoon. It wasn't that hard with three sets of hands, but Jerome likes to rearrange things seventy times to see what works best."

"You must have loved that."

"Majority rules came into play a lot." He squeezes my shoulder. "You wanna lie down or stay in your chair?"

"Um, I think I need to use the bathroom."

"Okay, give me a minute to make sure everything is ready, and I'll get you sorted out." He rushes down the hall. It's good we have separate bathrooms.

While I wait, I take in the reorganized space.

This hospital-style bed looks a lot comfier than the one I was just sleeping in, but it also reminds me that I'm far from okay. My favorite quilt decorates the bed. The one my mom had made when I was a teenager. I always refused to get rid of my old sports jerseys and shirts even after I'd long outgrown them. So for my sixteenth birthday, she had them made into a quilt. It's the last birthday gift I ever got from her and it goes with me almost everywhere.

Despite the fact that I'm closing in on thirty, I still keep it on my bed, and I often bring it out to the living room to cuddle under when we're watching TV. My favorite pillows are piled up on top of it, and a few of the magazines and books from my nightstand are on the table beside it.

I'm not much of a crier, but I find myself on the verge of tears for what feels like the hundredth time since I woke with half my body wrapped in fiberglass casts, unable to manage even the simplest, everyday tasks. I take a few deep, steadying breaths, reminding myself to stay strong and that I'll get through this like I've gotten through everything else, one challenge at a time.

Declan returns and wheels me down the hall, already having learned exactly how to maneuver to get me into the bathroom. There's one of those things over top of the toilet with handrails on it—something I associate with the frail and elderly. At the hospital I had a catheter for the first few days, but as soon as I could manage getting out of bed and getting to the bathroom—with the help of a nurse and often my sisters—the doctor removed it.

I look at the toilet and then at Declan. He claps once. "You ready to do this?"

"As ready as I'm going to be, I guess." He comes around the side with my bad leg, and I hook my good arm around his neck. Once my grip is solid, he slides both of his arms around my back and helps hoist me out of the wheelchair. It's awkward at best. And my ribs are ridiculously sore.

Living together means we're close, but we've never been particularly touchy, apart from when we were trying to get the ball from each other during soccer practice.

This is different, though. I'm not used to needing help with banal things like going to the bathroom. My chest comes flush with his, hard edges and angles warm against mine. It's not clinical like it was with the nurses. Maybe because he's my friend and there's more body-to-body contact?

It takes some maneuvering, but we finally mange to get me over to the toilet. I drop down with a groan, my body stiff and sore, partly from the accident, partly because I've been lying in the same position for hours on end, and other than the limited physical therapy, there's been minimal movement, so everything is that much more taxing.

I'm seated, with my pants still pulled up. Declan steps back, eyes bouncing around before he finally blows out a breath. "Uh, do you need help with the . . ." He motions to my lower half.

"No. I can get it," I say quickly, willing my cheeks not to turn red. "I'll let you know when I'm done."

"Okay, I'll wait in the hall, then?" It's more question than statement, and he thumbs over his shoulder.

"If you want to grab my phone, I can text you when I'm done. Better than you standing out there listening to me pee, right?" Based on how we both look away, my attempt at a joke falls flat.

"I'll be right back." Declan rushes out of the bathroom and returns a moment later, phone in hand. He leaves it on the counter and closes the door behind him. While I was in the hospital, they had me in one of those horrible open-back gowns. I couldn't get a pair of underwear over my cast, so Harley, being the ingenious and smart sister that she is, grabbed a few pairs of my bikini bottoms that tie up at the sides.

It meant needing someone to retie it for me once I was done, but that was a lot easier to manage when it was my sister, less so now that I have to depend on Declan.

It takes quite a bit of effort to get my modified sweats down over my butt—we cut the left leg off at the upper thigh so the hole was wide enough to pull over my cast—along with my bikini bottoms. It might make sense for me to wear long nightshirts and forgo the panties until I don't need help in this department.

On the upside, I'm happy to be in the privacy of my own home, in a familiar bathroom that doesn't smell like cleaning supplies and the awful soap hospitals have. And I don't have to wipe with the crappy, single-ply, rough toilet paper anymore. Once I'm done with my business, I consider trying to get into the wheelchair on my own.

My usable arm and leg are weak, though, and I'm so freaking exhausted. I give up on that idea three seconds after I have it and text Declan instead. He's in the bathroom almost as soon as I hit send. Once I'm back in the chair, he wheels me over to the sink, pumps soap into my hand, and then realizes I can't even wash it without assistance.

As he takes my hand between his, working the soap into a lather, I consider how much of a challenge it's going to be on bath days. I figure I can go a few days without one, just until I have a little more control over my body. And I can wipe myself down daily with a washcloth.

"Ave? Is everything all right?"

"Huh?" I've been staring at my hand, which is already dry. "Sorry, spaced out there for a second."

"You want me to make you something to eat? You must be pretty sick of that hospital food." He wheels me back to the living room, where my new bed is set up.

"Uh, yeah, sure. That might be nice. Can you help me into the bed first, though? I think I'm about done with sitting up for now."

"Of course. Yeah. You feeling worn out?"

"It's a lot to take in, you know?"

Declan lowers the bedrail and hoists me out of the chair. I'm in ragdoll territory, exhaustion sweeping over me. It takes what's left of my energy to keep my good arm wrapped around his neck while he lifts me up and helps get me situated on the mattress. I stretch out, happy to be lying down again, at least for now.

Declan fusses with the pillows, arranging them so my casted leg is elevated and so is my arm.

He turns on the TV and hands me the remote. "Anything in particular that you'd like to eat?"

"Um . . ." I consider all of my favorites and what isn't going to take long to make because I'm feeling like I might need a nap soon. "Oh! How about grilled peanut butter and honey?"

"I can definitely do that. I DVR'd a bunch of your favorite shows. Why don't you find something you want to watch, and I'll make you that sandwich?"

I flip through the recorded shows and settle on *The Bachelor.* Mostly we watch sports, and more specifically soccer, but I also like romantic comedies, and I have a thing for this particular reality show. I've missed a couple of episodes while I've been in the hospital, so now is a good time to catch up.

I settle back in my bed and let my eyes fall closed as the opening credits roll.

The whole drive home and bathroom experience must have worn me right out because the next time I open my eyes, the sun has gone down. The TV is still on, but the sound is low and it's an infomercial. I've obviously been out for hours.

Declan is stretched out on the couch, but his eyes are closed. I wonder how he's been sleeping this past week. I imagine not well, considering he basically refused to leave my hospital room apart from the two times they sent him home to change and shower.

My sandwich sits untouched on the table beside me, along with a glass of water. I'm guessing the sandwich is probably cold and the water is warm. I reach over and pick up one of the triangles, noting that he's cut it exactly the way I like it, into three sections, once diagonally and then again through half, creating three triangles, one of which is bigger than the other two.

I'm right. It's cold and the bottom is soggy, but I take a bite anyway. My mom used to make me grilled peanut butter and honey sandwiches when I was a kid. It was my very favorite thing to eat, and only she could seem to make it the right way. When she passed away, I started making them myself, but they were never quite as good.

It doesn't matter that it's cold, or the bottom is all soft, it's still the most delicious thing I've eaten in more than a week. I scarf down the rest of it, drain my lukewarm water, and lean back against my pillow again. I hate that something as simple as eating wears me out, but I close my eyes again, too tired to even bother wiping the crumbs off my chest before I pass out.

The next couple of days are a rough transition from hospital nurses to Nurse Declan. I understand that he doesn't want to leave me alone out here in the living room, but every time I shift or move or so much as make a noise that isn't an exhale, he practically jumps off the couch, and that in turn startles me awake. Two days in, we're both ridiculously bitchy from all the broken sleep, and I'm on the verge of snapping. So I tell him that his sleep farts are disgusting and they keep waking me up because they're so rancid. It's a lie, but it does the trick.

It's tough to find any kind of balance. I'm not used to this version of Declan, always hovering, always fussing.

I struggle not to cringe with every move, because each time it happens—which is often—it incites another round of apologies from him.

On day number three, Declan seems more ramped up than usual. He's been working from home and spends a lot of time with his laptop on the couch. When he has to make calls, he moves to his bedroom so he doesn't disrupt my frequent naps or my TV bingeing.

While Declan takes a call, I occupy myself by checking the Spark House social media accounts. Usually Harley is the one who takes care of that stuff, but with me off until I've healed enough that I can take care of my basic needs, she's had to take over a lot of my duties. It means she's behind on responding to some of the messages. I take it upon myself to answer all the most pressing ones, and to answer any of the questions in the comments as well.

My sisters have been by every day to make sure I'm doing okay. I love them, but between them and Declan, I'm feeling ridiculously babied. It sure is motivation for getting my mobility back as quickly as possible.

Declan returns to the living room, all shifty-eyed, with his hands shoved in his pockets.

"What's up?"

He bites his bottom lip, chewing three times before he releases it. It's one of his major tells that he's nervous about something.

I raise a brow and wait.

"Tomorrow is Monday."

"Okay." Since I've been home, the days all blend together. I've basically been binge-watching TV shows because my brain is too mushy from the pain meds to be able to do anything that requires actual focus or attention. I can maybe make it through a chapter in a book before my mind starts to wander and I have trouble remembering what I just read.

"The guys were hoping they could come over. They want to see you, and I've been putting them off 'cause I don't want to it to be more than you can handle." He removes his hands from his pockets and rocks back on his heels.

It'll be beer and wings and sports and loudness. Things I've missed. Something normal when all I've had is not normal. "I can totally handle it."

"Are you sure? Mark can always go to Jerome's place if it's better for you."

"It would be great. I'd love to see the guys, and it's nice to have something to look forward to."

"Okay." His shoulders come down from his ears. "I'll let them know. We can make a list of things you want, and I'll get the guys to pick up snacks and stuff."

"Candy. I want candy, and chips. And chocolate-dipped Oreos, barbecue kettle chips. Oh, and gummy bears! And Jerome has to bring his bacon-wrapped jalapeño poppers. And nachos, let's make nachos!"

Declan smiles for what seems like the first time in days. "Looks like your appetite is coming back."

"Hanging with you and the guys always makes me hungry."

My buoyant mood takes a graceless swan dive when I have to use the bathroom. I'm getting better at the whole thing, and the awkward has come down a level or seven since we've done the routine so many times now.

It's also a lot easier now that I'm only wearing long nightshirts and I've given up on underwear and pants until the pain is more manageable and I'm strong enough to do it on my own.

I catch my reflection in the vanity mirror—something I've tried not to pay much attention to since I have two mostly healed, but still discolored black eyes. Green and yellow bruises color my cheeks from when the airbag deployed. On the upside, my nose isn't broken.

I reach up and touch my hair. I haven't bathed since I've been home, apart from running a wet washcloth over my exposed limbs. My hair is disgusting, and I'm sure I must stink.

I'm worried about how difficult the whole bathing situation is going to be. And how much help I'm going to need from Declan to be able to manage it. I don't know how long I sit there, but eventually Declan knocks. "Ave, everything okay in there? You need some help?"

"I'm fine."

"Are you ready for me, or . . ." He trails off.

"Just give me a minute." I'm even more horrified when tears of frustration prick at my eyes. I try to stifle them, but they keep coming.

"Ave? Are you sure everything is okay? I'm coming in." He throws open the door. My hair is pulled up in a messy ponytail so I can't hide my face behind it, not that I would want to, considering how greasy it is. His eyes go wide. "What's wrong? What's going on? Does something hurt? Do I need to call the doctor? I'll call the doctor." He scrambles for his phone.

I hold up my hand. "I don't need the doctor."

"Then what's wrong?"

"I need to fucking bathe, that's what's wrong!" I snap.

"Oh. Okay. I can set that up for you. I'll get everything ready and it'll be fine," he says gently, as if he's speaking to an upset toddler. Which is pretty much how I'm feeling.

And I go off, because I'm frustrated and tired and I hate this. "It's not going to be fine, though, is it, Declan? I can't get into the tub on my own. I can't do anything on my own. I can barely pee on my own. Do you have any idea how humiliating this is?" I motion to my broken, beat-up body.

"I know this is hard for you—"

"Do *not* tell me you know how this is. You don't. I hate this! I hate being dependent on someone else to take care of my basic needs. I can't make my own cereal because I can't stand up long enough to get a bowl. I can't make myself a sandwich. I can't, I can't, *I can't*!" I slam my fist down on the counter.

"Avery, stop, you're going to hurt your hand." He rushes forward and grabs my wrist before I can slam my fist down again.

"Let me go!" I scream, completely irrational, out of control mentally, emotionally, because my physical body isn't mine to command right now.

I try to wrench free, but his grip tightens. "I'm sorry, Ave. I'm so sorry."

"It wouldn't be like this if you weren't such a selfish fuck boy." I spit the words at him and they have the intended effect, piercing him like knives. I'm angry and lashing out. Aggravated because I'm confined and he's not.

He drops to his knees, bringing my clenched fist to his forehead as he bows forward. "I know. I fucked up, Ave, and I'm so sorry. I made a really shitty mistake, and I wish I could take it back. Every day, every time I look at you, every time I see you in pain, I know it's my fault, and I hate myself for it. I should've gotten my ass out of bed and gone with you. I should've made sure you had my SUV. I shouldn't have gone out. I shouldn't have brought anyone home."

"Yeah, well, *should've* doesn't get me out of this mess, does it?" I yank my hand free, pissed off, wishing I could stop my mouth from running, but wanting to inflict some kind of pain on Declan that matches my own. And I'm succeeding. That it gives me some sense of vindication makes me feel horrible.

"I know, and I'm sorry. I hate that I did this to you. You're my best friend, and I love you, and it kills me to see you like this."

"Why? Why did you have to go out and find a hookup when you knew we had a drive ahead of us the next morning?" It doesn't make sense. We were looking forward to the trip, and then he went and screwed it all up for both of us.

He turns away, so I can only see his profile and not his eyes. His jaw tics and he exhales heavily. "I don't know. I made a bad call, and now it's going to haunt me for the rest of my life, because the end result is that I broke you."

I feel his remorse, but my frustration overshadows everything, particularly since his answer doesn't tell me anything. What makes everything worse is that all I want is to be left alone for a while, but I can't get myself out of this bathroom without help. "At least it's nothing permanent, right?" It comes out bitter and with venomous bite. I'm not being a very nice version of myself.

"I know how much you hate having to rely on someone else, Ave, and I'm sorry that it's me you have to lean on right now, but please let me help you however I can. I'll do whatever you need me to. Do you want me to call your sisters and see if one of them can come over to help with the bath? Tell me what you want me to do, and I'll do it," he pleads.

I close my eyes on a long sigh, hating myself for taking this out on him. "Don't call my sisters."

If London thinks this is too much for Declan to handle, then she'll most definitely try to get me to move in with her and Harley. They're already under enough emotional and mental strain as it is without me to help manage Spark House. I can't be dependent on them to take care of me too. There is a lot that I want for Spark House and that can't happen if their attention is on me.

"Let's get this shower thing figured out, so I'm clean and frustrated instead of filthy and frustrated."

9

SHOWER TIME

AVERY

I manage to get myself into a pair of bikini bottoms and a top, but I require Declan's help to tie the one side and fasten the clasp in the back. The bath bench has been moved into my bathroom shower, and Declan helps me into the tub and hands me the removable handheld showerhead.

I'm inordinately thankful for waterproof casts. I can't soak in a tub or anything, but at least I can get clean without worrying about keeping them out of the spray. "I've got it from here. I'll let you know when I'm done." I'm calmer than I was before, still frustrated, but not quite as heated.

"Okay, call me if you need me for anything." He closes the door behind him, and I exhale a slow, steadying breath.

This is so much harder than I thought it was going to be.

The hot water feels like heaven, though. I set my body poof in my lap, squirt some shower gel on it, inhaling the sweet vanilla scent—so much more appealing than the generic crap at the hospital. I take my time washing away several days' worth of grime. I can't move very fast regardless, but this is the first time I've had a shower in the privacy of my own home since the accident, so I'm going to enjoy it, challenge or not.

I spend longer than necessary between my thighs; even with the cleansing wipes I've been using post-bathroom trips, my lady bits can use the extra attention. I exhale a shuddering breath as my fingers skim over sensitive parts. I have no idea how long it's going to be before I can get myself off. My dominant hand is casted, and everything is awkward and unnatural with my left hand. I shut that line of thinking down, aware it's not helpful with my already dour mood.

I manage to shave my leg and under one arm, but I can't get a grip on the razor with the casted hand because my thumb is stiff, and I have very limited range of motion.

I give up and move on to my hair, which proves to be another difficult task. One-handed hair washing is a serious pain in the ass. I can't adjust the spray properly, and my hair is so dirty it needs a solid lather and more than one round of shampoo for it to feel properly clean. Beyond that, keeping my arm above my head makes my ribs ache. I end up with soap in my eyes and shout my displeasure, dropping the showerhead. It clatters into the tub with a loud bang, my shampoo topples over, and it has a domino effect, sending a bunch of bottles tumbling into the bottom of the tub.

The showerhead bumps around and spins out of control, spraying across the vanity and floor. It's a damn mess.

Declan doesn't bother knocking, just busts right in, eyes wide and frantic. "What happened?" His timing couldn't be more perfect; the showerhead does a spin, spraying him across the chest. His bare chest.

"I got shampoo in my eye."

I have my palm pressed against the affected eye, but my other, unaffected eye skims over Declan, taking in all the ridiculously defined muscles.

The showerhead does another twirl, and this time the spray gets him in the crotch, pulling my gaze down past the V that disappears under the waistband of his swim trunks. He raises a defensive hand and rushes across the room, nearly losing his footing on the slippery tile floor. He makes it to the bath mat and grabs the edge of the tub to steady himself.

Before the showerhead can make another full rotation, he nabs it and sets it back in the holder.

"Why are you in your bathing suit?" And why is my voice so pitchy?

"I wanted to be prepared in case you needed my help." His eyes roam over me, stopping at my head.

I can make out my reflection in the mirror across the room. I resemble a drowned rat with a half-lathered head.

His eyes dart around, and he rubs the back of his neck. "Can I help with your hair?"

I feel awful that I lashed out at him, especially when I know he already blames himself for my current situation. I can struggle through and do a half-assed job, or I can let him help—alleviating my own frustration and some of his guilt. So I concede.

"Yeah, okay, thanks. That'd be great."

"Okay. Good. That's good." He nods twice and then steps into the tub behind me. He carefully tips my head back so he can wet my hair without getting water or soap in my eyes. "Wanna hold this while I lather you up?" He nudges my hand with the showerhead.

I take it from him, and he grabs the shampoo bottle. It squirt-farts when he squeezes it and we both chuckle, some of the tension easing. He rubs his palms together before he smooths them over my hair.

It's been awkward getting used to having him help me get to the bathroom. I'm also forever grateful for the gag gift of Poo-Pourri Jerome gave us last year before the Super Bowl, because that stuff really does work.

But this is different, less about function and necessity and more about my limitations. It makes me feel even more vulnerable. I expect him to rush through the whole process, but instead, he takes his time. He works the shampoo into a lather, thumbs pressing into the spot at the base of my skull, anchoring there. He rubs slow circles while firmly but gently massaging my scalp.

I groan, the tension in my neck starting to ease. I drop my head back farther and bump against Declan's stomach. I jerk back up and mumble, "Sorry."

"Don't apologize." He tips my head back again until it rests against him. "Just relax. Your body took a real beating, you're probably all out of whack, huh?"

"It's awkward with all the extra stuff attached to my limbs." I raise my casted arm. "It'll be easier when my body is working a little better, and I can do more than rot my brain with bad TV."

"I know the downtime is hard to manage, but maybe when we see the doctor on Monday, they'll give you some exercises or something. I'm sure they're going to want to increase physical therapy soon, even with the casts."

"I'm almost looking forward to that." Almost, but not quite. I remember what it was like when I broke my ankle all those years ago. I thought being on crutches for six weeks was brutal, but it has nothing on this, or the months I had to spend in rehab before I could get back on the soccer field. Even then, it took a while before I felt comfortable on the field again and totally in control of my body.

Declan runs his thumbs down the back of my neck and then works his way back up until he reaches my temples. I hum my appreciation, almost disappointed when he takes the showerhead from me and rinses my hair. He moves on to conditioner, repeating the entire process, massaging my scalp and the back of my neck before he finger-combs my hair.

"Man, you're good at this," I murmur.

"Lots of practice with my hands." He holds one in front of my face, ring finger and thumb bent in and the other three straight—giving me *the shocker* sign. I bat his hand away.

"That's nasty! I do not want to think about you doing that to one of your randoms when your fingers are in my hair!"

"I'm kidding! It's a joke." He gives the back of my neck a squeeze. "But it's nice to be able to get a rise out of you again. You've been pretty subdued since the accident, and I was worried maybe it was permanent."

"Not permanent, just all the meds make me dopey. But the pain isn't as bad as it was, so I should be able to cut my dose down and maybe use my brain again soon."

"You want me to wash your back after I'm done with your hair?" He begins the process of rinsing out the conditioner.

When Declan offered to help me with the shower, I anticipated it would be a little awkward and clinical. But this is the opposite of that—it's comforting and soothing, like a warm blanket on a cold winter's night.

"Ave?"

I shake my head, realizing I've been lost in my thoughts. "Sure, yeah, that'd be great."

He doesn't reach for the body poof; instead, he lathers up his hands and smooths them down the sides of my neck and over my shoulders. "Can I unclasp this?" He tugs at the back of my bikini. "You'll need me to help you out of it anyway, right? It'll be easier to get your back if it's already out of the way."

I hesitate for a fraction of a second before I say, "Uh, yeah, sure."

Even with soapy hands, he manages to get it open with one quick flick. I bar my arm across my chest and his palms move down my back, thumbs on either side of my spine, pressing firmly.

My eyes roll up and I relax further, dropping my head. "Oh man, that feels freaking awesome."

His hands are warm and soft, but strong. It's been ages since I've had a massage, and even longer since I've been touched by anyone for any reason other than necessity, or a hug from my sisters. This feels . . . different. He rubs slow, lulling circles, rhythmic and almost sensual.

"I'll rub your back for you after your bath, if you want." His thumbs follow the curve of my spine all the way to the base of my neck.

"Really?" It's a half groan.

"Yeah, for sure. We can put on a rom-com, I'll make you something to eat and give you a back massage."

"Guilt is a strong motivator for you, isn't it? Not that I'm going to say no to any of that." I curl forward, humming when he hits a particularly tight spot between my shoulders.

His hands still for a moment before he runs them back up my spine and kneads my shoulders. Suddenly his chest is pressed against my back, warm and so solid. He wraps his arms gently around me. The connection sends a shock through me that I feel everywhere, from the crown of my head all the way to my toes.

His lips touch my temple, and I feel the warmth of his breath against my cheek. "I will never forgive myself for this, Ave, but maybe if I can take good care of you, I might have a chance at you forgiving me for being a selfish, thoughtless, insecure asshole." I don't have time to react before he releases me and turns off the water. "Let me get you a towel."

He drapes one over my shoulders and grabs another for my hair before he wraps himself up and tells me he'll be right back with a nightshirt. I sit there, feeling a little . . . stunned maybe. I don't know how to categorize everything I'm feeling right now. I chalk it up to the medication and Declan's new role in this uncharted territory of our relationship.

While I wait for him to return, I shuck off my bikini bottoms, wrap one towel around my torso, and use the other to dry my hair one-handed as best I can.

He returns less than a minute later with one of my long tank-style nightshirts and helps me into it. I keep a towel wrapped around my shoulders because my hair is still dripping.

Once I'm back in the chair, he wheels me to the living room and helps get me situated in my favorite spot in the corner of the couch. Then he makes sure I have all the pillows I need and that my arm and leg are comfortable.

He disappears down the hall and returns a minute later with my hairbrush and offers to brush it.

"I'm sorry I lashed out earlier. I was frustrated and taking it out on you."

He pauses his brushing and settles a hand on my shoulder.

"You weren't wrong, though. I was being selfish and thoughtless. If I'd just been responsible, I would've been with you. It would have been me driving and you wouldn't have been in that accident."

I cover his hand with mine and squeeze. "You can't know that, though, Declan. The exact same thing could've happened, and what if you'd been hurt too? Then it would be me feeling guilty for making you come with me. I don't blame you for this; you were just a convenient outlet for my frustration. So please, Declan, don't feel responsible for this, because you are not the one who put me here. That guy in the white pickup did."

His hand slips out from under mine, and he resumes brushing, working his way up to the crown. "I wish I hadn't let you down."

"You didn't, though."

His voice wavers the tiniest bit. "But I did. We were supposed to go together, and I flaked out on you."

I tip my head back and meet his sad gaze. "People make mistakes, Declan. It could have gone a lot of ways. Please don't beat yourself up over this. I'm going to be fine, slightly bionic, but fine. I've been through worse and come out the other side, and so have you. I'm sorry I blew up at you. All I need is a little forgiveness and then we can move past it."

"There's nothing to forgive." He bows forward and presses his warm lips against my forehead. They linger there for several seconds.

He exhales a ragged breath and straightens, clearing his throat before he says, "I'm hungry. Want a grilled peanut butter sandwich?"

"Um, sure."

He's already heading for the kitchen.

He gets me a glass of water and makes me a sandwich. Once the food is handled, he scooches me forward so he can sit behind me and make good on that back rub.

"I thought you were giving me lip service and you'd call it quits at the sandwich," I tease.

"Pfft. As if I'd dangle a carrot like that and then back out." He pushes my nightshirt up and reaches for the jar of coconut oil.

"What're you doing?"

"It's easier to massage with oil." He opens the jar one-handed—a skill I need to learn—and digs out a clump with his fingers.

"Ew! Why didn't you use a spoon?"

"I just finished making you a sandwich. My hands are clean."

"But I cook with that!"

"I touched your sandwich and you don't seem to be complaining about that."

"It's not the same."

"I'm not going to lick my fingers and dip them back in," he reminds me.

I take a bite of my sandwich and shut my mouth, because he's about to do something nice for me. I make a mental note to get new coconut oil when I'm back in cooking mode, though.

The movie plays in the background, and I'm only partially paying attention to it while I eat my sandwich and Declan works the knots out of my back.

I slump forward on the pile of pillows. "You really are great at this." I rest my chin on the pillow, groaning my contentment as he works on a particularly tight spot between my shoulder blades. His hands are sure and the pressure steady.

"I took a two-day massage course back in college."

"Really? Why?"

"Honestly?" His thumbs smooth up either side of my spine and back down again. "It seemed like a solid lead into foreplay."

I bark out a laugh and then cough and groan because it makes my ribs hurt. "Only you would take a massage course so you could seduce women. It's not like you need the help; you're plenty good at it without all the bonus stuff."

"Yeah, but I figure since I can't give the women I take out anything of substance, I might as well give them the kind of good time they'll remember, you know?" His tone is somewhat teasing, but underneath it there's a layer of hardness, and if I dig even further, sadness too.

"You're not incapable of substance," I mutter, eyes at half-mast, lulled by the way Declan's hands move over my back. "We've been friends for years; you're insanely loyal."

"It's not the same as a relationship, though. Sex can become a weapon, and my parents used it on each other for years. I never want to put anyone else through that or have someone I care about disappoint me in such an extreme way. Sex is great as long as there aren't any feelings tied to it, then it's dangerous and complicated."

I don't think he means it as a warning, but part of me interprets it that way. Especially when I consider how much closer we've become recently. Couple that with the forced physical proximity and how well Declan has been taking care of me, and I can see how easy it would be to cross the lines of friendship. I clear my throat and make my response purposefully light. "Well, if one day you decide it's okay for feelings and sex to mix, you'll make some woman a great boyfriend. You grill a mean steak, you clean, you give massages, and you watch rom-coms. You're like the ideal boyfriend candidate."

I want to slap myself for the last part, especially when Declan pulls my nightshirt back down. But then he leans forward, and his warm, bare chest is suddenly pressed against my back, like earlier in the shower. And just like before, he wraps his arms gently around me, and that warmth courses through my veins.

I breathe in the scent of his aftershave and his deodorant. The clean laundry detergent smell mingles with my shampoo and body wash. I have to remind myself that he's my best friend. That whatever I'm feeling is probably related to my lack of ability to manage my own needs.

"You're the only person I would do this for." I feel his warm exhalation on the back of my neck and then the soft press of his lips at the top of my spine. He releases me and slides out from behind me, jumping over the back of the couch. "I gotta take a leak. Be right back."

The sudden loss of his proximity and his body heat makes me shiver. And for some reason, I feel that loss as more than a drop in temperature. It settles in my chest too.

10

FRIEND ZONE

DECLAN

I really need my body not to be an asshole. I stand with my fists propped on the vanity as I will my erection to deflate. "What the hell is wrong with you?" I growl at my reflection.

Half of my best friend is wrapped in fiberglass. Her body is covered in bruises. She can't even wash her own hair, and I have a hard-on over rubbing her back. It doesn't make any damn sense. Maybe it's a guilt hard-on. Maybe I should let the guys take shots at my junk with a soccer ball the next time we play. Which won't be for a long time. Not for me. I refuse to get back on the field until Avery can get back out there with me.

I run a hand down my face—my bruise-free, undamaged face—and work at getting a handle on myself and my stupid hormones. Every time I look at Avery, I'm reminded of my stupidity. Of the selfish choice I made.

I think about the way she looked when I first walked into

that hospital room. How puffy her face was, the black and blue bruises that colored her eyes and her cheeks, the full cast on her left leg and the one on her right arm. The way they had her in traction to keep her stable. How frail and broken she looked. How scared I'd been. It does the trick, deflating my traitorous, inconsiderate erection. When I'm under control again, I return to the living room. Avery is snuggled into the corner of the couch, arm propped on a pillow, leg elevated, head lolling forward—totally passed out while *How to Lose a Guy in Ten Days* plays on the screen.

The bruises are starting to heal, and she's starting to look more like herself again. Even as battered and beat up as she is, she's still beautiful—broken, but breathtaking nonetheless. I shake my head, trying to understand what the hell my problem is these days.

I don't want to wake her, so I let her sleep through the rest of the movie before I move her back to her bed and tell her I'm sorry for the thousandth time.

The next day I spend hours in the kitchen making all of Avery's favorite foods and enlist the guys to pick up things like chips and candy and her preferred chocolate bars. She can't drink, so I make sure we have root beer and stuff to make smoothies, since that's her jam.

Just before the guys come over, I help her move from her bed to her corner of the couch—which I've already arranged so she's comfortable and has everything she needs.

Jerome and Mark arrive after six with pizza, beer, and a whole bunch of bags. They envelop her in awkward hugs.

"Guys, be gentle," I warn.

"It's fine, D. I'm good," she assures me and pats the couch, inviting the guys to take a seat. "Tell me what's going on. Did you guys play against the Jockstraps last week? Did you kick their asses?"

"We sure did, won by two goals. But everyone misses you." Jerome pulls a giant cellophane-wrapped basket out of one of the bags and sets it on the coffee table. It's filled with all of Avery's favorite snacks. "Everyone chipped in and got you a recovery package. There's a card too."

"Oh wow! This is awesome!" She manages to tear the card open with one hand, reading through all the names and "*get better soon*" and "*we miss you*" messages from the team.

Her eyes get all watery, and she sniffles, holding the card to her chest. "This is so great. Tell everyone I said thanks. Deck, can you grab me a pair of scissors so I can get into this and check out all the stuff?"

"I can open it for you if you want," Jerome offers.

"No, no. I'd like to do it. It'll take longer, but it's good for me to do things on my own, even if it's as simple as opening a basket of goodies."

My stomach twists at her somewhat embarrassed smile.

I grab the scissors from the kitchen and hand them to her. The guys are crowded around her, Mark sitting on the edge of the coffee table and Jerome on her right.

Her tongue peeks out, and she uses her leg to brace the basket and her casted arm to stabilize as she snips through the ribbon and peels the cellophane back. It takes her forever to get into it, but she doesn't ask for help. It's obvious that we all want to offer assistance, but the guys bite their tongues, because this is Avery and she's always been the kind of person who likes to do things on her own.

There's a very distinct theme, and most of the food items include peanuts or peanut butter. Under the treats are some non-food items. She pulls out a face mask and some lotions and girly things.

"A few of the girls thought you could use some pampering stuff for when you're starting to feel better," Mark offers.

"We didn't want to discourage them, even though you're not really into that," Jerome adds.

"It's really sweet, and by the time I'm back on my feet, I may very well want to be pampered. Declan's doing a pretty good job of that, actually. I'm sure he'd be happy to help me manage a face mask and a foot scrub, right, D?" Her smile is sly and knowing.

"I'll do one with you; that's how much of a team player I am."

Mark gives me a look I can't quite decipher. I feel exposed and transparent today, like they can see through me. Which doesn't make a lot of sense since I'm not doing anything wrong. I'm taking care of my best friend because she needs me. Yesterday's reaction was a fluke. She was emotional and so was I. That's all there was to it.

Eventually Avery needs to use the bathroom. She moves aside all the pillows and the blankets, intent on doing as much on her own as she can before she lets me step in to help.

She can almost manage getting from the couch into the chair on her own now. It's only a matter of time before she's ready for crutches, and then she'll be able to get around a lot easier on her own. For now, I'm serving my penance and feel like I have some value. It doesn't seem to matter that I know she's right; even if I'd been the one driving, she might very well be in the same state or worse. The fact that I wasn't there when she needed me still weighs heavy on my conscience.

I wheel her to the bathroom, making sure she has her phone. "You doing okay? Feeling tired or anything?" I ask once the guys are out of earshot.

"No, I'm good. It's nice to have them here. Makes me feel normal." We have the bathroom routine down and most of her modesty has gone out the window at this point.

I help her over to the toilet, and once she's seated, she braces her foot on the floor and lifts enough to tug her nightshirt free. She's wearing one of my old oversized hoodies over it—we cut off the sleeve so we can get her casted arm through it easily. The bulk hides her chest and the fact that she's braless, which is her most frequent state—apart from when she occasionally tames her boobs with one of those strapless, claspless numbers that look a lot like a bandana or whatever. It's also often what she wears when we manage the shower situation.

"Tell me if you're getting tired and I'll kick them out, okay?" I maneuver the chair so it's not in the way.

"It's the first time I've had the energy to stay awake past eight since I came home. I can sleep in tomorrow. I'll text when I need you again." She shoos me out the door.

The guys are half watching the game, half talking between themselves, at least until I return to the living room, which is when the conversation grinds to a halt.

"Anyone need a beer?"

I'm hoping this is one of Avery's quicker bathroom trips, although none of them are fast considering how much she likes to try to do everything herself. She almost pulled the wheelchair on top of herself yesterday. She's pretty damn stubborn when she wants to be, and I highly anticipate that she'll try some maverick shit tonight.

When no one answers, I glance over my shoulder to find both of them staring at me. "What?"

"What all does Avery need help with?" Mark asks, eyebrow raised.

"She's only got the use of one arm and one leg." I uncap a beer and take a long swig. This is why I was apprehensive about having the guys over—that they would see exactly how much assistance Avery needs.

"So basically everything?" Jerome asks.

I cross the room and drop down on the couch. "It's only for the next few weeks. Until she has some mobility back."

Jerome, who is the most laid-back, slides an arm behind his head and leans back into the cushions. "So if she needs help with the bathroom, I'm guessing she also needs help with the shower?"

"Well, yeah, she can't really do much on her own right now." I don't like their raised eyebrows and pursed lips. "She can't wash her own hair, and she's been frustrated enough with the whole process that she's mentioned more than once hacking it all off. I'd prefer if she doesn't make drastic, emotional choices because she's desperate to have her independence back. So I'm making it easier for her wherever I can, since it's my goddamn fault she's in the state she's in."

Jerome raises a hand. "Whoa, no one's blaming you for this, Deck."

"Yeah, well, we all know if I'd been with her, there's a good chance she wouldn't be in this state." It's better for me to lay it all out before they do.

Mark blows out a breath. "You can't know that. We get that you feel bad about what happened, but we're worried about how much you're taking on here."

"What is that supposed to mean?"

"She got hurt and you blame yourself. You're spending a lot of time together and she's relying on you for a lot of things. It changes the dynamic of the relationship," Jerome says.

I focus on my bottle. "Nothing has changed, apart from the fact that she's not capable of taking care of herself the way she likes to. That's it. And that's for the short-term. Soon she'll be back on her feet and everything will be exactly how it was before." But as I say it, I know it's not really true, especially since we've been in more intimate situations than we ever have before. I'm just not ready to face what that means quite yet.

Thankfully my phone pings with a message from her, so they don't have a chance to grill me any further about it. I set my beer on the table and head to the bathroom. When I get there, I find Avery already sitting in her chair.

"Look what I did!" She's wearing a wide smile that lights up her entire face.

I can't decide if I'm proud or pissed off, or something else entirely. "If you'd fallen, you could have hurt yourself. I think you have enough broken parts already, don't you?"

"It's like a two-foot drop to the floor, Deck." She rolls her eyes. "Come on, you should be excited about this! It means I'm one step closer to being able to handle the bathroom on my own."

"Maybe next time let me supervise, just until you get the all clear from the doctor that you can start doing wheelchair acrobatics." I make light of it, not wanting to take away her win. I want her to get better, but I also want to be there for her, because even though I know I didn't cause this, I still feel awful that she was alone when it happened.

11

STABILIZE

AVERY

The days that follow bleed into each other, but Declan and I establish a routine. Physical therapy starts after the first doctor's appointment. It's nothing strenuous, but as the bruises heal and my ribs stop aching, my mobility and my independence slowly return. After the second appointment the doctor gives me the go-ahead to use a crutch to get around. I'm still weeks away from having my arm and my leg back, but we're making gains, and my doctor is pleased by my progress.

I'm stretched out in the back seat of Declan's SUV, eyes closed the entire duration of the ride home. After my parents' car accident I used to have full-on panic attacks whenever anyone mentioned a car ride. I stopped taking public transit to school and rode my bike, at least until the weather turned nasty. I'm already worried about what the drive to Spark House is going to look like by the time I'm able to drive again, and how I'm going to be able to manage the anxiety. But that's something for another day.

By the time we get home I have a tension headache, and any thought I had of trying out my new crutch has disappeared in the wake of my throbbing temples and tight shoulders.

"You okay?" Declan asks as he helps me into the wheelchair out of habit, not necessity.

"The car rides stress me out." I knead the back of my neck.

"I'll rub your shoulders when we get up to the condo." He wheels me into the elevator and hits the button for the twelfth floor. It's empty apart from us, so the second the doors slide closed, he moves my hair aside and presses his thumbs into the spot at the base of my skull that always makes me purr like a cat.

"You weren't kidding, you're tighter than a guitar string." He rubs the spot until we reach our floor, then wheels me into the condo.

As soon as we're inside, he gets the couch set up for me. I've graduated from spending the majority of my time in the hospital bed to rotating between it and the couch. My ass is probably going to be pancake flat after eight weeks of sitting on it.

I try to tell myself that the excitement I feel right now has nothing to do with the massage I'm about to get and everything to do with getting a little more of my mobility back. Once I'm seated, I pull my shirt over my head. He takes his spot behind me and pushes my bandeau bra down, giving him full access to my back. At this point I've given up on modesty for the most part with Declan, but I use my shirt to cover my chest and lean on the pillow in my lap while he grabs the lavender-scented oil and squirts some into his palms.

"Thank you for doing this," I mumble, body already relaxing as his palms smooth up my back.

"It's the least I can do. Maybe we need to get out a bit more now that you're starting to feel better. We can go for short rides, get you used to being in a car again, work on taming that fear?" His thumbs sweep down the length of my spine.

"Yeah, maybe, but I need a few days to get my head around that. Just thinking about it makes my back feel tight."

"I figure if we make a plan and we talk it out, you might be less anxious about it? We could get Dairy Queen drive-thru. Does a chocolate peanut butter milkshake and a greasy burger and fries sound good? We could go on the way home from your next physical therapy appointment. Or if you want to go sooner, we could do your exercises together and then make the trip. It's only about a mile away, nice and short, with a great reward attached to it." He gives my shoulders a squeeze, finds a tight spot, and focuses his attention there.

"I haven't had a milkshake in forever." I close my eyes, allowing myself to relax into his touch.

While my shoulders soften under his hands, other parts of me start to tighten. I find my mind wandering and my body reacting. It's been happening more and more lately, especially when he's giving me one of his massages or when we're in the shower. Basically, every time he touches me for purposes other than bathroom trips. I try to push those thoughts out of my head. He's my best friend and currently my primary caregiver. Imagining him massaging other parts of my body isn't helpful.

The problem is, it's been weeks since I've had an orgasm. Although I haven't felt particularly sexy lately, the more I heal and the better I start to feel, the more my body reminds me that

I have other needs. When I'm healthy and functional, and not hopped-up on pain meds, I'm typically the kind of person who self-satisfies at least three or more times a week.

I'm shocked out of my increasingly dirty thoughts by a knock at the door. "You expecting a delivery or something?" It's approaching dinner, maybe Declan planned ahead and ordered in.

"Uh, nope, maybe your sisters decided to stop by?"

"Maybe?" Although they generally message in advance and ask for a list of things I might need, mostly stuff that I could ask Declan to get for me, but would prefer not to. I've taken to ordering groceries online and having them delivered so I can take something off Declan's to-do list, which is a lot longer with me being dependent on him.

My sisters are supposed to come over tomorrow night so we can talk about the event they're planning. This one is a bachelorette party for a very sporty bride, which would've been right up my alley. I'm doing what I can from home, researching the things they'll need, ordering in items, but I don't love that I can't be there planning the event like I normally would.

Spark House has always been my baby. I knew even before I went to college that I wanted to take it over. I love planning events, seeing people come together and unify. It doesn't matter what the event is, giving people a place to celebrate their accomplishments or life milestones makes me happy. And because my sisters and I are so close, I always assumed that Spark House was their dream as well. But without me there, I'm beginning to see that maybe that isn't true.

I can sense London's stress whenever I ask how everything is going with Spark House. Event planning isn't either of my sisters' strong suit—London loves creating centerpieces and other do-it-yourself crafts for the events, and Harley is great at setup and social media—but the actual planning isn't easy on them. Mostly they tell me not to worry and that they have it handled, which I guess I have to trust.

Declan carefully slides out from behind me and grabs a couple of tissues so he can wipe the oil off his hands. He waits until I pull my shirt over my head before he crosses to the door and checks the peephole. His shoulders tighten and he shakes his head imperceptibly.

"Did one of those door-to-door guys make it in the building again?" It happens every once in a while.

"Uh, no." He cringes, possibly because I'm loud, and opens the door with some reluctance. All it takes is the sound of a high-pitched nasally voice on the other side for me to understand why he's talking to the person through a three-inch gap.

"Hey, Decky! I thought I'd stop by and see what you're up to! I just got back from LA, and I figured you might wanna hang out!"

"Uh, now really isn't a good time, Becky," Declan says quietly.

Becky lives two floors below us. She's a model, and every single thing she says ends in an exclamation mark. Including her orgasms, which I've had the displeasure of listening to on more than one occasion when she's invited herself over for a booty call. It also drives me up the wall that she calls Declan "Decky."

"No problem. I'm around for a few days before I have to take off for Spain! I got a hot new tattoo and I'd love to show you!"

I can practically feel her exaggerated wink.

If my wheelchair wasn't on the other side of the couch, I would 100 percent try to get my ass out of this room so I don't have to listen to her horrible voice, or Declan planning his next hookup.

"Yeah, I'm not sure if that's gonna work out, but thanks for the offer."

"Oh, that's too bad. Do you have a girlfriend now or something?"

"Uh . . . or something. It's complicated." He rubs the back of his neck.

"Well, if you get tired of complicated, you know where to find me!"

"Uh, okay, thanks, Becky. See ya later."

"Bye-bye!"

Declan closes the door and remains facing it for several seconds before he finally slides the chain latch back into place and turns around. "I'm sorry about that."

"You can go if you really want to." I motion to the closed door, and for some reason my stomach knots. Declan has hooked up with lots of women over the course of our friendship. It's never bothered me before. Maybe it's because a woman literally showed up at our door offering herself to him, and there's no way I'll be getting any kind of gratification in the coming weeks. Or that he made my lady parts aware of their plight by giving me a back rub, of all things.

Declan arches a brow. "Uh, yeah, that's not gonna happen, Ave."

"Just because I can't get action doesn't mean everyone else shouldn't." And now I'm snippy.

"While I might agree that not *everyone* should have to go without action, I'm going to go ahead and say that if *anyone* shouldn't be getting their rocks off right now, it's me, especially considering the circumstances." He runs a hand through his hair. "Besides, she sounds like she's auditioning for a porn star role every time she comes, and I'm honestly not interested. Plus, I wouldn't subject you to that noise, and I'm not leaving you alone for an hour so I can unload somewhere other than the shower."

"Is that your whack-off location of choice?" I'm going for cheeky, but I'm not sure that's how it comes across.

He flops down on the couch beside me. "Makes the least mess, plus it's like double duty. Get clean and take care of business all at the same time. That way I can start my day with a clear head."

"But doesn't it make you tired? Like don't you want to pass out right after?"

"Right before bed, sure, but first thing in the morning it's like an espresso shot, wakes me right up. At night it's more like a sedative, helps me stop all the wheels from turning." He taps his temple.

"Huh. Well that's . . . enlightening." And not something I need to be thinking about right now.

Declan picks up the remote. "Wanna watch *50 First Dates*?"

"I'm more in the mood for action today. How about *Thor* or something?" I can't handle watching people falling in love and making out, not with my emotions and my hormones all over the place.

"You just want to see a shirtless Hemsworth." He scrolls through the movie options and stretches his other arm across the back of the couch.

"You're not wrong." I have a great love of all things Thor.

He tugs on my shoulder, pulling me into his side.

"Don't you have work to do today?" He's spent his entire morning with me at the doctor's, and I'm well aware that there are nights he stays up late so he can finish things he doesn't manage to get done during the day.

"Work isn't going anywhere. It can wait a couple of hours."

I rest my head on his shoulder, thinking about how nice this is, and how I'm going to miss it when things go back to normal.

"This woman is a total bridezilla! If ever there was an event you should be happy you can tap out of, it's this one!" London spears an almond-stuffed olive with a toothpick.

"She's that bad?" I pop a baby gherkin into my mouth and go back to folding Declan's laundry. It's not easy one-handed, but it's honestly the least I can do for him since he's doing so much for me.

"She's a step above 'that bad,'" London says.

"She seemed pretty normal in the initial emails."

"That's because you were dealing with her sister, who's actually reasonable." Harley tucks her hair behind her ears and crosses her legs like it's carpet time in kindergarten. "Last week she cc'd the bride, and the shit hit the fan."

"Holy crap, why didn't you tell me?" As soon as the words are out of my mouth, I realize I already have the answer.

London raises a brow.

Over the past week I've been able to wean myself off the painkillers. Am I still uncomfortable? Sure. But I'm healing, and I'd rather things hurt a little than feel like my brain is made of mush. "You know you can start bringing me back in on the planning side of things. I can do more than answer emails and like social media posts. Let me make some phone calls. I can talk to the bride, maybe smooth things over. My body might not work, but my brain and my mouth do."

"We know. We just don't want you to dive back in full tilt, which is exactly how you kind of do things." London folds a strip of paper between her fingers. She's obsessed with making origami stars. She keeps them in boxes at Spark House and uses them as table decorations at events. I'm sure she could fill a bathtub with them, at the very least. I keep telling her she should open an Etsy store since she's so crafty. From penis piñatas to paper stars, she can turn almost anything into something beautiful. She keeps saying she'd love to but doesn't have the time.

I motion to my leg and hold up my casted arm. "I can't really jump into anything full tilt, but I'm feeling so much better, and I'd like to ease back in. Let me help where I can. What are bridezilla's major issues? Let's problem solve." I've missed this. Over the past few weeks the focus has solely been on healing, and I need to feel useful, like I have value.

"I think it would be easier to tell you what *isn't* an issue," Harley mumbles.

London shoots her a look and Harley shrugs. "Well, it's true, and we could honestly use the help."

"Oh man, this must be really bad. Why don't we go over what you have prepared and what we can change to make her happy?"

"A personality transplant might be effective," London gripes, finally giving in a little, maybe because of Harley's honesty.

I bark out a laugh. "Well, since we're not in the personality transplant field, let's see what other options we have."

It feels good to be doing something other than binge-watching terrible TV shows and movies.

It also means Declan was able to go into work today and run some necessary errands. As much as he tells me he's happy to work from home, I'm aware this hasn't been easy on either of us. Being productive feels amazing.

"She's worried the obstacle course is going to be too hard,

and she doesn't want to end up with an injury right before the wedding."

I flip through my tablet, scanning the timeline with a frown. "The bachelorette party is two months before the wedding, though."

"That is correct," Harley says with pursed lips and a long exhale through her nose.

"And she's worried about injuries that last two months?" I recognize the irony considering my predicament, but running an obstacle course and being in a car accident are not the same thing.

"She's been watching wedding disaster videos, and now she's freaking out about everything," London says.

I roll my eyes. "Why do people do that?" Although, to be quite honest, I'd been obsessively looking at the research about multiple breaks and the lasting impacts this accident could have on my body. It was making me anxious, so I had to stop.

"People like to control the uncontrollable," Harley says.

She's not wrong, considering it's what I've been trying to do since they released me from the hospital. I'm beginning to see exactly how much of a challenge things at Spark House have been for my sisters. I'm usually the one talking clients off the ledge.

"Okay, so let's fix what we can so she's more comfortable. Since we're hosting the bachelorette party and the wedding, we need to make sure the bride feels good about whatever we have planned," I say. "Is her mother still taking the lead on the wedding preparations or has that changed?"

"Mom is still the go-to, for now, but the closer we get to the bachelorette party, the more involved the bride gets. Which I totally understand. Unfortunately she keeps changing her mind about things, and you know how hard it is to rush order stuff, not to mention expensive." London tosses another star on the coffee table, adding to the small pile she's created while we've been chatting.

"Okay, so she's worried the current obstacle course has too much potential for bruising. What if we do something water-oriented instead?"

London's eyes light up. "That might work. We did that event last year for the water polo team. Maybe we can recycle some of that stuff?"

"We might be able to. Water courses can be fairly simple, and we can use the indoor pool."

"Then we don't have to worry about the weather." London nods. "I love this already. Oh! Remember when we went to the Dominican Republic back when we were in college for winter break and they had that blow-up slide thing? That would be fun and safe, wouldn't it?"

"Yes! That's exactly what I was thinking." I tap my temple and grin at London, who already looks infinitely less stressed-out. "And this bride loves basketball, right?"

"She does. Total fanatic," Harley says.

"Okay, so we can make that part of the whole water setup. And we can use beach balls instead of basketballs, that way no one ends up with a black eye." If I could clap my hands, I totally would. "It'll be fun and easy and virtually impossible for anyone to get hurt."

"That is a fantastic idea!" Harley does the clapping for me.

I grab my iPad and use the speech-to-text function to search for inflatable slides. "It looks like we're in luck! Since it's the end of the season, they have a twenty-five percent off sale." I pass the device to Harley, who passes it to London.

"Oh! This is perfect. And it keeps the party under budget without cutting into profit, which is great because I was starting to worry we were going to end up way over, and I'd have to pull from the fountain budget to cover things while we wait for the balance of the payment, but it looks like we'll be fine."

"What about the alumni association? That contract should help balance things out, right?"

London's smile drops, and she waves a hand around in the air. "Oh, it'll be fine, especially now that we have a new plan, and this is a much cheaper option than anything else they've proposed. Besides, you know me, I always try to stay under budget. Anyway, have I mentioned how glad we are you're not all drugged up on painkillers anymore? We really needed your brain for this one." London melts back into her chair. "Honestly, I had no idea how much work went into the customer relations side of things. I have a new appreciation for how much time you spend fielding phone calls."

"Just start passing things over to me. I'll make phone calls, that way you can focus on the other stuff. And soon I'll be able to come back at least part-time. Maybe when I see the doctor this week, I can ask about coming in a couple of days a week?"

"I'm not going to lie, it would be great to have you around, especially to deal with client requests and issues." London bites her nail, looking cautiously optimistic.

"I'll ask my doctor what's reasonable, and we can go from there." I shift around on the couch, adjusting my leg on the stack of pillows.

"Do you want us to take you to your next appointment?" London asks.

"It's okay, Declan and I already have things set up. Besides, the back of his SUV has way more room than your Mini." Since the accident, she's been incredibly protective. I think it comes from a place of fear, but I haven't broached it with her, aware she's under more pressure than usual with Spark House.

"Okay, well, let us know if anything changes."

"I will." I roll my head on my shoulders, stretching my neck. The hardest part about having broken limbs is how unbalanced my body is. You never really know how hard it is to be down an arm and a leg until you can't use the ones you have. "Honestly, at this point the boredom is really the biggest obstacle, so being able to come back to Spark House, even if it's only once a week, would be great."

"Well, if you feel up to it, maybe you could start documenting your recovery more regularly?" Harley suggests. "The posts you've put up over the past couple of weeks have gotten great traction."

London nods her agreement. "We've had a lot of people asking about you. I bet they'd love more regular updates."

"Do you really think people want to know what shows I've been binging while my bones are healing, or the challenge of washing my hair with one hand?" I'm half joking, but at the same time, it doesn't actually sound like a bad idea.

"Honestly? Yup." Harley's eyes dart around, and she taps on the arm of the chair. "People love the personal posts, and they love it when they see people overcome adversity. Those physical therapy videos you posted last week had more than three thousand views."

"That's because I videoed Declan doing shirtless push-ups." And not the regular kind. The ones where he pushes up, claps, and then alternates one arm and then the other. It was impressive.

"Declan's push-ups aside, I think it would be a really great way to show our followers that you're doing well. And it'll help keep you occupied while you're recovering and give us extra content for our social media."

She holds out her phone and shows me a post she put up less than an hour ago. It's of me, on the couch, hair pulled up in a messy bun, my tablet in my lap, laughing at something Harley or London said.

It already has close to a thousand likes and a hundred comments, many of them wishing me well and happy to see that I'm back in action.

"We can call it your recovery journal. Maybe you can start with a couple of days a week on your profile and you can share it with the Spark House account. If you find it therapeutic, you can post more often," Harley says, her expression hopeful.

"I love the idea." And it's a great way for me to contribute in a meaningful way. For the first time since I came home from the hospital, I have something to be genuinely excited about and a sense of purpose again.

12

I PROBABLY SHOULD HAVE KNOCKED FIRST

DECLAN

I try to time getting home from work and running errands so that I don't run into London and Harley. Is it a wuss move? Yup. Do I feel bad about avoiding them? Not particularly, no.

I can handle Harley because, well, she's Harley. She's soft and sweet and understanding and forgiving. London and I pre-Avery's accident used to get along fine, but London post-accident is like an angry mama bear. I get it, the three of them are super tight and always have been, and the accident scared them.

So I understand why London is pissed at me, but it's been weeks and I still get the death glare every time I see her. Our regularly scheduled finance meeting is coming up, and suffice it to say, I'm not looking forward to it. I sent London the latest reports and told her they were not going to have the margin they planned for. But London has been dodging me, quick to tell me we can deal with things later, when she isn't pulling double duty.

Avery said it really isn't like London to hold a grudge and reassures me that she'll get over it. I'm not so sure I agree, but I'm figuring by the end of the next decade, she may find it in her heart to forgive me. Hopefully. If I'm lucky.

Thankfully, they're getting ready to leave when I walk in the door, so I don't have to deal with London's frostiness for too long.

"We'll be back on Thursday morning, okay? And remember, if you need us to handle appointments, or you want us to pick up any other *things* you might need, just let us know." London leans down to hug her sister. "You're almost out of crunchy peanut butter, FYI."

I'm not sure what kind of *things* Avery might need that I can't get for her, but I hold up a grocery bag, pleased with myself for noticing that we were low on the PB before I left this morning. "I picked some up on the way home."

"Oh, well that's good." London almost seems disappointed by my competence and thoughtfulness.

"We still on for that finance meeting, or do you need a little more time to get things together?" I ask.

"Let me get back to you on that." London turns back to Avery

"Sure thing. I just don't want to get too behind on the quarterly."

"Is there anything I can do to help?" Avery asks.

"Oh no, I've got it handled." She waves Avery's worry away. "We'll call you tomorrow to check in. And as soon as you get the go-ahead, we can plan an afternoon for you to come over or come to Spark House, or whatever you want. I'm sure you're ready for a change of scenery."

I relax a little once Avery's sisters leave. It's as if I'm being carefully observed when they're here, and it makes me antsy.

While I prepare dinner, Avery fills me in on her visit with her sisters.

"Harley suggested I start a recovery journal, but more of a visual one that I can share on our social media."

"That sounds cool; more like something that Harley would do, though, isn't it?" I chop vegetables for the salad, making sure the pieces are all bite-sized.

"It usually is, but I've been helping out with that a bit since I've been home."

"Oh?" I pause my chopping. "I didn't realize that."

"Other than physical therapy and doctor's appointments, I'm lying around, waiting to heal, so I started managing some of the social media posts for Harley. She has this whole system set up where she creates posts and puts them in a document with the text and images. I followed her lead and started scheduling things for her and I, uh . . . posted a couple of videos last week."

I resume my chopping. "Videos? Of what?"

"Oh, you know." She waves her phone around in the air and mutters, "Physical therapy stuff. You doing push-ups."

I nearly take off the end of my finger and set the knife down so I can give her my full attention. "Did you say me doing push-ups?"

Her grin is cheeky, but she flushes, which is a very un-Avery reaction. "You were showing off. Besides, our followers loved it, and it takes some of the pressure off Harley. Plus it gives me something productive to do that isn't watching TV and trying to fold laundry one-handed." She motions over to the couch where a basket sits.

For the first time, I notice that it's not her laundry, it's mine. "You don't have to fold my laundry."

"I didn't do a great job. And I figured you'd rather not have to put them on the refresh cycle and forget about them again."

"Thanks, that was nice of you. And it reminds me that I should drop my stuff off at the dry cleaners after dinner. If they're still open."

"It's already there. And I scheduled delivery."

"How did you get my stuff to the dry cleaners?"

"I had London and Harley take me. Anyway, when we go to the doctor's this week, I was thinking to ask about phasing in a day a week at Spark House."

I slide the chopped veggies into the frying pan and nod slowly. "If you think you're ready for that and you don't feel like it's going to set you back, I think that's a great idea."

"One day a week isn't too much, and the sooner I'm back to work, the better it's going to be for our bottom line. You know how London worries about the finances. She should feel better about that soon, though, especially with the alumni association coming on board."

I bite my tongue. After avoiding the conversation, London finally spilled the beans a couple of days ago that they didn't get the alumni contract, which explains why London is worried about staying under budget. I wanted to tell Avery right away, but London insisted that they wait, worried she'd try and jump straight back into working full-time and potentially set back her recovery. I don't quite agree this is the right way to handle things, but I can see her point, so I'm keeping my mouth shut for now. "Well, London always is more conservative when it comes to money and runs a tight ship. Now she's dealing with the other side of things, so . . ."

Avery makes a face. "Yeah, she likes working with other businesses, but problem-solving with bridezilla isn't her favorite."

"I don't know how you manage to keep your cool through this kind of thing. Sounds like a good reason not to get married." I bring the plates over to the couch. Avery has her lap tray set up, and I've cut the chicken into manageable-sized bites.

I learned that lesson the first time I made something that required a knife and fork and reduced her to tears of frustration. I can handle a lot of things, but seeing Avery cry is akin to drinking bleach. She doesn't get emotional to the point of tears often, and she hates it when she loses control like that. She's strong and proud and stoic in the face of a challenge, so seeing her break down over something as simple as not being able to cut her own food is not something I'd ever like to repeat.

She inhales deeply. "Oh man, this smells amazing. Please don't be offended if I can't finish it, though. London and Harley brought a charcuterie board with them, and I really went to town on it, especially all the stuff covered in chocolate." She stabs a piece of chicken parm. "And a bridezilla is not a reason to swear off marriage. Besides, it would be a travesty if you didn't share your culinary skill set with another person."

"I don't need to get married to do that." I motion to her as she pops the bite in her mouth and groans her food delight. "Case in point. And my relationship history should be enough of a red flag to send any smart woman running the other way."

Avery gives me a sidelong glancc. "Hookups don't really count as relationships, Deck."

I point a forkful of fusilli at her—spaghetti is on hold until she has the use of both hands again. "My point exactly."

"Just because you haven't had a relationship with substance doesn't mean you'd be bad in one."

"You grew up in a house with two parents who loved each other and treated each other with respect and consideration. My parents revenge-screwed their friends to piss each other off." Their relationship is like something out of a soap opera. It goes on and on, back and forth, and three decades later, they still haven't figured out that not talking to each other would be best for everyone, particularly me. "And I don't do emotional connections."

Talking about my lack of relationships with depth has never bothered me before, but then things have changed recently. Especially with how much time Avery and I have been spending together, and how much I seem to like it. We've always hung out a lot, but there is a certain level of intimacy that I'm not used to. And I'm reluctant to admit it, but I'm not immune to the way all that forced contact and proximity affects me.

That I willingly give her massages on a nearly daily basis without expecting anything in return—like a penis massage—says a lot about where I'm at with Avery, and I'd prefer to keep my head in the sand.

"We have an emotional connection." She points at me and goes back to eating the dinner she didn't think she'd be able to finish.

"It's not the same." I'm not wrong. My friendship with Avery means far more to me than every single girlfriend I've ever had combined. The possibility of messing that up with my hormones practically makes me break out in hives.

"Maybe not, but just pointing out that you're capable of them, is all." She nudges a piece of paper on the coffee table with her toe. "Oh, I got a little carried away and finished the first twenty across words, so it's your turn." Her smile holds an apology.

I'm grateful for the change of topic. "You've got some catching up to do so you might as well double down while you can. I can't tell you how much it's sucked having all these half-started crossword puzzles hanging around."

"You could've just done them, and don't get too excited. It looks like a kindergartner filled it out, so if you can't read something, ask me and I'll try to decipher my own writing for you, but no promises." Sharing the weekly crossword from the newspaper has been our thing since college.

"I have the ones you missed saved, and I only did the first ten down on them, so you can jump in on those when you're ready."

"You saved them?"

"Well, yeah. That's our thing, right?"

She tips her head, a small smile pulling at the corner of her full lips. "Yeah, I guess it is. How frustrating was it for you to only be able to finish them partway and then have to stop and wait for me to be lucid enough to finish my part?"

I shrug. I ended up buying a crossword puzzle book and finished half of all the puzzles since Avery and I always share them. I do some of the down, she works on the across, and we usually stop after the first ten words, but with her out of commission, they've been sitting there, waiting for her.

I figure if her life is on hold, most of the things in mine should be too.

Since Avery moved back into her bedroom, having mastered the art of getting in and out of her bed with the assistance of a crutch, the living room is now back to its pre-accident state. The hospital bed has been returned, and most of the furniture has been moved to its original place, with a few modifications so there are more straight lines for her to travel.

As Avery's injuries heal and she regains her mobility, her independence returns. At this point, she's managing to get to and from the bathroom on her own. She would love to be rid of the wheelchair, but her muscles fatigue easily, and it's a lot of work moving around a body with one arm and one leg out of commission.

It's Wednesday morning and I'm not heading into the office until later, but I still get up at the usual time so I can fit in a short workout. I use the treadmill in the gym in the building and head back to our condo to finish off with mat exercises.

I'm in the middle of a set of crunches when I notice Avery standing at the end of the hallway, her phone in her hand, aimed at me. "What are you doing?"

"Entertaining my followers. I saved the last video in my highlights, and it has over six thousand views. I figured they could use another hit of your abs. Maybe you should do a few burpees, just for fun."

"No one does burpees for fun, but I'll do a few for the sake of your entertainment." I roll to a sitting position and grab the towel at my side, swiping it over my face before I stand up and roll my head on my shoulders. "Ready for the gun show?" I waggle my brows and flex one of my biceps.

She shakes her head, but she's smirking. "Stop stalling, McCormick, and show us what you got."

I do a set of burpees, my sweatpants slipping lower and lower. I stop before I lose them and flash Avery. "How was that?"

"Good." She clears her throat. Her gaze moves slowly from

my waist back up to my face. "The fans will appreciate your dedication."

"I'm gonna jump in the shower. You want pancakes or something for breakfast?" I grab the towel from the floor.

"Yeah. Sounds good." She nods a few times, eyes bouncing around, face a little flushed.

"Do you need my help with anything first?"

She blinks a couple of times. "Uh, no. I'm good. I'll get changed and put on a pot of coffee."

"Sounds good." I brush by her on my way to my bedroom. Usually she'd be grossed out by the fact that I'm sweaty, but today she seems distracted. "You okay?"

"Yeah. Fine. Just burpee envy."

"Don't worry, Ave, you'll be back to hating burpees soon enough." I kiss her temple and head down the hall.

Fifteen minutes later I'm showered, and I pass Avery's closed bedroom door on the way to the kitchen, but pause when I hear a soft groan. I wait a few seconds, unsure if I'm imagining things, or maybe I stepped on the spot on the floor that creaks, but ten seconds later she groans again, longer and lower this time.

Worried she's hurt herself trying to get to the bathroom and isn't within reach of her phone, I wrench the door open. At first I'm confused, because Avery's expression isn't one I can read. At least until another low sound escapes her, and what I'm finally seeing makes more sense. It's also 100 percent not what I expect. And Avery most definitely did not hurt herself trying to get to the bathroom. At all.

Her nightshirt is pushed up high, exposing a few inches of toned stomach and a thin sheet covers most of the lower half of her body. Her uncasted leg is bent with her knee and calf peeking out from under the sheet. Her head is thrown back, exposing the smooth expanse of her throat. Her good arm is hidden under the sheets, but the angle and the way the sheets are moving tell me exactly where her hand is and exactly what she's doing under there.

She's so focused that she doesn't notice me standing in her doorway. And I'm so shocked, and maybe a little concerned, or enthralled by how aggressively her hand is moving under that sheet, that all I can seem to do is gawk.

She groans again, and this time it's one I'm familiar with because I've heard it a lot since the accident. Frustration.

"Come on!" The slap is unexpected and based on the sound, she isn't hitting the mattress.

I jump back, bashing my elbow into the doorjamb.

Her eyes pop open and her head lifts, gaze locking with mine.

"Shit! Sorry! I thought you'd hurt yourself." I back out of the room, slamming the door shut.

"What the fuck. What happened to knocking?" she yells from the other side.

"I'm really sorry!" I shout back.

I should move away from her door, but I don't. Instead, I stand there, like a dumbstruck idiot, with my hand still on the knob, trying to wrap my brain around what I walked in on. I don't know why I'm so surprised. I take care of my own needs at least once a day, so why wouldn't Avery do the same?

I've seen the black packages that come in the mail for her periodically, which indicates that she's managing her needs. Not once have I allowed myself to think about what that might look like or sound like. But now I've seen and heard it, and based on what's going on below the waist, my body would very much like to witness that again. I shake my head, trying to make the images disappear and force my body to calm the heck down. "I'll get breakfast started." I figure the best way to deal with this is to go about things like normal and pretend it didn't happen.

I've managed to get my body under control again by the time Avery appears in the kitchen.

"Hey!" I cringe at the high, almost-prepubescent pitch of my voice and the excessive chipperness.

All I get in return is a grunt. She adjusts her crutch under her arm, hops a couple of times as she finds her balance and opens the cupboard door.

"What do you need? I can help."

She wobbles, and an elbow gets me in the side as she reaches up to open the cupboard. "I got it, thanks."

She finally manages to grab the knob, but she loses her hold on her crutch in the process and hops perilously on one foot. I catch it before it hits the ground and wrap my other arm around her waist to keep her steady.

"I'm really sorry, Ave. I thought maybe you'd fallen and hurt yourself. I should've knocked first."

"I should've locked my door," she mumbles, face red, refusing to meet my gaze.

"You don't need to be embarrassed about it, okay? We all masturbate." I pull down a coffee mug and move around to her other side to grab the carafe. The last thing I need is Avery spilling hot coffee on herself.

"Please, Deck, I'm good without the pro–self-exploration pep talk."

"It's a good thing you're getting your drive back, right? It means you're healing." I fight a cringe. There's a solid chance I'm making things worse. While we've jokingly talked about my masturbation habits in the not-so-distant past, talking about it and witnessing it firsthand are two totally different things.

"Seriously, Declan, can you please drop it? The cheerleading isn't really all that helpful." She dumps a heaping spoon of sugar into her coffee and stirs it aggressively. Coffee sloshes over the side of the cup.

"You're not mad at me, are you? It was an honest mistake." I can't read her right now.

She sighs and tosses the spoon into the sink. "I'm not mad at you. I'm frustrated."

That doesn't make a whole lot of sense. "Shouldn't you be relaxed?"

"Yes, Declan, I should be relaxed, but I'm not because I couldn't finish. I can't maneuver properly and it's too freaking awkward to manage dual stimulation."

"Dual stimulation?" I have no idea what she's talking about, and I'm pretty sure where my mind has gone can't be right.

Her face turns red. "Both buttons need to be pressed at the same time."

"Both buttons?" *What the hell kind of high-tech vibrator is she using?*

"The G-spot and the bean! I don't even know why I'm explaining this to you. It's the girl equivalent of blue balls!" She waves her left hand around. "I'm probably not going to have a freaking orgasm until this stupid cast comes off, unless you're planning to help me out with that too!" She spins around, leaving her coffee on the counter, and clomp-crutches back down the hall to her room, slamming the door behind her.

I don't yell after her to stop, or try to apologize again. Frankly, I'm stunned and working to process all of this information.

I'm not sure how to deal with a sexually frustrated Avery, especially if it means I'm going to spend the next few weeks having my head bitten off on a daily basis. If this morning's reaction is anything to go on, and her frustration grows over time—I'm imagining what it would be like not to be able to take care of my own needs for more than a month, and the prospect of that looks pretty damn grim—then I'm thinking the coming weeks are going to be rough.

This morning is definitely not going how I thought it would. And now, faced with what I walked in on, my body is telling me something I've been trying very hard to deny—I have feelings for Avery. Non-platonic, very unfriend-like, and nowhere in the realm of brotherly.

I don't want her to be embarrassed or angry, so I steel my resolve and head down the hall, prepared to face her—with her coffee in hand, of course.

This time I knock on her door. "Ave? I have your coffee." I'm met with silence. "Can I come in?"

I can almost hear her sigh. "Yeah."

I poke my head in the door and find Avery sitting in bed, laptop tray in front of her, tapping away on the keyboard, her face red, her gaze unable to meet mine.

"Are you okay?" I glance around the room as I set her coffee on the nightstand, trying not to visualize what I walked in on not that long ago.

She pauses her typing and arches a brow. "Do you actually want the truth or do you want me to tell you I'm fine?"

13

IT'S A GREAT IDEA

AVERY

Declan is standing beside my bed with his hands jammed into his sweatpants pockets. It's basically all he wears these days. Gray sweats that, depending on how he's standing or sitting, sometimes give me a great view of what he's packing behind that fabric.

I've been trying and failing not to notice how good he looks in those sweats, but this morning was the straw that broke the camel's back, and apparently my resolve. I've been trying to tell myself it's deprivation that makes him more appealing these days, but that's a lie. We've been spending so much time together and he's been so attentive, so good about anticipating all of my needs, there to motivate me with physical therapy, with everything really, that it's become impossible not to see him through different eyes. And realize that what I'm feeling has been there all along. I just pushed those feelings down and tried to suffocate them.

He clears his throat. "I don't want you to lie, but I don't want to make you uncomfortable either."

I sigh in defeat. "Unless you have the sudden magical ability to make me spontaneously orgasm, I don't know that there is anything you can actually do." I try to make it sound like a joke, but I'm not sure I'm successful. Spontaneous orgasms would be a great superpower, though.

"Uh, I was thinking maybe we could get some ice cream or something." He chuckles nervously.

"At nine thirty in the morning?"

"What about chocolate chip pancakes, then? Chocolate is supposed to be a good substitute for orgasms, isn't it?"

I arch a brow. "If you'd gone without an orgasm for weeks, would chocolate be a reasonable substitute for you?"

He makes a face. "Not really, no."

I consider how much longer it's going to be before I can get myself off on my own again, especially with my preferred arm in a cast and my limited mobility. I have a couple more weeks before the cast on my arm comes off, and even then, I'll need rehab before my hand is up for the task. It's an unreasonable length of time to go without an orgasm.

Especially not with Declan still helping me with showers and doing shirtless burpees, looking more and more delicious with every passing day. The attraction I once felt back when we were freshman in college seems to have found its way out of the friendship box I stuffed it into years ago.

I bite my nail as heat creeps into my cheeks. Declan and I have been more touchy-feely lately. We used to sit at opposite ends of the couch, but now he's always next to me and keeps his arm around me. And whenever we pass each other, I find myself reaching out. But it's gone beyond that. When he's done rubbing my back, he'll often pull me back against his chest and snuggle with me for a while. There's been more than one occasion where I've *felt* him. It's excited me more than I care to admit.

"Maybe you could help me." The words pop out, more accidental than purposeful, but it's too late to call them back.

Declan blinks at me. "I'm sorry, what?"

I swallow down my mortification. "Nothing. Never mind. I'm kidding. Obviously."

He crosses the room to come to the edge of the bed, his expression shifting from shock to something I can't read. "I don't think you are."

"Just forget I said anything. I'm frustrated and talking out of my ass."

"What's the longest you've gone without an orgasm?"

"I don't know. Like the first seventeen years of my life." I'm embarrassed, and I don't want to get into this with him, but at the same time I do.

"I don't mean when you first had an orgasm. What's the longest you've gone since then?" His voice is quiet and low, and the way he's looking at me makes it hard to hold his gaze, so I stare at his fingers, gliding across the fabric near my leg.

"Until this accident, maybe three days, but I had the flu and I could barely get out of bed."

"I imagine that's pretty uncomfortable, then." His fingertips graze my knee and my skin breaks out in a wave of goose bumps.

"It is," I whisper.

"Avery." His voice is gravelly.

I lift my head slowly, gaze dragging along his forearm, catching at his waist, where I can very much see the effect this conversation is having on him. "I can't focus on anything," I admit. "It's such a distraction." He's a distraction. The kind that makes my current predicament even worse. "Just forget I said anything. I'll deal." Or die of embarrassment.

Declan's chest rises and falls with every uneasy breath, and he rubs his fingers over his bottom lip. His throat bobs with a nervous swallow. "Ask me again. I wasn't ready before." His heavy, fiery gaze meets mine.

I don't know what's happening here, but I feel powerless to stop the words from pouring out, and I'm not even sure I'd want to if I could. "Will you help me?"

"Be explicit, Avery. Ask me for exactly what you want so I know we're on the same page."

"I've already said it. Why do you need me to say it again?"

"You're in a very vulnerable position. I don't ever want to take advantage of you, so you need to be very sure about what you want."

"I want you to touch me," I say but can't meet his eyes.

He puts a finger under my chin and gently urges me to raise my head so I meet his gaze. "If we're going to do this, we need to talk about it. Let me be very clear that it won't be like when I help you out with showers or back rubs."

"You don't have to—" I'm terrified. I'm the one who put this on the table, but I didn't think about the consequences of actually going through with it.

"Listen." He cups my cheek in his palm and covers my lips with his thumb. "I'm telling you if we do this, it won't be because I only want to help you, which obviously I do. If we go through with this, it's because I want to be the one who makes you feel good. Because I may need it as much as you do."

"Oh." I breathe the word.

He smiles a little; it's nervous and maybe slightly chagrined. "Yes, oh. So, now that you know where I stand, tell me, what do you want?"

We stare at each other for a few heavy heartbeats, and his thumb strokes along the edge of my jaw. "I want you to touch me and make me feel good. Give me the release I need."

"Because you think I can help?" There's a waver in his voice, a hint of vulnerability.

"Because you're my best friend and I trust you. And because I want it to be you." I pause and bite my lip. "And because I'm attracted to you, and I don't know how many more showers I can handle without losing my mind."

He laughs a little. "I feel exactly the same way, about all of those things."

"Can I have five minutes in the shower alone to get ready?" I'm already zinging below the waist.

"You can have whatever you need." He kisses my temple. "You tell me when you're ready for me and I'll be waiting."

14

I'LL MAKE IT BETTER FOR YOU

DECLAN

I glance at the clock again. Avery has been in there for seven minutes now. I rushed to my room, had the world's fastest shower to rinse off the workout sweat, and put on a pair of swim shorts. Now I'm sitting on the edge of her bed, waiting for her to call me into the bathroom.

This isn't a good idea. I know it's not.

But I can't deny this attraction anymore.

More than that, I don't want to.

All the feelings and thoughts I've kept a lid on since I first met her are suddenly popping out like those stupid Whac-A-Mole things that are nearly impossible to bop on the head before they go back into hiding.

Except this time, all my feelings are right in front of me. Clear and painfully obvious. I don't know when things shifted, but they have. And now I'm sitting here, waiting for her to call me into the bathroom so our relationship can be irreparably changed.

If I hadn't interrupted her, I wouldn't be sitting outside her bathroom, listening to the shower, waiting for her to call me in. I can't decide if that is a good thing or a very bad thing.

"You can come in now!" she shouts.

I'm not sure if I imagine the uncertainty in her voice, or if it's in my head.

I brace my hands on my knees and push up off the edge of her bed. My excitement and anxiety spike as I cross the room. There's no going back now. For better or worse, this is going to happen.

I push open the door, expecting her to be dressed the same way she always is for shower time: in a pair of side-tie bikini bottoms and one of those tube bra things.

Except that's not at all how she's dressed.

Avery is naked. Totally, gloriously naked. And wet.

Wet and naked.

I've been in the shower with Avery countless times since she's come home from the hospital. I've seen her in bathing suits plenty of times. But this is very, very different. She's bare and vulnerable.

Her gaze darts from my face to her lap, where she's holding the showerhead, aiming it at the bottom of the tub.

"You're fucking gorgeous, Avery." My voice is gritty.

She peeks up at me, uncertainty and desire mixing with her nerves. So of course she makes a joke. "I think the casts really add to my allure."

"They make you badass and a warrior." I cross the room and climb over the edge of the tub and wrap my arms around her from behind. Bending, I kiss her temple. "You're in charge, Avery. Whatever you need, I'll give it to you."

"Okay." She exhales a tremulous breath and tips her chin down, focusing on her feet. I note the almost imperceptible shake in her hand, her peaked nipples, and the way the toes on her unbroken leg curl when my lips brush her cheek.

I give in to the urge to touch her in the ways I've tried not to think about over the past few years. I drag my fingers along her shoulder, up the side of her neck, watching her skin pebble under my touch. I continue along her throat, cupping under her chin so I can tip it up.

I move closer so her crown rests against my diaphragm. Her lids lift and she meets my gaze.

I stroke along the edge of her jaw. "Can I start by washing your hair?" It seems like a better choice than just jumping right into things. Besides, I have a feeling the hair washing gets Avery a little ramped up, and I want her to be that way because she's turned on, not because she's anxious and worried or embarrassed.

She nods once, and I release her chin, rinse her hair, and lather it up with shampoo. I have to force myself to slow down and take my time. I run my thumbs down the back of her neck and skim the sensitive spot behind her ear. She melts into my touch, head tipping back, eyes falling closed. Her good hand flutters in the air and lands at the base of her throat, then slides down, fingertips dragging gently over a peaked nipple before it skims across her stomach and settles on her upper thigh.

I rinse out the shampoo and finger-comb her hair before I twist it and pull it over her shoulder.

Her fingertips press into the top of her thigh and her throat bobs with a heavy swallow.

"Tell me how you're feeling," I murmur.

"Nervous, desperate, turned on," she whispers.

"It's okay to want some relief." I sweep my fingers down the side of her neck. "But if you want me to stop at any point, just tell me, okay?"

"Okay." She nods once. "But I already know I'm not going to want you to stop."

"Tell me where you want me to touch you."

Her hand drifts up, fingers brushing over her nipple. "Here would be nice."

She sucks in a quick breath when I circle the other nipple and pinch it between my thumb and finger, tugging gently. I move in closer, my chest pressed against her warm back, and bend until my mouth is beside her ear again. "How's that, Avery? Does it feel good?"

She makes a deep sound, almost like a purr, as she arches into my touch.

"Is that a yes? Or a no?"

I start to move my hand away, but she whispers, "Yes. It's a yes. I want more. Please."

"I should keep touching you?" I drag my lips along her skin, biting gently when I reach the base of her neck, tasting her skin for the first time. She's sweet and warm under my tongue. Addicting. Enthralling.

"Yes, please." Her hand comes up, fingers twining in my hair as she tips her head, giving me better access to her neck. "I like that. Do it again."

"Which part? This?" I tug her nipple. "Or this?" And drag my teeth across her skin.

She groans. "Both."

I nibble my way up her neck. "What now?"

"I want you to make me feel good."

I allow my fingers to travel slowly down between her breasts and over her stomach. "Like this?"

She bites her bottom lip. "Yes, please, exactly like that."

"Avery." I circle her navel and her muscles jump and tighten, but this time it seems more like anticipation than uncertainty.

"Mmm." She shifts her hips, and the fingers still twined in my hair tighten as I take her earlobe between my teeth and tug. I slide my free hand under her chin and tip it toward me.

My lips sweep across her cheek until I reach the corner of her mouth. She stills and sucks in a quick breath. "Declan?" She drags her tongue across her bottom lip, so soft and full and inviting. Wisps of uncertainty float away as her gaze lifts to mine.

"Can I kiss you? Would that be okay?"

"Please. Yes." She tugs on the back of my neck, pulling me closer.

I brush my lips over hers, tentative at first. At the same time I ease my hand lower, dipping between her thighs.

Her mouth opens on a gasp, and I slant mine over hers, sliding my tongue inside, stroking against hers in the same rhythm as my fingers swirling around her sensitive skin.

"Oh, that's . . ." Her nails dig into the back of my neck, and she rolls her hips. "Yes, please. Don't stop doing that," she murmurs against my lips.

I chuckle and continue to tease her, taking my cues from the way her soft moans grow deeper, her lazy hip rolls become jerky, and her sounds grow needier.

"It's not going to be enough. I won't be able to finish," she groans into my mouth, biting my bottom lip.

"Hey." I disengage from the kiss, thumb smoothing back and forth across the edge of her jaw. "We have nothing but time, and

I promised I'd take care of you, and I will. Tell me what you need so I can give it to you."

"I need more." She almost seems apologetic, which I don't quite understand.

I press the heel of my palm against that sensitive, swollen nub and curl my fingers.

I'm rewarded with a gasp of surprise followed by another sweet moan.

And then it clicks: This is what Avery meant about hitting both buttons at the same time.

"Is that better?" I shift, kneeling on the edge the tub, and nip along her jaw again, amazed at how natural it feels to be like this with Avery. I love how soft she is, how we both seem to give ourselves over to the intimacy of it.

"Yes, so much better, thank you." She skims my forearm, following a thick vein all the way down.

She covers my hand with hers, pushing down, grinding harder against my palm.

"You need more, still?" I murmur in her ear.

She bites her lip and nods, hand curling over mine.

"You tell me when it's enough, okay, baby?"

She nods, her hand still covering mine, adding pressure. We kiss and move together, Avery rolling her hips, her body pliant and liquid, her hums and gasps tell me she's getting closer. And then she goes rigid; a low, primal moan bubbles up and breaks free. She shifts to grip the edge of the seat, forearm taut as she struggles to maintain some kind of control over her body.

"Let go, baby, you know you want to." I bite her shoulder, and like I promised, she comes, shaking and groaning. "So sexy," I murmur in her ear as her body goes lax and she melts against me.

"Holy crap." Her head lolls and she nuzzles into my neck. I kiss her cheek and back down to her mouth, and she opens for me, tongue stroking in slow, leisurely sweeps for long minutes before we finally part. I could keep going, but the water is growing tepid, so I turn off the shower and grab her a towel.

For a moment I worry that things are going to suddenly become awkward and uncomfortable, but she smiles up at me. "Thank you, I feel so much better."

"Absolutely my pleasure." I lean in and kiss her quickly on the lips, lingering for a second. "I'll be right back."

"Where are you going?" she calls after me.

"To get your chair."

She scoffs. "I can manage getting from here to my dresser, I just need your help getting out of the tub."

I nab a towel to wrap around my own hips, and hopefully conceal the issue I'm currently rocking below the waist. "Most of the time I might agree with you, but you're looking pretty boneless right now, so let's not kill your afterglow with too much exertion."

She sighs but doesn't argue, maybe seeing my point.

I bring her chair into the bathroom and help her out of the tub, wheeling her to her bedroom.

"I can help you get dressed." I grab the panties and bra set neatly on the edge of the vanity and bring them to her.

"I can manage on my own."

"Let me rephrase. I'd like to help you get dressed."

"You don't have to worry about me getting all sketchy on you, Declan," she says softly.

"That's not what I'm worried about."

"But you are worried about something," she presses.

There's a shift in the energy between us. The atmosphere is

heavier now, laden down with new knowledge. There's chemistry between us, the kind that's going to be impossible to ignore moving forward, because judging by what happened in the shower, sex with Avery would be mind-blowing. But I have no idea how far we're going to take this, or even how far we should. So I deflect with humor.

"I'm worried about you falling on your face while you're trying to put these on and breaking your perfect nose." I drop to my knee in front of her and slide the underwear carefully up her casted leg.

Getting underwear on is a bit of a feat with a broken leg and a cast that ends mid-thigh. It's not a problem getting it over her foot and her shin, even her knee isn't too bad, but Avery is an athlete and an avid soccer player, so she's got some serious thigh muscles and that means it takes some work getting them over the last six inches. Normally this is when I'd leave Avery to manage on her own.

But this time I don't.

15

NOT WHAT I EXPECTED, BUT I LIKE IT

AVERY

Everything and nothing has changed.

The energy around us is charged and electric as his hands disappear under the towel, along with my panties. My horrible, ugly granny panties. Which, based on what's happening inside Declan's swim shorts, he doesn't seem to mind.

He takes my hand and places it on his shoulder. "Lift for me." His voice is low and husky, and his tongue sweeps out to wet his bottom lip.

It makes me wonder what it would feel like to have his mouth where his fingers were not that long ago. It also makes me wonder if that's likely to happen in the near future. And whether it's a good idea to continue down this path.

I plant my foot on the floor and brace my hand on his shoulder, tilting my hips so he can pull my underpants up. I expect him to back out of my personal space as soon as my rear hits the chair again, but that's not what happens.

Declan's fingertips trail up my sides, causing my skin to pebble in a wave. He pauses when he reaches my breast, eyes lifting to meet mine. "May I?"

I glance at the clock on the nightstand. I have lots of time before Harley is supposed to be here. I suppress a grin. "Sure, go ahead."

He cups my breasts in his palms, thumbs brushing over the already taut nipples and leans in, nuzzling between them before he turns his head and bites the swell. His dark hair tickles my skin, a stark contrast to the way his stubbled chin chafes against my breast. "Hi there," he murmurs into my chest.

I laugh, because what other response is there? "Obviously you're a boob man."

"I'm an everything man, but yours are particularly glorious, and I didn't get a chance to properly appreciate them in the shower, so I figured I could do that now, before I finish helping you get dressed." He kisses his way over the swell, circling my nipple with the tip of his nose before his lips brush over it. "If that's okay with you."

"It's definitely okay with me."

My chuckle fades and becomes a soft sigh as his lips part and his mouth closes over the puckered tip. His tongue sweeps in a slow, sensual circle, tasting me before he sucks gently. I exhale a shuddering breath as my nerve endings light up again, the sensation traveling down between my legs. He switches breasts, thumb and finger teasing the abandoned wet peak as he lavishes the same attention on the other one.

Declan braces his hands on the arms of my chair, lips skimming my neck, teeth nipping at my jaw. I tip my head in the opposite direction, opening for him as he slants his mouth over mine. I sink into the lazy kiss and let it coat me like warm chocolate syrup.

Eventually he releases my mouth and backs up only far enough that he can meet my gaze with an earnest one of his own. "I'm here for you whenever you need me, Avery, whatever you need me for."

I shiver at his words, but don't have the chance to respond because my phone pings with a message, breaking the heavy tension.

"That's Harley." Declan passes me the phone, and I quickly scan the message. "She's going to be here in twenty minutes and I'm not even close to ready."

"I'll leave your nipples alone and help you get dressed." He pushes to a stand and adjusts himself. I can see the outline of the ridge pressing against the blue material of his swim trunks. If we had more time, I'd offer to return the favor.

Declan helps me into my bra, adjusting the cups at least three times before he brings me my dress. My casted arm goes through first, then my working arm before he pulls it over my head and helps me smooth it down.

"Do you want me to blow-dry your hair for you while you work on this?" He makes a circular motion around his face.

I don't have the time or the ability to do much with it on my own. "I can pull it up in a ponytail."

"I can still dry it for you; there's a bit of a chill this morning."

I fully anticipate the hair drying experience to be something of a cluster, since I doubt he's had much experience in this area, if any at all. But he's surprisingly gentle and adept.

While he manages the hair dryer, I swipe a coat of mascara on my lashes, dust my lids in neutral shadow, and dab a little concealer under my eyes and across the bridge of my nose, hiding the faded remnants of the yellowed bruises.

"Okay, I need to know where you learned how to blow-dry hair, because that is not a skill set typically honed by any men other than stylists."

Declan chuckles. "That's a bit of a sexist stereotype, isn't it?" He takes the rounded brush and slowly drags it down the length of my hair, the dryer following along.

"Based on all the pictures I've seen, you've never had long hair, so unless you secretly studied to be a stylist back in the day, I'm going to go ahead and say this is a skill set you've acquired for another reason."

"When I was a kid, my great-grandmother lived next door to us. She had really long hair, like down to her butt, even though she was in her eighties. When I was really little, like preschool age, I used to go over there and hang out while she watched *The Price Is Right*."

"Aww, that's sweet."

"Well, she used to give me these candies that were coated in powdered sugar. They were imported from England and whenever she got to the end of a tin, she'd let me eat all the powdered sugar at the bottom, so don't give me too much credit." His expression softens and his gaze takes on that faraway quality, as if he's reliving those childhood memories. "I always went there when my parents were fighting, which was often. Anyway, when she was in her late eighties, she fell and sprained her wrist. You know how bad sprains can be and how long they can take to heal."

I sure do. And so does Declan. We've both sustained a variety of minor injuries over the years. It's part of the deal when you play a lot of sports, even if they're recreational.

"My parents didn't want the responsibility of helping her with her hair every day. She would brush it, then braid it, and pin it to the top of her head like a crown. It was part of her daily routine, and I hated the idea of her cutting off all of that hair. It was part of who she was. I started getting up extra early in the morning, so I could go over there and help her before I had to go to school."

"That is honestly the sweetest thing I've ever heard." Declan has always been an intensely loyal friend. He may be relationship averse, but the people he cares about always come first with him.

Declan shrugs. "She always gave me a treat to pack in my lunch, like a chocolate bar, or something my parents never would have been okay with. It'd never make it to my lunch, either, because I'd eat it on the walk to school and be all hopped-up on sugar."

"Still, that's pretty awesome. You two must have been tight."

Declan nods. "Oh yeah, I spent a lot of time there, and she was really patient with me about the braids. They turned out like shit for the first few weeks, but after a while I got good at it. When she was ninety, she fell again and broke the same wrist she sprained with the first fall. That was when my parents decided she should probably go into a home. She was super pissed, like man, she felt betrayed, but they got her a spot in the place right down the street from us, so I still went and visited her a lot. She was an awesome great-grandmother and a safe place for me growing up."

In all the years I've known Declan, he's never really opened up about his family, and maybe now I understand a bit better as to why. With parents who fought and philandered on each other relentlessly, I can only imagine how desperate Declan would have been to have some kind of stable role model in his life.

"She sounds like a wonderful woman."

"You would have loved her, and she would have loved you. I still miss her, even though she's been gone more than a decade." He turns off the hair dryer, unplugs it, and sets it on the vanity to cool. "Okay, you're looking sexy as hell, and Harley is going to be here any minute. You want me to help get the rest of your stuff ready, so you don't have to keep her waiting?"

"That'd be great." I let him gather my purse and my crutch and wheel me out to the living room, a little sad that he's so quick to turn off his emotions, especially when I feel like he's given me a little piece of himself after such an intimate morning together.

He rushes to change into a pair of jeans and a T-shirt before Harley arrives, and insists on helping me to the car.

"Don't let her overexert herself, and twenty minutes max on the crutches at a time, or she'll fatigue her muscles too quickly and she'll be sore," Declan tells her on the trip down to the lobby.

I'm a little annoyed by all the mother bird restrictions Declan is laying out for me. "I'm not a kid. I know my limits."

Harley and Declan exchange a glance.

"Knowing and abiding by them are two totally different things," Harley says.

"Whatever, I'll be fine."

Declan squeezes my shoulder. "I know you will, because Harley won't let you push yourself too hard today. Have fun, be safe, and don't overdo it. Send me dinner requests, and I'll make sure we're all stocked up." He helps me into the back seat—I'm still not particularly comfortable in a car, let alone the front seat, not that I can fit in easily with my cast. "Message when you get to Spark House, so I know you're safe, okay?"

"Okay."

For a moment I think he's going to lean in and kiss me, but he backs out and closes the door gently. He and Harley have a brief conversation. They're too quiet for me to make out what they're saying, but I assume it's about what I can and can't do.

A minute later Harley slides into the driver's seat. Her gaze meets mine in the rearview mirror. "You okay back there?"

"Yup." I give her a thumbs-up as she pulls away from the curb and heads for the exit.

I glance back at Declan, still standing on the sidewalk, one thumb hooked into his jeans, the other sweeping back and forth across his bottom lip before he lifts it in a parting wave.

The way my heart skips a beat makes me question how big the can of worms I've opened is after this morning. Especially considering how much I already want it to happen again.

16

BACK IN THE SADDLE

AVERY

"So." I don't have to see her face to see the arch in her brow. "How are things going with Declan?"

"Fine. Why?" My voice is pitchy, and I spit the words out too quickly. I can also feel my face heating up.

Harley chuckles knowingly. "Your poker face needs a lot of work."

Now that the orgasm is over, and I'm no longer riding the high, I can see how this could be a new level of complication for Declan and me to deal with, particularly since he's currently my primary caregiver. But I'm starting to get my mobility back, little by little, so I won't need to rely on him quite as much.

"What is that supposed to mean?"

"It means your face is all red, and you look like the cat who ate the canary."

I debate whether I want to say anything to Harley about what happened this morning. The three of us don't generally keep secrets from one another, and I'm not entirely sure I'll be able to keep it from either of my sisters, even if I wanted to.

"Maybe it should wait until we get to Spark House. What kind of mood is London in this morning?"

"Oh my God! Does this mean you two hooked up?" Harley's eyes light up like it's Christmas baking day—which incidentally is her favorite time of year. Any time she can make cookies and tarts, she's a happy camper.

"Do I look like I'm in any kind of condition to entertain a hookup?" I motion to my half-casted form.

"Something happened though, right? Like something had to have happened. Did you make out? Did he kiss you? Was there groping?"

"I'm answering none of these questions right now."

She hits the brakes a little harder than necessary when a light changes yellow—she's been driving extra cautiously on my behalf, aware I'm still nervous. She glances in the rearview mirror and claps excitedly. "Something totally went down! Your face is so red right now. This is so exciting!"

"You sound like you've been waiting for this to happen," I mutter.

She gives me an incredulous look. "Seriously, Ave?"

"Seriously what?"

"Oh come on, you two have been friends for years and you freaking live together. I sort of expected something to happen a lot sooner, but times of crisis have a way of either pulling people apart or bringing them closer together." Her expression turns wistful for a moment.

"I don't think London is going to be nearly as excited about this as you are. And you never answered my question about what kind of mood she's in."

Harley glances at me briefly before she focuses on the road again. "She's a little stressed out."

"Is that why it's just you picking me up, or is there more to it?" I press. "Did something happen with that photographer guy she's been seeing?"

"It's not about Daniel. They're still seeing each other." Harley taps the wheel with a sigh. "I need to tell you something."

"This doesn't sound good." Anxiety makes my throat tight. "Did something happen?"

"It's more like something didn't happen." She makes a face. "We didn't get the alumni account for your university."

"What? Why not? It was practically in the bag; my meeting was supposed to be a formality."

"Yeah, I know. But it was a formality when you were involved. We pitched your ideas, but without your knowledge to back it all up, and with the uncertainty of when you'd be able to work on the project, they didn't feel good about making the commitment. London was crushed, and she's been afraid to tell you because she doesn't want you to be upset with her."

"Why would I be upset with her?" Am I disappointed? Sure. But it's not her fault it didn't work out.

"Because her pitch flopped. She's really struggling, Ave. And I don't want to put this on you because you have enough to deal with, but I don't think either of us realized exactly how much weight you pull at Spark House until you weren't there to pull it. This is your passion and it always has been. You live and breathe Spark House. You make everything look so easy and effortless, when really it's not."

She's not wrong. Until this accident, the only thing I did other than work was hang out with Declan and the guys and play rec soccer. Even now, with my being stuck at home, I'm still trying to get stuff done, although it's not as easy doing it remotely. Still, I don't want my sisters to feel like losing the alumni account means they've somehow failed. "I just talk a good game."

"Uh, that's absolutely not true. You have an incredible presence and people are drawn to you. That's a fact." She blows out a breath. "So yeah, that's where London's at this morning."

"So maybe I should keep my mouth shut about Declan, then."

"You can try, but I doubt you'll be successful. London will pick up on something, and if you keep it from her, it'll hurt her feelings. You and I both know how sensitive she is."

Harley's not wrong. London is incredibly sensitive. She just hides it well.

Harley makes a right onto the long, winding driveway leading to Spark House, the massive mansion-style hotel we've turned into a unique event space. Pink ribbons adorn the lampposts and huge, tacky metallic pink unicorns are interspersed between them.

"It looks like we're prepping for a six-year-old's birthday party, not a bachelorette," I remark.

"Just you wait until you see the food and cake designs. I have never met an adult woman so in love with pink and unicorns, makes me wonder if she was either deprived as a kid or totally overindulged."

"Maybe both?"

"Probably. In the past few days we've learned that she's a bit of a hypochondriac, and her love of sports was an exaggeration. Apparently, she and her sister don't always see eye to eye on things."

"Oh man, this sounds like it's going to be messy."

"It's possible. According to the maid of honor, our lovely bride threw her sister's bachelorette party. She invited a hundred people, most of them *her* friends, not her sister's, and took her to a dance club and got her super shit-faced."

"Oh no."

"It gets better."

"Do you mean worse?"

"Absolutely. So when the bride-to-be's sister was getting married, she had asked for a weekend getaway with her closest friends because she *hates* bars. And her sister, the current bride, didn't bother to invite any of them."

"Which makes this a revenge bachelorette party?" This could be a complete nightmare. "I can't believe you didn't say anything to me about this until now. No wonder London is so stressed."

"Well, we just found out about the previous bachelorette party over the weekend. Apparently, the sister has been keeping the maid of honor from saying anything because she's got some dirt on her. Anyway, it's a total soap opera, but I think we've got it mostly under control."

"Is all the pink part of the revenge or what?"

"Oh no, that's legitimately what the bride wants. She actually asked if we could dye a white horse pink and put a horn on it so she can ride it like a magical unicorn princess."

"You told her no, right?"

Harley gives me one of her famous looks. "I informed her that we couldn't do that to a horse, but if she'd like to take her dog to the salon and see if they'd be willing to take on that challenge, we would happily find him a unicorn costume."

I give my head a shake. "And what does the groom have to say about that?"

"Not a lot, really. He has the backbone of an amoeba. It's very clear that she's the dominant one in that relationship."

"I'm so sorry you and London have had to deal with this on your own. I'm glad I'm finally back, at least in some capacity. You two are going to need a vacation when this is all over."

"We'll be fine. And London has managed the stress surprisingly well. Although, she has made about five million of those star things. I'm literally finding them everywhere. It's almost like the sky is falling. But it would be great to have your input on some of the events coming up later in the fall."

"All I want is to be productive again. I wish I could help London with the creative stuff, but I'm not great at it with two hands, let alone one."

"That's London's Zen place anyway. She would spend all day making centerpieces if she could." She parks in the spot right in front of Spark House and reaches over to squeeze my hand. "I'm really glad you're on the mend. I can't tell you how scared we were."

"I know." I squeeze her hand back. "Me too."

Her eyes go all soft and watery. Out of the three of us, Harley is the most prone to showing emotion. If she starts to cry, I'll probably end up doing the same. "I put mascara on today and I have no idea if it's waterproof or not, so don't you dare get weepy on me."

She waves me off and gets out of the car, grabbing my chair from the trunk. I'd love to be able to crutch around, but thanks to freaking Declan with his don't-overdo-it speech, I doubt Harley will make it that easy for me. Besides, she and London have already been through a broken, pinned ankle with me before, so it's not as though they don't know what I'm like during recovery.

As soon as I'm given the go-ahead, I tend to push myself too hard, too fast. Since they know that, they're bound to put up a few roadblocks so I don't overdo it and set myself back.

"What about the crutch?" I ask as I pull myself out of the back seat and pivot so I can drop down into the chair.

"You can have that later." She wheels me up the ramp and hits the button, so the door opens automatically for us.

I inhale a deep breath and exhale on a sigh as I take in the familiar sights, sounds, and smells of Spark House and then frown. "Does it smell like cotton candy in here?"

"Indeed, it does."

"Does that mean there's also a cotton candy machine somewhere around here?"

"Also, a yes."

In addition to the gaudy pink and unicorn theme, there's a carnival-style component to this bachelorette party that will continue through the wedding theme. Because that's where these two met, at a carnival, on the Ferris wheel.

It really sounded like a fun, sweet, meet-cute. Her friend chickened out because she's afraid of heights. His date got sick on the Tilt-A-Whirl and ended up going home, so there they were, in line together, ready to look over the cityscape alone, until the ride attendant made the assumption that they were a couple and forced them into the same carriage. And the rest is gaudy pink and carnival history.

Which we are fully embracing this weekend for what may be an epically hellish bachelorette party. "The weirdness of this might be on par with the hobbyhorse expo." It's a full-on assault to the senses.

"I think it might surpass it, if I'm going to be honest. I can't wait until you see the cake." She wheels me across the foyer, past a massive Pepto-Bismol pink flower arrangement to the dining and event room.

We head for the office, where I'm sure we'll find what is likely to be a very stressed-out London based on what Harley has told me this morning. I don't think we ever planned for a scenario like this, and maybe I didn't do a good enough job setting things up in the first place to make it easy for Harley and London to manage.

Harley wheels me into the office. We don't spend much time in here during events, but when we're in the planning stages, it's the hub of Spark House. We each have a desk arranged in a way that makes it look more like a chilled-out library than an actual office.

I don't particularly love having to sit behind a desk all formal-like, so beyond my desk is a set of huge, comfy chairs close to the windows that overlook the sprawling gardens outside. There's also an adjustable standing desk facing the windows and a yoga ball that I can sit on when the chair isn't working for me and neither is standing.

Harley's space looks like it belongs to a very organized teacher, and London's has a placard that says LADY BOSS on it. We got it for her as a Christmas present. While I tend to be the face of events, London manages all the things behind the scenes: liaising with companies to get great deals on supplies, coming up with cool ideas to complement the theme of whatever event we're hosting. Very lady boss behavior, even though she doesn't necessarily like the title.

London is sitting at her desk, a pile of tiny stars in front of her, which after hearing Harley say how many there are around their house, tells me that this is her way of coping with stress. "I'm sorry, but that's not what we agreed upon. I have the email right here. If you're not going to honor the price, I'm happy to negotiate with another vendor. We have five weddings planned through the end of this year and we're looking at least another fifteen next year, so I'm not interested in working with a company that says one thing and then does another. Especially when it puts our reputation on the line." She spins around, eyes going wide when she sees me. She holds up a finger. "I'm more than happy to forward you the email citing the price. There's been no miscommunication on my end. Maybe it would be wise to speak with Claude, as I've dealt with him on the past two events." She picks up a star and drops it in a glass jar where it joins its sisters. "I'll need an answer by the end of the day, or unfortunately I'll have to go with a different vendor. I'm sure you understand how delays such as these can impact the success of an event."

Her smile holds strain, but her tone is sweet. Almost admonishing. London is very good at getting what we need at a very fair price. "Of course, I sincerely appreciate you getting to the bottom of it so quickly. I'll speak to you later. Have a lovely afternoon."

She ends the call and rounds her desk, leaning down to give me an awkward hug. "I cannot tell you how much we miss you around here."

"I miss being here." Although based on the way London schooled that supplier, she's holding her own.

"Netflix bingefest getting old?" She leans against her desk and crosses one heeled foot over the other.

What I wouldn't give to wear a pair of shoes right now, even heels. I'm currently sporting a single Birkenstock. My toenails could really use a fresh coat of polish. "It was fine when I was medicated and my brain was firing on one cylinder, but now that I'm not in a complete fog and my brain is actually functioning, binge-watching shows is not all that exhilarating. On the upside, I can use a crutch to move around now, so I'm not completely reliant on Declan for every little thing. At least when I'm not being monitored by the crutch police." I thumb over my shoulder at Harley.

"Just making sure you don't overdo it on your first day back."

"Since you're moving around so much easier, why don't you come stay with us for a few days? A change of scenery." London frees a strip of pink paper and starts folding it.

"It's really fine. We're not getting on each other's nerves."

"Sort of seems like it might be the opposite, based on what I witnessed this morning." Harley smirks.

London's eyes narrow. "What does that mean? What did you witness?"

"She didn't witness anything." I can feel my face turning red, though, just like it did in the car with Harley.

"Lies. You said you'd spill the beans when we got here. We're here, so start talking." Harley drops into the chair across from me and cocks a brow expectantly.

I sigh. I don't want to keep secrets from my sisters, but London's continued disdain for Declan is a problem. One I can't ignore forever. I guess this is a reasonable test. "Declan walked in on me while I was masturbating this morning."

Harley slaps her palm over her mouth and mumbles, "How mortified were you?"

"Exceedingly," I say dryly.

"That has to be difficult with your left hand." Leave it to London to focus on the technical challenges.

Harley props her chin on her fist. "What did Declan do?"

"He apologized."

"That can't be all that happened."

"Well, I couldn't finish, because as London pointed out, I only have the use of my left hand. So obviously I was bitchy about the whole thing. And he felt bad about walking in, so I made a comment about him helping me out." It seemed offhand at the time, but now, with a little distance and perspective, I'm aware this has been building for a while.

"You did not!" London's voice is an ear-piercing shriek.

"Oh yes, you did!" Harley slaps the arm of her chair, eyes lighting up with excitement while London's shutter with concern.

"I did."

"And? Did he take you up on the offer?" Harley waves a hand around in the air. "Never mind, your face totally says it all. How was it?"

"It was nice to get some relief." It was more than nice, and more than just relief. It's been ages since I've connected with anyone the way I did with Declan this morning. I think about the way he whispered in my ear, how it felt to have him kiss me, how I'd been nervous at first, thinking it was going to be awkward and weird, but it wasn't either of those things. It felt amazingly natural and right. Kissing him wasn't strange, it was euphoric, and just thinking about it makes my thighs clench.

"Oh, come on, Ave! It was *nice?* I need some details. This is Declan we're talking about. He's gotten around more than a joint at a high school party."

She's not wrong. He was the worst during college and has settled down some, but his love life has always been prolific. "He's very skilled with his hands."

Harley leans forward in her chair, knees bouncing with her excitement. "Is he a good kisser?"

"Seriously? Why are you revved up about this?"

Harley gives me her *get real* look. "You've been friends forever. I honestly thought you two were finally going to acknowledge you have feelings for each other when you moved in together, but that didn't happen. Until now."

"Whoa, whoa." I hold up a hand. "Don't get ahead of yourself. I have no idea where this is going, if anywhere." Although based on what he said this morning, at the very least Declan would like to explore the chemistry we have, and so would I.

"Uh-huh, okay, whatever you say." Harley crosses her arms and smirks.

London's brow is furrowed with worry. "Are you sure this is a good idea, Ave? I mean, I understand we all have needs, but is he only going to be taking care of yours or is this going to be a mutual exchange?" In the very short time we've been talking about this, London has amassed a small collection of rainbow stars on her desk.

"It happened once. It's not a big deal." I try to brush it off, not wanting London's worry to rub off on me.

"So does that mean it's not going to happen again?" she asks.

I lift a shoulder and let it fall. "I don't know. Maybe it will, maybe it won't, but we're adults making adult decisions."

"I get that, and I fully agree that it's your decision to make, but he's taking care of you beyond helping you with your orgasm problems. You're relying on him a lot right now. What if he wants more?"

"That's not going to happen. Declan doesn't do relationships."

"Okay, but what if you do?" Her expression is earnest.

"I can deal with my feelings."

"So say it's a one-time thing and it doesn't happen again.

How will you feel when he inevitably brings someone home in the future?" London presses.

"He's not going to bring home a random." Although, I hadn't really thought beyond the next several weeks. The only times he's been out since I came home from the hospital has been to go into work while my sisters are over or to run to the store if I've forgotten something important in my online shopping. Which was pretty much every time when I first came home from the hospital and my brain was in a fog.

There have been no Saturday club nights. No nights out with the guys, no visits with Becky from two floors down. At least not that I'm aware of. "Stop being a buzzkill, London."

"A buzzkill?" Her expression shifts to hurt. "As if it isn't hard enough on you being in this chair, now you're adding all this"—she flails—"this potential complication. Excuse me for worrying about you!"

"I'm a big girl, London. I can manage my expectations. And I think this is less about you worrying and more about you still blaming Declan for what happened. You need to let it go."

The muffled sound of my phone ringing comes from my purse. I fish it out of my bag and check the screen. It's Declan.

I answer the call and bring my phone to my ear. "Hey, what's up?"

"Thank fuck. I was worried. Don't do that to me." His voice is high and panicked.

"What?" I'm a little confused by his tone.

"You said you'd message when you got to Spark House. It's been forty-five minutes, and it doesn't take that long to get there even if you're going under the speed limit on back roads."

"Oh! I'm so sorry. We got to chatting and I totally forgot."

"It's okay. It's fine. I was just worried. I'm going into the office for a few hours, so if you want to let me know when you're going to be home, I can try to time it so that we arrive at the same time."

"Okay, sure. That works for me."

"Great. Have a nice relaxing day, Ave." He ends the call on a cocky laugh, and I slip my phone back in my bag.

London sighs. "I'm sorry for raining on your orgasm parade."

"I know you worry." I wave the apology away. "Tell me about Daniel. How are things there?"

"He's good. Nice. He's a fan of buying me flowers and sending me things from the places he visits. He's out of town this week, but I'm supposed to see him when he gets back. He's asked if I would stay at his place for a weekend, but I'm on the fence as to whether that's a good idea."

"Why wouldn't that be a good idea?"

"Well, a weekend implies more than one night, and I'm not sure how I feel about two nights. Anyway, it's something to think about."

"It could mean a weekend of sex, and as someone who hasn't had it in a really long time, I have to say, it's definitely worth thinking about." Harley and I exchange a look, and I can tell she's biting her tongue. Every time London gets into a relationship she shifts from "fun London" to this serious version. Like all of a sudden being with someone means she's no longer allowed to have fun. It creates weird tension that we don't always know how to manage.

"Anyway. Moving on. Let's talk business." She clears her throat and picks up her tablet. "Should we go check out the pool obstacle course setup?"

Harley wheels me through the grand foyer and down the hall toward the indoor pool. It's Olympic-sized and the entire room is a half dome of curved glass. It's beautiful and serene. I can't wait to have at least my arm back, so I can make use of it again.

At one end of the pool is a massive inflatable slide, and the pool is set up with two floating obstacles that the participants will have to master to move on. "We set it up just like you explained, and Harley and I ran the course the other day to work out the kinks, but since it's neither of our strong suits, we figured it would be good to get your input." London flips a pen nervously between her fingers.

"It looks good, but it's hard to say unless I see it in action."

"I figured you'd say that." Harley pats me on the shoulder and pulls her dress over her head. She's wearing a bathing suit underneath.

"Have you been wearing that this entire time?"

"Yeah. I put it on this morning because I already knew London was going to make me run the course again."

"I'm not making you do anything. I told you I'd run it," London replies.

"But you also mentioned how you'd had your nails done and how bad the chemicals were for them, so I totally took that as a hint that you'd like me to run it instead. And honestly, I don't mind. It's actually a lot of fun."

Harley runs the course, and I make suggestions on tweaks for distance between the obstacles and dropping the number of beach ball baskets they have to score from five to three for the sake of timeliness.

"I'm glad you could come in today; it's great having your brain for these kinds of things." London's obviously trying to smooth things over.

"Me too. I'm looking forward to being able to take on more. And it won't be long until I have my arm back, which will make everything so much easier."

After Harley finishes the obstacle course—for the fourth time—she begs to be done because she's exhausted and starving. London wheels me back to the office and orders lunch while Harley gets showered and changed.

While we're waiting, London gets a call from one of the companies she's reached out to recently regarding a marketing partnership. Normally she and I would confer about these kinds of things, but I wasn't here to have the discussion, so it's clear she took matters into her own hands, which are nervously twisting behind her back. "They're dedicated to sourcing environmentally responsible products and reducing their carbon footprint. If I can convince them to work with us, it could open Spark House to a whole new client base like you talked about before the accident. It could be a really amazing way to gain a new revenue stream, especially since I didn't get the alumni contract."

"Harley told me. I'm sorry, London."

She shakes her head. "I'm the one who's sorry. If you had been there, it wouldn't have been a question, but they wanted to wait until you were back before they committed to anything."

I give her hand a squeeze. "I can reach out in a few weeks and see if they'll reconsider."

"Sure, that'd be great. But in the meantime I have a meeting next week with Go Green, and it all looks really promising."

This is so hard for all three of us, not wanting to step on one another's toes, having to shift roles. Usually I'm the one in charge, and now London has had to jump in with both feet. It means she likely doesn't have the time she'd like to focus on the details. I make a mental note to get her Etsy site set up for her since she isn't the best at making time for herself. She needs a place to channel her creativity and an outlet for her stress.

"Can I say something?" London's fingernails drum on the desk.

"Sure, of course."

"I'm sorry I got on you about Declan. I know you're capable of making your own choices. I just don't want you to get hurt. This whole thing, you being in the accident, it brought up a lot of the same fears and worries I had when Mom and Dad died. I don't ever want to lose you, and it felt like we came close this time." Her smile is sad.

"You can't get rid of me that easily." I reach out and give her hand a squeeze.

"Maybe when you're feeling up to it, you could come stay the night at our place? We could have a girls' night. Just the three of us?"

"That sounds great. I'd love that."

"Okay." Her smile widens.

Sometimes I wonder how hard it is for her to always be in the middle. Always trying to keep the peace. Forever the mediator.

17

NEVER TOO MUCH OF A GOOD THING

AVERY

Harley gets me up to the condo, but we stop at the dry cleaners on the way home to pick up Declan's suits and make another stop at the grocery story to grab a few ready-to-go meals. I'm able to manage simple things in the kitchen, and although being down a hand means I lack the dexterity to prepare anything elaborate, if I can make meal prep easier on Declan, I absolutely will.

Declan isn't back from the office yet, and Harley asks half a dozen times if I want her to stay, but it's been a long day and I know she has stuff she needs to do in preparation for the event this weekend.

I forgot to message Declan before I left Spark House, so I fire one off to let him know I'm already at the condo. Message sent, I crutch down the hall to my bedroom to change. I've gotten used to not wearing bras with straps and going commando most of the time, so a bra, underwear, and a dress is a lot to handle.

I also take a moment to freshen up below the waist, on the off chance what happened this morning happens again this evening. I don't know what to expect, if anything. I'm as nervous as I am excited. I push London's worries aside. Declan and I have a great foundation of friendship, and this shift, while unexpected, is something I think I'd like to explore more of.

The change-and-clean-myself-up routine takes almost half an hour, but at least I'm feeling fresh and relaxed by the time I crutch back out to the living room. I grab a bottle of water and a snack and make myself comfortable on the couch.

Declan has left the crossword for me, having finished the next ten words down. I turn on the TV for background noise and check my phone, but there are no new messages. It's closing in on seven and I haven't had dinner, so I polish off a box of crackers and work on the crossword for a while.

I must pass out, because I'm startled awake by the sound of something being knocked off the coffee table.

"Hey, sorry, I didn't mean to wake you up. I messaged like half an hour ago, but I guess I know why I didn't get a reply." He winks and kicks off his dress shoes.

He's wearing a black suit with a white button-up and a pinstriped purple tie. I'm aware that Declan is a good-looking guy—he has a strong jawline, high cheekbones, full lips, thick dark hair, and gorgeous blue eyes. But today I finally understand why women lose their shit over him, because not only is he very, very easy on the eyes, he's also incredibly adept with his hands, and good lord can he kiss.

I swipe my hand across my mouth to make sure I haven't been drooling in my sleep. "Guess I must've been tired. What time is it?"

"It's almost eight." He picks the remote up off the floor and sets it on the edge of the couch.

"Oh wow, you're late getting home. Did you have a lot of work you needed to catch up on?" I feel a slight pang of guilt over the number of times Declan has helped get me into bed and then resumed working. Often, he'll set his laptop aside when we're watching movies so he can rub my back. I wonder how behind working from home has put him. I make a mental note to stay on top of his dry cleaning and the groceries so he doesn't have to. And his laundry.

"Nah, I just hadn't heard from you when the guys were leaving, so I figured I could grab a beer with them. Have you eaten yet? I brought you dinner." He shrugs out of his suit jacket and tosses it on the lounger before he loosens his tie and undoes the top two buttons on his dress shirt.

"Have you eaten already?"

"I had a few wings at the bar, but I saved myself for you. Let me grab some plates."

"Sure. Okay." My stomach does a flip when he winks again and heads for the kitchen. A couple of minutes later he returns with plates, cutlery, and two bottles of beer. "You think you can handle one of these?"

I nod. "What'd you bring home? That smells amazing."

"Your favorite." He unpacks the bag and flips open the lid on the top box.

"Oh man, is that lobster-bacon mac and cheese?" My mouth starts watering instantly.

"Sure is." He spoons half the contents onto a plate and sets it on my lap tray.

"I love you so much right now," I mumble around a forkful of cheesy pasta, groaning as the flavors hit my tongue.

He quirks a brow. "As much as you did this morning?"

I blink a couple of times and use sarcasm to try to hide my surprise at his casual mention. "It's a toss-up."

"That orgasm was better than this pasta." He stabs a spiral noodle and smirks. "At least it looked like it from where I was standing."

"Can your inflated ego, Deck. I haven't had an orgasm in weeks. Sitting on the washing machine during the spin cycle would be almost as good as this." I find a chunk of lobster and pop it into my mouth, savoring the delicate flavors. I love comfort food, and there's nothing better than lobster-bacon mac and cheese.

"Do you think I should try again? Maybe see if I can do better the second time around?"

"And what if you can't do better?" My nipples tighten under my shirt and the muscles below my waist clench at the memory of what happened between us this morning.

He lifts a shoulder in a semi-uncertain shrug. "Practice makes perfect, doesn't it? Besides"—he drags his tongue across his bottom lip and points at my chest—"based on what's happening under your shirt, you might like that idea as much as I do."

I rap his knuckles with my fork. "Or I might be really excited about this." I shovel another forkful of pasta into my mouth.

"I didn't know lobster fetishes were a thing."

Both of our phones ping at the same time, lighting up with a message from our group chat. Several more messages follow, Jerome chiming in after Mark.

"You cool with it if the guys come over Monday night to watch the game?" Declan taps his bottom lip, something he does when he's nervous.

"Yeah, of course, why wouldn't I be?"

"Just checking." He sets the food aside and flips the other box open. He always gets the peppercorn steak and fettuccini.

"Are *you* okay with the guys coming over?"

"Oh yeah, of course." He nods a bunch of times and focuses on twirling noodles on his fork.

"It sounds like there's a but coming."

"I think we should probably keep what's going on between us."

I pause with my fork halfway to my mouth. "Uh, it's not like I'm going to tell the guys you're giving me orgasms because I'm incapable of giving myself one."

"Yeah, no, I know. I just mean, I don't think they'd like it is all, so we should act like nothing is going on when they're here."

I set my fork down and give Declan my full attention. His ears are going red, and he's been spinning the same noodles on his fork since he brought this up. "You don't think they'd like it if they knew I was having orgasms?" I'm playing dumb, because I know if I push hard enough, Declan will crack and come out with it already.

He gives me a look. "No, Ave."

"Are you worried it will make things awkward?" I'm trying to figure out why he's suddenly so sketched out.

"I don't want to rock the boat, especially when you're still healing." He runs his hand through his hair. "I like all this time I get with you right now. I like that I get to take care of you and make you feel good. I don't want there to be drama with the guys to mess it up, you know?"

I'm trying to understand why he's so adamant about keeping this from the guys. "Why do you think there would be drama?"

"They'll have questions. They'll want to know what the deal is and what we're doing." He threads his fingers through mine and brings my knuckles to his lips.

"What exactly are we doing here, Deck?" The question comes out an uncertain whisper. I'm acutely aware of the way my body is already reacting to his touch. My skin tingles as his lips move along my knuckles, soft and sweet, and an ache swells and settles between my thighs. It makes me both nervous and needy.

"I don't know. I guess it really depends on what you want this to be." He flips my hand over and presses his lips to the inside of my wrist. "But I don't think the guys need to know about how well I'm taking care of you."

I huff a laugh. "It only happened once, maybe it was fluke."

It's Declan's turn to chuckle. "That sounds a lot like a challenge." He unthreads our twined fingers and tugs at the edge of the blanket covering my legs. "Should I give it another shot? See if it was a one-time thing or not?"

I lift my shoulder in a careless shrug. "I guess it wouldn't hurt to at least see, would it?"

"Probably a good idea, really. That way we'll know for sure if it was a fluke or not." His fingers drift up the outside of my thigh and slide under my nightshirt.

"You're probably right." I bend my knee and the blanket slips off my leg. We both look down as his hand moves higher, curving inward, the fabric bunching as he goes.

His fingertips brush over me, skimming the sensitive skin.

A soft moan escapes my lips.

Declan's lips meet the edge of my jaw. "Fuck, Ave, that has to be my new favorite sound."

"Oh, yes please." I shift, giving him better access.

"Definitely just a fluke since it doesn't seem like you're enjoying this much." He bites my earlobe on a low chuckle.

"Stop talking smack. Your ego is going to ruin this for me." I grab the back of his neck and twist my head until our lips meet.

We tilt our heads, mouths opening to accept each other. Every sensation is heightened, my awareness magnified. This is about so much more than physical gratification, at least for me.

Maybe I should have expected this level of connection. In a lot of ways it makes sense since we know each other so well, but the intensity of the emotion isn't something I anticipated. Want and need take over. I pull him closer and lift my hips, seeking more of his touch, wanting more pressure.

"Did you think about me today? About how good I made you feel?" he whispers against my lips as his fingers tease and explore.

"Deck." I try to pull his mouth back to mine, but he shakes his head.

"Don't wanna admit it? Think it's gonna go to my head?"

I groan in frustration and at his soft touch.

His grin is devilish and his eyes darken, but under that lurks another emotion that I recognize as vulnerability. "Just tell me, Ave, that's all I want."

"Yes. I thought about you all day." About how good he makes me feel, about how I want more of this closeness, about how I can see the possibility of how good we can be together.

"Me too." His mouth crashes down on mine, and he pushes me toward the shimmering bliss of an orgasm.

When I can feel myself tipping over the edge, he tears his

mouth from mine and his hand disappears from between my thighs. I groan my displeasure and try to pull him back, at least until he drops to his knees on the floor, hitches my leg over his shoulder and brings me to orgasm, with his mouth this time.

I shudder when he licks my sensitive skin and laugh when he murmurs, "Good to know it wasn't a fluke."

18

ADVENTURES IN AVERY-SITTING

DECLAN

"We're going out." I toss one of Avery's bras into her lap, along with a pair of sweats, an oversized shirt, and a hoodie. It's a crisp fall day, the sun is shining, and if I don't get her out of the house, I'm going to try to get her out of her clothes.

"Huh?"

"Out. You and me. We're going to do something fun."

"Fun?" she parrots.

"Yes. Fun. Now get dressed." I turn around and head back down the hall.

"I think it would be more fun if you helped me get dressed!" she calls out.

"That kind of fun comes later!" I shout back. She's right, it would be a lot more fun. But over the past few days, there's been a lot of orgasms and not a lot else happening in this condo. I need to get some fresh air and some perspective, and my face and fingers out of Avery's sweet spot. So I planned an afternoon of activities, the kind that will hopefully wear us both out so I can rein my freaking hormones in.

I change into jeans and a sweatshirt. Check my messages to make sure I haven't missed anything important and return to the living room, where I find Avery sitting on the couch. Thankfully she's dressed. She's also pouting. "What if I don't want to do something fun?"

"Trust me, you do." I hold out a hand and wait for her to take it so I can pull her up and pass her the crutch. "Besides, weren't you complaining about not having enough material for your recovery journal? You sitting on the couch doing crosswords isn't exactly riveting, so I thought a change of scenery would help. And there's ice cream at the end."

Avery's eyes light up. "Ooh, what kind of ice cream?"

"Whatever kind you want."

Avery is the only person I know who will willingly eat ice cream in the dead of winter. It doesn't matter that it's October, or that her teeth will likely be chattering by the time she's done with her cone. Her love of ice cream supersedes any and all weather conditions.

Avery could probably manage to get into the front of my SUV if we moved the passenger seat as far back as possible, but she's still super nervous about driving anywhere, so the back seat it is for now.

I pass her my phone. "Why don't you pick a playlist?"

"How far are we going?" The hint of panic isn't unexpected.

"Not far, I promise." I planned out today's activities so we're in the car for short periods of time, but long enough to push Avery out of her comfort zone a little. Anything I can do to distract her should make her feel better about the whole thing.

Avery scrolls through my music. "Wait, you have a playlist with my name on it?"

"Well yeah, for when we go on road trips and stuff. That way we don't have to change stations every ten minutes because there's a song you don't approve of on the radio, or commercials."

Avery cues up the playlist and keeps on scrolling. In the past she used to keep herself entertained by going through my contact list. I always put notes beside the women who rotated in and out of my life, most of them for very brief periods of time. Some of them had names like the Screamer, the Yodeler, the Bendy Yogi, the Ass Slapper. It used to be funny, and now the thought of her going through that list is embarrassing. "What're you doing?"

"Just checking out your other playlists and your IG account. Based on the number of pictures you have of pizza and wings from Tony's, you could be a paid sponsor."

"If it gets me free pizza out of the deal, I'd be down for a sponsorship."

I make a right and pull into the parking lot of our first stop for today.

"Mini putt?" Avery sounds somewhat skeptical. She holds up her arm and taps her casted leg. "How is that going to work?"

"I'm here to be your extra set of hands." I wave mine in the air and waggle my brows. "But they're for putting purposes only until we get home."

Avery side-eyes me. "I better get an orgasm for every hole in one I manage."

"I can definitely get on board with that."

I cut the engine and hop out of the driver's seat so I can help her get out of the SUV. She doesn't need much in the way of assistance anymore. And her arm is almost healed now, so she can at least use the cast to brace herself, if nothing else.

I pay for two rounds of mini putt, and we join a few families with young kids on the putting green. I take a couple of pictures of Avery trying to set up her ball, and then a video of her working out the logistics of putting while balanced on one leg and relying on her nondominant hand. "And up next is world-class putter Avery Spark. Avery is facing some unique challenges and is currently using a new move called the flamingo putt. Trademarking that baby now because I'm positive it's going to be the mini putt move of the century."

She looks half-annoyed, half-amused. "Is the commentary necessary?"

"It absolutely is, Miss Spark. How else will the world be able to identify the magic that is the flamingo if we don't capture it on film? You are witnessing history right here, the flamingo, trademarked."

Avery shakes her head but focuses on the ball, expression turning serious as she swings a couple of times. Avery has always been super competitive, and she hates losing. It's why I love playing on the same team with her.

She hits the ball down the strip of turf, and it circles the hole once, nearly jumps out, but manages to circle again before it falls in.

"Hole in one on the first try, ladies and gentlemen! If ever there was a lesson to be learned here, it's that Avery Spark can overcome any obstacle!" I end the video and hand Avery the crutch.

"That's orgasm number one. And don't think I won't keep a running tally." She smirks.

"I absolutely expect you to cash in on every single one of those." I kiss the end of her nose, then look around, remembering that we're in a public place.

Avery doesn't seem to notice or care. "Can I see the video?" she asks as we move to the next hole and I set up my ball since I'm up first.

"Sure." I pass her my phone and tee up. It takes me three shots before I land the ball in the hole, but I don't really care. All I want is to give Avery a reason to smile.

We spend the next hour running through the course. After about seven holes Avery's game starts to suffer, likely because it takes a lot of physical energy for her to maintain her balance, and while she's been using her crutch more and more, and doing all the doctor recommended exercises, she's still spent the past month doing more sitting and lying down than moving around.

She's determined, though, and we finish the eighteenth hole, although it takes her seven shots to get the ball in. On the way home we stop for ice cream—as promised—and by the time we get up to the condo, she's bagged and ends up passing out on the couch.

By ten she's still sawing logs, so I carry her to bed and leave a snack for her, in case she wakes up hungry.

Two days later I knock on Avery's door at 10 a.m. She's usually up by now, and while I've been a regular provider of the orgasms as of late, I still respect her privacy.

"I'm decent; you can come in," she calls out.

I throw the door open. "Well, that's unfortunate."

She's sitting up in bed, hair a mess, laptop settled on her lap pad, three chocolate-covered granola bar wrappers strewn across her comforter. There's a smear of chocolate on her right cheek.

"Breakfast of champions, I see."

"They were in my nightstand and only one month expired. Getting out of bed was far too much work, and I already have enough of that to deal with so I figured, what harm could it do?" She covers her mouth and stifles a yawn.

"Have you had a coffee yet?" I nod to the mug on the nightstand.

I know the answer to that is no because I've been sitting at the dining room table since seven, and she has yet to make an appearance. She picks up the mug—it's from yesterday—and brings it to her lips. She tips it back and makes a face as she sets it down.

"How about this? I will get you a beautiful, fresh, not cold and twenty-four-hours'-old coffee, if you finish whatever you're doing and get dressed."

She groans and rolls her eyes like a teenager. "What do you have planned now? My legs still ache from mini putt."

"Today will be way more chill. And we'll bring the chair along. Get your ass out of bed so we can make some IG-worthy videos. The last one has like five thousand likes and hundreds of comments."

"Really? Last I checked, it had one thousand likes."

"When was that? Two hours after you posted? Get your ass in gear. We have videos to make."

Less than half an hour later I find a parking spot in one of the local parks that's about a ten-minute drive away. My goal is to get Avery comfortable with car rides so that by the time she's ready to get behind the wheel, she doesn't have a full-on panic attack.

"What are we doing here?"

"We're going to chill and enjoy some nature." I pull the wheelchair out of the SUV and set it up for her.

She looks like she wants to argue for a moment but drops into it with a sigh. "Are you trying for an inspirational video scene with this?"

I'm aware she's still sore from mini putt. I'm also aware she's annoyed that mini putt makes her this sore. But her body has been through hell, so my plan is to slowly and carefully ease her back into physical activity, one outing at a time. Today it's the park.

I bring along her crutch because I know she's going to want to walk on her own without me pushing her around. It never occurred to me before her accident how hard it must be to manage with a wheelchair. Even when it's temporary, it's an entire adjustment of her daily life. Doorways can be too narrow, turns too tight, hills too steep. Everything requires more planning and time.

So being out here in the open is a good place to feel less confined by her restrictions and give her a taste of what she's going to get back once she's healed.

I wheel her over to the baseball diamonds, where we would sometimes go to run bases or toss balls to each other when we first moved to Colorado Springs. There's a kid's team practicing, and in true Avery form, she shouts her praise every time one of the kids makes contact with a ball.

I take some videos of her for her journal. Once the kids vacate the diamond, I wheel her to the pitcher's mound.

"What are you doing?"

"You're gonna pitch, I'm gonna hit, and we'll see how it goes." I toss her a whiffle ball.

She snatches it out of the air. "I guess it's a good thing I can't really hurt you with this thing, because I doubt I have the best aim with this arm."

"We'll see about that. You said you were going to suck at mini putt, and you kicked my ass for the first nine holes."

"Yeah, but I circled the drain in the last nine."

"Because you were tired. Stop making excuses and start pitching." I pick up a bat, tap the home plate, and settle into a batter stance. If there's a sport, Avery's played it at least once. Baseball might not be her favorite team sport to play, but it doesn't mean she's not good at it.

Her first toss is a little low, but I still manage to hit it, sending it out into left field. She pitches half a dozen balls, her aim improving with each throw. When we run out of balls, I jog out onto the field and collect them, and when I return, Avery has moved from the pitcher's mound to home plate, which is what I was hoping for.

She pushes up out of her chair, arm outstretched to help her find her balance.

"You want your crutch to start?" I drop the balls at the pitcher's mound and jog over to her.

"Might be a good idea." She puts a hand on my shoulder, and I wrap my arm around her waist as she hops twice, finding her balance. Even once she's steady, neither of us lets go right away.

"Thank you for this."

"Anything for you. You know that." I lean in and give her a quick peck on the cheek.

Once she's steady, I pass the crutch to her and wait for her to get situated before I hand her the bat. When I'm confident she has her balance, I jog back to the pitcher's mound to set up the camera again before I start tossing balls. She misses the first one and nearly loses her crutch, but after a couple more swings and some corrections on my part, we finally get a rhythm going.

Each hit is stronger than the last, and by the time we get to the last few balls, she's back to balancing on one foot and hitting whiffle balls into the thicket of trees at the edge of the field.

"I feel like you're doing that on purpose," I call to her as I pick up the final ball and toss it a couple of times before I wind up.

"My aim is off." She raises the bat and gets into position.

This time when I throw the ball, I add a little curve and, as expected, she hits it right where the last four balls have gone—into the trees.

While I round up the whiffle balls, I hand Avery my phone so she can post some video clips. It takes me nearly twenty minutes to find all the balls this time.

"Are we going another round?" she asks when I finally jog back with the last one.

I check the time. "We should probably head back since the guys are supposed to be over in a couple of hours, and the last thing I want is you passing out before dinner again."

19

LOOSE LIPS SINK SHIPS

DECLAN

"Can you please stop smirking?" Avery elbows me in the side while blushing.

"I wasn't smirking." I rub a hand over my mouth to hide my smile.

"You one hundred percent were. You might as well wear a shirt that reads 'I'm a master at multiple orgasms.'" If she could prop a fist on her hip she would, but since she's standing in the kitchen with her crutch under her arm, balanced on her good foot, all she can manage to do is glare.

"I wouldn't say I'm a master, more like extremely proficient."

She tries to jab me in the side of the thigh with her crutch, but I block it and nearly set her off balance. I grab her around the waist to help steady her, then pull her in close. I nuzzle into her neck, smiling even wider when she melts against me.

I've always been aware of Avery's hotness level, but after Sam demolished her heart, I compartmentalized that knowledge and filed it away under fantasies never to indulge in. She's my best friend, and I care about her just as much, if not more, than my family. Probably more, actually, since my parents are pretty huge assholes. I'm very glad I'm an only child and don't have any siblings who are also as fucked up about relationships as I am.

And that right there is another reason I shouldn't have taken this as far as I have, but my logic shorted out. Maybe I should have stopped after that first time, or the second, or third, or fourth. But I can't deny her, and I honestly don't want to.

Everything about this situation with Avery is different. And I find myself wanting things I'm not sure I'm capable of handling. Like monogamy and stability and something *real*.

I kiss my way up the side of her neck. "You're pretty wound up, Ave, maybe I need to calm you down before the guys get here."

"They're supposed to be here in less than ten minutes."

"I bet I can get you off in five. Let me try." I slide my fingers under the hem of her shorts. She's not wearing underwear.

"Do not start something you can't finish, Declan. I have no interest in spending the next four hours being all hot and bothered because you gave me the girl equivalent of blue balls."

"Blue balls are physically painful." I would know, I suffered through them until Avery put her foot down and insisted this was not a one-way street. That happened three days into whatever it is we're doing. She decided if she was getting off I should be too. And then she cited that it would be good for her forearm strength. It was hard to argue her point.

"And so is being left hanging halfway to an orgasm, at least for me. You seriously need to rein it in if you don't want the guys to figure out that you're taking a very involved, hands-on approach to tending to my every need."

"And my mouth is also very involved, don't forget about that." I nibble along the edge of her jaw.

"Please." She tips her head to the side, giving me better access, a contradiction to her previous warning and her now-pleading tone. "It's not fair to play with me like this when you're not going to be able to do anything about it for hours."

I've learned a lot about Avery's needs since I started taking care of the most intimate one. I've also learned that she has an incredibly high sex drive, and that once it's tended to, instead of waning, it seems to grow exponentially. The whole experience can be likened to opening a box of your favorite cookies and being unable to stop yourself from going back again and again until you realize you've eaten the entire package.

The thing is, there is no end to Avery's box of cookies—yes, the pun is intentional—and the more I get, the more I want. And the more I offer, the more she seems to crave it and me. So it's becoming a bit of an addiction for both of us. I assume this insatiable need will wane after a while, and we'll dial it back, but for now, well, I'm all for pushing her buttons.

"That's the point, babe, because it means when I finally get my mouth and hands on you later tonight, you're going to be utterly insatiable, and I'll be the one who gives you everything you need."

The buzzer goes off, signaling that the guys are in the lobby, waiting to be let in. I cup Avery's cheek in my palm and tip her head to the side, pressing my lips to hers. "Come on, babe, let me in."

For several long seconds her lips remain pursed.

"I wouldn't push your buttons if I didn't know how much you love it," I whisper and suck her bottom lip between mine.

She relents, lips parting, tongue stroking out to meet mine.

The buzzer goes off again.

"It's going to be a long evening." She pushes on my chest. "I'll let them in. And you need to be on your best behavior unless you want to let the cat out of the bag."

"What'd you do with that container of peanut butter brownies?" Jerome riffles through the bags of snacks sitting on the floor beside the coffee table.

I'm currently sitting in the recliner on the opposite side of the room from Avery; otherwise, I'm liable to do something that will give us away. As it is, I've caught myself almost calling her babe at least three times in the past few hours.

"I haven't seen it. I thought it was in with the Funyuns." Mark loads up another nacho chip and sets it on his plate.

"You mean this container?" Avery holds up an empty Tupperware with a lazy grin.

She's only had one beer, but her eyes are droopy and her blinks a little slow. I assume it has to do with this afternoon's batting practice.

Jerome's eyes flare. "Did you eat *all* of those?"

Avery makes a face. "They're my favorite. Sorry. I didn't want to share, even though they tasted a little weird."

"Oh shit." Jerome and Mark give each other a look.

"Oh shit what?" I ask.

Jerome runs his hands down his thighs. "Uh, those were pot brownies."

Avery isn't on painkillers anymore, thank God, but she's never been much of one for any kind of medication or recreational drugs. Usually she's a two-beer max kind of drinker. It was helpful back in college when the rest of us used to get shit-faced and she was the designated driver.

"How many were in there?" It's a pretty big container.

"Four, I think?"

"I guess that explains why I'm so thirsty." Avery licks her lips and makes a smacking sound. "My mouth is super dry."

"Isn't orange juice supposed to help counteract the effects of THC?" Mark asks.

"Oh! I would love some orange juice right now! So refreshing!"

"I'll get you a glass." I push out of the recliner.

"Yay! You're the best, Deck!" Avery bounces a couple of times, tipping a bowl of popcorn over, kernels spilling in her lap and onto the floor. "Uh-oh, looks like I made a mess." Avery tries to lean over to right the bowl, but ends up sending it tumbling to the floor.

"It's okay, Ave, I'll get it." Mark sweeps popcorn off the couch cushions into the bowl while Avery tries to aim pieces into it from where she's sitting. Mostly she misses and gets Mark in the face. Or maybe that's the point.

"Oh man, this is going to be entertaining." Jerome chuckles as the giggles set in for Avery.

"You should tape this! It'll be like another in-prational video. In-spatial video." She makes a duck face and waves her hand around in the air. "You know what I mean."

I cross my arms. "This is pretty far from inspirational, Ave."

She stops aiming for the bowl and chucks popcorn at Mark, trying to get it to land in his hoodie. "Come on! Look at how good my aim is!" She beans him on the forehead and the cheek, and a kernel ends up in his beer glass, sending her into hysterics that has tears streaming down her face.

I pour orange juice into a plastic glass, because I don't trust that she's going to be able to manage anything breakable at this point. "Nice work," I mutter to Jerome as I pass him.

"Here, take a sip of this." I hand the glass over to Avery, who's still laughing, but it's died down to a reasonable giggle.

"Thanks, Deck, you're the best nurse-friend ever. You take such great care of me." The orange juice sloshes precariously close to the rim of the glass as she raises it. She tips it before she reaches her mouth and ends up pouring half the glass down the front of her hoodie—which is actually my hoodie.

"Oh shit!" She looks down at the front of her shirt like she can't figure out what just happened. "I guess I missed."

I take the glass before she can spill the rest of it and set it on the side table. "Maybe a straw would be a good idea."

"I didn't even get to taste it. I'm super thirsty." She licks her fingers. "I think I need a new shirt, and maybe a different blanket."

"I'll help you out of the hoodie," I tell Avery. "Jerome, can you get me a wet cloth, please?"

Getting Avery out of the hoodie isn't particularly easy, and the orange juice that hasn't soaked in yet ends up dripping all over the blanket in her lap. Under the hoodie she's wearing one of her long nightshirts, and she's braless, as evidenced by the fact that her nipples are visible against the fabric.

I pull my own hoodie over my head and help her into it while Mark grabs a different blanket and Jerome brings a wet cloth so Avery can wipe her hands and anything else that's bound to be sticky.

Once she's cleaned up, I go in search of a straw and a cup, preferably with a lid. She has a bunch of those reusable ones with the metal straws. I'm a little worried she's going to bite it and chip a tooth, but I can't find any paper straws.

She drains the entire glass in thirty seconds and asks for a refill. "Where's my phone? If Declan won't video me, I'll do it myself."

"We're not recording this for your recovery journal," I tell her as I fill her glass.

"I know that, silly." She rolls her eyes exaggeratedly. "I just want to record it for me. I have all these thoughts, and I want to get them out before I forget them."

Mark is about to reach for her phone, but I shake my head. "Fine. I'll use my phone."

I pass her the glass of juice and pull mine out of my pocket.

"Are you recording?" she asks around the straw.

"Yup." I'm not, but she doesn't need to know that.

"No, you're not. Hit the record button."

"Fine." I give in, because I know she's not going to give up until I do. Tomorrow I can show her the evidence, and she'll thank me for not letting her video herself.

She slurps her orange juice and waits for me to follow through. Halfway through the glass, she makes a face. "Don't we have any of the other bendy straws? Can you check for one, Deck? My head is so heavy and it's really hard to drink like this."

She slumps down in the cushions. I can't imagine it's comfortable. "I can't get you a bendy straw and record you at the same time."

"Oh, hmm. Yeah. That's true."

"Want me to put a pillow behind your head?" Mark offers.

"Sure, maybe that'll help."

Mark grabs one of the throw cushions that ended up on the floor, and Avery struggles to lift her head off the cushion. I grab her juice so she doesn't drop it.

"Seriously, why is my head so freaking heavy? Is it magnetic and the cushion is keeping it pinned? I can't even lift it. Mark, you need to try to slide it behind my head, 'kay?"

"Dude, she's a mess," Jerome mutters.

I lower the phone, but Avery points at me. "Hey! I have things I need to say!"

"We could voice record." I hit a button, intending to stop recording.

"It needs to be a video," she insists.

Mark is still trying to get the cushion behind Avery's head. "Ave, you're literally pushing your head back into the couch, just relax."

"But I'm not! It's really this heavy. I think there's a magnetic field. I'm like Magneto head right now. What if I can't ever get up off this couch because my head is stuck?" Her eyes go wide.

I keep holding the phone up, so she at least thinks I'm recording. "Hey, Ave, I have your orange juice."

"Oh! Yay!"

I hold it far enough away that she has to lean forward to get it, giving Mark enough room to put the pillow behind her. When she leans back, she slides even farther down the couch and her chin meets her chest.

"I don't think this is going to work. I'm going to end up with a neck crick." Avery tries to get the straw to her mouth, but it's facing the wrong way. "This is the worst! Who designed this? My head feels like a boulder. How much does a head weigh, Deck? Mine is like two hundred pounds right now. I feel like

I'm sinking into the couch. Do you think the couch is made of quicksand? What if I become part of the couch?"

"You're not going to become part of the couch, Ave. I promise none of us would let that happen." I sit on the edge of the chaise lounge and turn the straw around to face the other way. "Here, try this."

"Ooh! That's better. I don't know why they make these straws so tricky. The paper ones are the worst. I miss plastic bendy straws. Like I get it, they're not good for the environment, but you can't chew on the paper ones, and they start to disintegrate almost right away, which is super annoying because no one wants paper bits in their orange juice."

"Paper bits in orange juice is just wrong," I agree, still holding the phone up.

"Right? Anyone who is against plastic straws is basically a devil worshipper! I mean, the plastic bendy straws are so much fun. And are these metal ones really better for the environment? Like sure, they're not going to harm the turtles, but they could harm something else." She punctuates that statement with a long slurp. "What if you dropped it in the ocean, and a big fish ate it and then they couldn't poop it out? Then he'd have a metal straw sitting in his belly until his stomach acid dissolved it. Do you think that would cause heartburn? I bet it would. So see, metal straws aren't better for the big fish at all!"

Avery chases the straw around in her glass and takes another aggressive gulp before continuing her weed-brownie-fueled rant. "And turtles are cute and all, but they're super stinky. And some of them bite, which isn't cute at all. Sometimes I really miss the fun, non-environmentally friendly versions of the less fun things we have to use now, especially plastic bendy straws. I wonder if you can get them on the black market. I bet you can. Can someone pass me my phone?"

Jerome is laughing so hard, he's not even making sounds anymore.

"Would you like me to look it up for you so you can keep drinking your juice?" I ask.

"Oh yes, that'd be awesome. This is the best orange juice I've ever had. But do you know what would make it better?" She cocks a knowing brow.

"A plastic bendy straw?"

"Exactly! What if I accidentally try to chew on the end of this thing and chip my freaking tooth? What if a turtle tried to chew on it and chipped his tooth? Turtles aren't the only important species out there. People matter too!"

Avery finally seems to realize that the guys are dying of laughter.

"What's so funny? Why are you guys laughing? This is super serious. I need bendy straws in my life, and the turtles are making it impossible!"

Avery rants about the lack of bendy straws in her life and the unfortunate odor of turtles, and then she goes so far as to question whether climate change even exists. Which I'm aware isn't at all how she really feels.

Unfortunately, I'm not allowed to put my phone down until she's done. It isn't until I finally look at the screen that I realize that instead of stopping the video, I've been recording the entire time. Avery takes my phone out of my hand and mumbles about sending it to herself. I have my doubts that she'll even be able to manage that feat considering the way she jabs at the screen.

After a minute she gives up and tells me I need to make sure

I send it to her. Then she announces that she has to pee. "Can you get me my crutch, Nurse Declan?"

"It's probably easier if I wheel you there, don't you think?" I honestly don't think she'll be able to balance at all in her current state.

"Hmm, maybe you're right. I feel like my butt has magnets in it and wants to stay on this couch." She tries to lean forward, but flops back against the cushions. "If I had a peen like the rest of you, then I could just whip it out and aim for a bucket. Peens are weird but convenient, vags not so much."

Avery is a rag doll, so getting her off the couch is a struggle. Her face ends up mashed against my neck.

"You smell yummy," she mutters. "Way better than a turtle."

"Well, that's reassuring since turtles are apparently super stinky."

"They're adorable but gross. You're not gross, though. You're the opposite of gross. I don't know why I never really noticed how not gross you are before you became my nurse."

"Maybe you could tell me about that later, when everyone goes home," I whisper in her ear as I help shift her into her wheelchair.

"Okay, that sounds like fun."

I'm not sure I trust in her ability to manage the bathroom without assistance, so I stand outside the door and wait until she calls me back in.

She doesn't even bother to pull her shorts back up, so I take them off for her and drop them on the floor, leaving her in a long nightshirt and one of my oversized hoodies. "I think I might need to go to bed. My head is still so heavy, but light, like a lead balloon," she tells me as I help move her back to her chair.

"Okay, want to say good night to the guys, then?"

"Yeah, that'd be good." She nods once, head loose and floppy.

I wheel her back out to the living room where she mumbles a garbled, less than perfectly coherent good night. "Next time I won't eat all the special brownies." The words are slurred.

"Sorry I didn't warn you about them," Jerome says.

"S'okay. I bet I'm going to sleep like a baby. Not a colicky baby, one of those babies that sleeps through the night." She pats my hand and tips her chin up, trying to look at me, but I'm standing behind her. "Can you stay with me tonight? In my room? I still feel like my body is a magnet."

"Why don't we get you settled and see how you feel once you're in bed?" I don't like the hot feeling creeping up my spine, or the fact that Mark and Jerome are bearing witness to this. "I'll be right back," I tell the guys.

"You need help?" Mark asks.

"Nah, man, we're good. It'll just take a minute." I spin her wheelchair around, heading for the hallway to her bedroom.

"I think I'm too tired for full service tonight, which is too bad, 'cause I was really looking forward to it." She pats the back of my hand again.

I shush her and rush her down the hall, so we're out of earshot of the guys.

I help get her into bed and she keeps on with the chatter. "I really wanted another orgasm tonight, but I'm so tired. I think I'd probably fall asleep on you and that would be embarrassing. And a lot of wasted effort."

"Shh, Ave, it's okay."

"I think I'll probably appreciate it more tomorrow. And I'll be able help you out too."

"Let's talk about it in the morning, 'kay, babe?" I kiss her forehead and tuck her in.

Her eyes are already closed, and she seems to be down for the count before I even have her comforter pulled all the way up. I leave her door open a crack and stand in the hallway for a few seconds, trying to gather myself before I face Jerome and Mark. I sincerely hope they didn't catch any of the telling comments she made.

Based on their cocked brows and inquisitive expressions, I'm guessing they did.

Mark is the first one to talk. "Wanna explain what 'full service' means?"

The real answer to that is no, I don't, but I don't think that's going to cut it. I hold up my hands in supplication. "It's not what you think."

"So you and Avery aren't screwing around?" Leave it to Jerome to be blunt.

I tuck my thumbs into my pockets so I don't run my hand through my hair, aware it's what I do when I'm stressed and having a conversation I don't like. "It's not like that."

"So what's it like then?" Mark asks.

"She only has one working hand, and it's her weak one. She needs help with everything." I don't know why I don't own up to it like I should.

"Seriously?" Mark looks incredulous. "You do realize there are toys out there that can do the same thing, without the added layer of complication."

And this, right here, is why I wanted to keep it between me and Avery. "She was frustrated. What was I supposed to do? She needed relief, and I helped her out because she asked me to, and

I will keep doing whatever the hell she needs me to until she tells me she doesn't anymore." I cross my arms, defensive and on edge.

Mark frowns. "Why are you trying to make it sound like some selfless act on your part?"

Jerome sighs. "If you have feelings for her and she has feelings for you, just own it, but don't stand here and pretend you're doing this just because she couldn't do it herself."

"Obviously I care about her. She's my best friend."

"We all care about her, man," Mark says. "But the last thing either of you needs is a broken heart to go along with all the other broken parts."

20

THE FREAKING TURTLES

AVERY

My brain is full of fog. I glance to the right and am surprised to find Declan's large body in my bed. The sheets are shoved down to his waist, bare chest rising and falling slowly.

I'd like to be able to appreciate the incredible view, but Declan never sleeps in my bed, so instead, all it does is incite panic and some questions. I catalogue the aches in my body. There's no unusual pain, so I don't think he's in my bed as a result of me hurting myself.

I try to remember what happened last night, but it's a haze. I had one beer and a lot of snacks. Peanut butter brownies that had a bit of an odd taste to them. And then a whole lot of orange juice, which isn't usually something I drink much of. That's typically Declan's go-to drink of choice.

My phone buzzes from my nightstand and I glance at the clock. It's late, closing in on eleven, and I don't often sleep past eight. I shimmy over a few inches and nab my phone, fumble it and nearly drop it on the floor. I manage to catch it with two fingers and fling it up onto my comforter-covered stomach.

My reaction time sucks this morning.

I close my eyes for a few seconds, finding it hard to keep them open. I must fall asleep again because I'm startled by the buzz on my pelvis. This time I manage to bring my phone to my face. I have an alarming number of missed calls and messages from my sisters. "What the hell?" I mutter, glancing over at Declan's relaxed, still passed-out form.

I bring up the group chat and scroll back to the beginning, skimming the conversation in reverse. There seems to be some kind of video that's caused a heck of a lot of drama, but I have no idea what my sisters are talking about.

I skip the messages and call Harley. I'm aware I'll likely get both of them on the line, but London seems to be the most upset, so I'd rather deal with Harley first if I can.

She answers halfway through the first ring. "We have big problems, Avery."

The fog that's been hanging around in my brain is quick to lift at her less-than-pleasant tone. "I gathered from the messages. Can you fill me in, though? Because last night is unclear."

"What the hell did you do last night that would make it unclear when you're recovering from broken freaking limbs?" She's loud and angry, which is not good. Harley rarely raises her voice.

I filter back through last night, and remember, just vaguely, when Jerome asked where the Tupperware had gone and how I'd polished off the entire container, despite the brownies tasting a little odd. "The guys came over to watch football. I had a beer because I'm not taking the painkillers anymore. Jerome brought some brownies of the special variety. I didn't know and ended up eating all of them."

"The special variety?"

"They were pot brownies. I was unaware and polished them all off, which I don't recommend doing, ever."

"Didn't they taste . . . weedy?"

"I thought they might have some zucchini in them or something."

"Well, pot brownies might explain your video rant." Harley doesn't sound amused.

"What video rant?" I rub my temples, still in the dark about the actual issue.

"You posted a video rant. Can you let us in, please, so we can have this conversation face-to-face? The latch is on and we've been standing outside your door for the last twenty minutes trying to get you to answer the door or your freaking phone."

"Oh crap, you're here?"

"Yeah."

"Is London with you?"

"Yes."

"Okay, give me a minute and I'll let you in." I end the call and leave a still sleeping Declan—I have no idea how he passes out so hard—in my bed while I hobble uncoordinatedly down the hall.

Neither of them looks impressed when I throw open the door. London doesn't say a word as she sashays past me, heels clipping on the hardwood.

Harley sighs and shakes her head as she looks me over. "I hope last night was worth it."

I follow her back down the hall and catch a glimpse of my reflection in the mirror. My hair is an insane wreck, still halfway up in a ponytail. My eyes are red-rimmed, there are pillow lines on my face, and I'm still wearing my sleep tank from last night. I'm also suddenly aware that it only covers my butt by a couple of inches, and I'm not wearing a bra or underwear.

The living room is a mess. The coffee table is littered with remnants of last night's snacks, empty chip bags, a bowl with chocolate wrappers, and an empty pizza box. There are crushed pieces of popcorn littering the floor around the couch where I normally sit. The kitchen counter is home to several empty beer bottles, a half-gallon jug of orange juice, which I'm guessing I polished off, and several dirty pint glasses.

London wrinkles her nose at the mess and props her fist on her hip. "What were you thinking when you posted that video?"

"I think you need to back this up a little because I still don't know what video you're talking about."

Harley's nostrils flare and London holds up a hand. "Last night you uploaded a video to the Spark House account where you ranted about bendy straws and turtles, among other things."

"That doesn't even make sense." I wrack my brain, trying to come up with a reason as to why turtles and bendy straws would even come up in conversation.

"Regardless of whether it makes sense or not, the company that was entertaining working with us backed out of the deal!" London says.

"Wait, what?" It takes me a few seconds to piece it together. Especially with my brain fog going on. And then I realize London is referring to Go Green, the company that she was trying to create a sponsorship connection with.

"Go Green backed out. They're not going to sponsor us anymore," Harley says quietly.

"I don't understand why they would back out over a rant about bendy straws and turtles?"

"Because you said anyone against bendy straws was a devil worshipper. Then you went on to say being able to use a bendy straw was more important than saving turtles from the environmental damage that they cause, which also happens to be one of the key freaking initiatives that Go Green has backed for the past several years," London states matter-of-factly. "The CEO spearheaded the entire campaign surrounding restaurants shifting to paper straws in order to prevent the unnecessary and inhumane death of the turtles."

"Oh. Well, that's not good."

"No, it really isn't. We needed that sponsorship after I lost the alumni contract, and now we're back to square one." London rubs her temples.

I sort of want to do the same thing, considering the way this is making my head pound.

"What's going on out here?" Declan appears at the end of the hall, wearing nothing but a pair of gray track pants. His hair is a mess, but instead of looking like something the cat dragged in, he's ridiculously delicious. He runs a hand through his hair, making his biceps pop.

London doesn't even look his way. "It's Spark House business; it doesn't involve you."

He crosses his arms. "Actually, since you're out here getting heated with Avery, in what happens to be *our* home, I think it does involve me."

"You know what, on second thought, you might be right,

because from what I understand, it was you and your friends who videoed her slamming environmentally responsible practices and allowed her to post it on our social media for all of our clients to see!" London's eyes flash with ire.

Declan's brow furrows. "What are you talking about? I would never have let Avery post a video like that."

"Well, someone must have, because it was up on the Spark House account for hours before we realized what was going on and pulled it down."

"Avery was a mess. I didn't think she'd actually post it."

"Why would you even take a video like that in the first place?" London asks.

"Honestly, it was an accident. Avery kept saying she had important things to say, and I thought I wasn't recording but I guess I was. She must have sent it to herself without me realizing it? I didn't think she would even be able to manage that considering the state she was in, so I can't imagine that she would have posted it intentionally." Declan gives me a worried look.

London squeezes the bridge of her nose. "Intentional or not, this cost us a massive sponsor and some amazing opportunities which, frankly, we could have used right now!"

"Maybe I can talk to the sponsor and explain what happened," I offer.

"What are you going to say? That you accidentally ate a whole bunch of weed brownies, and your boy toy videoed you ranting about how inconvenient it is that you can't use bendy straws when you're high? You are the one who has been pushing for expansion, Avery, and without a sponsor, that can't happen. We're barely keeping our heads above water as it is."

"We can't be in that bad of shape." At least I didn't think we were.

London looks at Harley and sighs. "We've had to turn down a couple of events because we couldn't make it work without you. And two prospective clients hinged on having the sponsorship funding with Go Green. Without that, it changes a lot of things. And before you say it, Declan, I told you taking out a loan is frivolous and not smart for our bottom line."

"Wait. Why is this the first I'm hearing about this? About any of this?"

Declan rubs the back of his neck. "I wanted to tell you, but London felt it wasn't a good idea."

London throws her hands in the air. "I wanted to be able to fix it! I wanted to prove that I could handle it on my own."

Declan raises a hand. "I know and I get it, but leaving her in the dark isn't exactly helpful either."

"I'd hoped we'd be able to get them to reconsider." London clasps her hands together, probably to keep from fidgeting since she doesn't have those star strips she usually keeps handy. "And I didn't want to put more pressure on you when you were already dealing with enough."

"You would have wanted to return to work if you'd known, and you would have set yourself back. You can try to deny it all you want, but we all know what you're like." Harley takes me by the arm and leads me to the couch. "You need to sit down; you're pale and the last thing we need is you passing out."

I sit, embarrassed and frustrated with this whole thing. I can see all sides, and I've made it worse because I got messed up last night and did something stupid. "My rant must have been pretty bad," I mutter.

Harley rubs my back, but doesn't answer my question, which I suppose is answer enough. "Declan, I appreciate that this is your place just as much as it's Avery's, but I think we could use a few minutes alone to sort out how we're going to move forward."

Declan defers to me. "Are you going to be okay?"

I nod.

"I'll be in my room, but if I hear raised voices again, I'm coming back out here." Declan turns around and walks down the hall, kneading his neck.

I flop back against the cushions. My mouth feels like it's full of cotton, and so does my head. "I should probably see this video so I can understand how bad things are."

I get about thirty seconds in before I turn it off. "How many people saw this before it came down?"

"Not that many," Harley says, looking away.

"At least a few hundred from what I saw before I could pull it from social media. But there were screenshots, and I think you may be a meme . . ."

I rub my hand over my face. There isn't going to be an easy fix for this. "I should reach out and explain the situation." Although I'm not sure how much good it will do since I was high out of my gourd. I could blame it on pain medication.

"I've already called. They are no longer interested in working with us, and I'm not sure what it would take to make them change their minds, so I think we need to move on. In the meantime, I'm looking into some not-for-profit environmental groups *we* can sponsor or feature to help us do damage control." London reaches into her purse and pulls out one of her star strips. She doesn't even have to look at it, just starts folding.

There are bags under her eyes and despite being put together, she seems slightly disheveled. I hate seeing them this stressed out, all because of me.

"I can't pretend to know how difficult this whole thing must be for you, Avery," London says gently. "I can imagine it must be a challenge to be reliant on another person so fully, and you have to be struggling with how little physical activity you've been getting, but getting stoned out of your mind on pot brownies isn't a good alternative based on the end result."

I feel awful that this has happened. "You're right, you have no idea what this is like for me, but the whole thing was an accident, from the pot brownies to the video."

"Why were the pot brownies even there? You're healing from multiple breaks. And why in the world did Declan agree to video you when you were in that state? He should have said no."

"He did say no, but I kept nagging him." I have very vague memories of telling him I had important things to say that I wouldn't remember tomorrow. "And like I said, I had no idea they were weed brownies, otherwise I wouldn't have eaten four of them and made an ass out of myself. It was a mistake, and I'm sorry, but you need to stop blaming everything on Declan. Declan is not the root of the problem. You're mad at me, but it's easier to be mad at him."

London blinks, taken aback, and remains silent for a few seconds before she finally says, "You know what, you're right. I am angry with you. We're all busting our asses, trying to make things work, and you're over here eating freaking pot brownies and undoing all of our hard work! Everyone is pandering to you and what you need, myself included, and that's obviously a mistake.

Spark House is *your* baby. We're over here trying to keep it afloat, and for what? Where's the fucking gratitude, Avery?"

It's my turn to be shocked. For a moment my back is up, at least until I let her words sink in. And I realize she's right. I may be doing little things here and there, but they're a two-woman show at Spark House. It's hard enough when it's the three of us. "I'm so sorry, London. You're absolutely right. I've been focused on me and only me. That needs to change. Let me try to fix it. Please."

Her shoulders come down from her ears, and I hold out my arm. She comes in for a hug, and it's in that moment that I understand how hard all of this has been on her, and how much we all rely on one another.

London and Harley have to leave for Spark House because, like every other Saturday, there's an event this weekend. I stare at the ceiling, trying to figure out what exactly I'm going to do about this situation.

It's less than ideal. London is right to be upset with me. And now I'm seeing that she's been doing all of this, not because she loves Spark House the way I do, but because she feels like she has to. And that's not how I want it to be.

The cushion beside mine dips and Declan's knee bumps against mine. "I'm really sorry, Ave. I didn't mean to mess things up for you."

If I could reach out and take his hand, I would, but he's sitting on the casted arm side, so I shimmy over and rest my head against his bicep and my casted arm on his thigh. He's still wearing jogging pants, but he's put a shirt on. "We'll get it sorted out." I don't know if it's a lie or not, but I don't want to shove more guilt down his throat when it's not his fault I acted like an idiot and did something stupid.

His lips find my temple. "Is there anything I can do to fix it?"

"Honestly? I don't know. London needs some time to calm down before I can really get any information out of her. She's been working on hooking us up with a sponsor for a while, and this one seemed really invested, so it's understandable she's disappointed. I don't even remember the video, let alone posting it, but obviously I did."

"I honestly thought I wasn't recording. I should have deleted it right away instead of letting you even look at it."

"You couldn't have known I would post it. It's my fault for pushing you to take it in the first place. I know how hard it is for you to say no to me right now." And I realize that *no one* wants to say no to me, which is its own problem. One I'm in a position to fix.

"You said you wanted to let loose and I didn't want to ruin it." He stretches his arm across the back of the couch, and his hand curves around my shoulder. "Do your sisters know what's going on between us?"

I need to tread carefully here, because this situation is already messy and I've got more than enough on my plate without sending Declan into a state of panic. "Harley sort of guessed that something happened. I just told her we were being casual about it."

"Right. Okay, yeah." He's quiet for a few seconds and my stomach drops. "This probably isn't the best time, but I need to tell you something."

I pull myself up so I can see his face. He looks worried, and maybe a little freaked-out. A freaked-out Declan isn't a good thing. "Did something happen?"

Like did he decide he wants to hook up with that Becky chick since giving each other handies and blowies isn't cutting it for him anymore? Or maybe he's not that into it and thinks we should stop messing around.

His eyes dart around. "So you said some things last night that you probably don't remember."

"What kind of things?" All I can do is hope that I didn't tell him I love him. Before we started hooking up, I wouldn't have thought twice about saying it. In fact I used to say it all the time, particularly when he brought me my favorite takeout or did something nice. We've been friends for a long time, and it goes without saying that I love him. And until recently I would have put it on the same level as the way I feel about my sisters, a sort of familial, platonic kind of love. But everything is different now.

And I don't feel platonic about my best friend anymore. In fact, if I'm honest with myself, it's very much the opposite of a platonic kind of love, so my level of panic is really damn high, and it was already at near-sonic levels after my sisters stopped by.

Declan blows out a breath. "You made a comment about not needing full service in front of the guys."

I slap my hand over my mouth. "I did not."

He cringes. "You did. And then you made some less than quiet comments about how you'd been looking forward to another orgasm."

"So they know, then?"

"Yeah. Like how your sisters know, I guess?" It's framed more like a question than an actual answer.

I bite my thumbnail, which needs desperately to be filed or I'm going to bite it off. "How did that go over?"

Declan shrugs. "As well as could be expected, I guess. They're concerned."

"About what?"

"You, mostly. They don't want me to fuck this up, and we both know I'm pretty good at doing that." He takes my hand gently and threads his fingers through mine to stop me from tearing my nail off. "Why don't I file these for you? I can even give painting them a shot if you want?"

It's a deflection from a heavy conversation Declan doesn't want to have. All of his fears build up in layers that weigh him down. It's something that needs to be addressed eventually, but I don't want to upset the delicate balance. Not right now. My biggest worry is that it will bury him, and us along with it. Whatever we are.

21

MISS INDEPENDENCE

AVERY

I'm currently sprawled out on the couch with my laptop and my tablet so I can research and make notes at the same time. I miss my desktop and split screen, but the casts make sitting in a computer chair nearly impossible.

"How's the research going? Want me to take notes for you?" Declan takes a seat beside me on the couch and peers at my screen.

"Not bad. I have a shortlist of companies that focus on the use of eco-friendly, recyclable products that don't harm animals in the area that I can reach out to. I've already emailed a few, but I'm thinking that calling some of these other ones would be a better idea."

"Easier than typing emails one-handed or having to edit speech to text?"

"And it's a bit more personal. Emails get lost, phone calls not as much. Besides, I have the time, so I might as well put it to good use."

"Yup, makes sense to me." He flips a pen between his fingers. "So I need to tell you something."

"What kind of something?"

"Remember that huge account I told you about a while ago?"

Declan works on a lot of big accounts. Spark House is actually one of his smallest portfolios. He's had a couple of offers from clients to manage them independently, but he likes the company he works for. "Sure. What's going on?"

"I landed Go Green's portfolio."

"Oh my gosh! That's amazing!" Go Green is a massive company, so landing the account is a big deal.

He nods. "It is. And while I can't guarantee that I might be able to get them to take you back on, I'm going to see if I can't at least try to feel them out about doing business with Spark House."

"You really don't need to do that."

"I know. But I can at least give it a shot. I know how much this has stressed London out."

"Oh no, is she still being cranky with you?" I figured she'd had more than enough time to get over being upset with Declan, especially with me on the mend.

"She's fine." He holds up a hand. "Not a warm teddy bear but not a prickly cactus either. She's stressed because she likes to have a nice buffer. And with losing the alumni contract and the sponsorship, and you being out of commission, things have slowed down a bit."

"Are her worries legitimate?"

Declan shakes his head and runs his thumb down the back

of my neck, as if he can sense the sudden tension in my body. Which I realize he probably can. "No, I just think she's being cautious."

"She's been pulling double duty. And doing all of these things that really aren't her favorite. She's so great at talking business, but ask her to problem solve or troubleshoot with emotional clients or pitch an event, and she gets so flustered. Plus, she really loves all the creative stuff. Maybe more than I actually realized." I point to the mason jar full of little stars that she makes every time she comes over. She leaves them in a pile on the side table, and each time I scoop them into the jar. It's mostly full now.

"Too bad making paper origami puff stars isn't a lucrative way to support yourself."

"Well, actually, look at what I put together." I pull up the Etsy store page I've been working on for London in my spare time.

Declan frowns and then his eyes flare. "Wait, London makes all of this? When the heck does she have time?"

"The store isn't live. And it's all the prototypes for centerpieces that she's made over the years. Or the stuff she does when she's hanging out and we're watching movies or whatever. I know she doesn't have time to set something like this up, and probably doesn't have time to work on it right now, but I figured I could do it for her, and then when she's ready to hit the button, she can."

"I think this is amazing, Avery."

"I hope she loves the idea. And I wanted to do something for Harley, too, so I've gone through her IG feed—not the Spark House one, but her personal one. She's always trying out Gran's and our mom's favorite recipes and posting pictures. I figured I could make her a special cookbook. I don't want them to have to shelve what they love because of what happened to me."

He kisses my temple.

"The little things always mean the most."

Six weeks post-accident I leave the doctor's office with one less cast. The doctor is also pleased with how well my leg is healing, so the cast only comes up to my knee now, and it's a walking cast, which means getting around is going to be infinitely easier and faster.

Declan helps me get into the front seat of his SUV. My right arm is weak, sore, and stiff, but it's functional, and that's something to smile about.

"I'm so excited to have a walking cast! This means I'll be able to manage stairs on my own again. Just a few more weeks and I'll be able to drive." I chew on my bottom lip, both nervous and eager for that potential development. I could actually drive now if I wanted to, but I'll feel a lot better about it when my arm is stronger.

While I can't wait to have my independence back, I'm aware that my PTSD around driving, particularly on the freeway and in the rain, is worse than ever. Thankfully there's more than one way to get to Spark House, including a slightly longer back road option. And I'll have Declan or my sisters there as support until I'm feeling confident behind the wheel again.

"Don't push too hard too fast, Ave." He gives my thigh a gentle squeeze.

"I'll take it easy. It's just nice to finally be able to start real rehab and move around without always needing help."

"You know I don't mind."

"I know and I appreciate that, but I don't think I've ever been so excited about the prospect of doing up my own bra."

He chuckles and pulls out of the parking lot. He had a million and one questions for the doctor about my walking cast, including what the limitations would be and what exercises I should be doing with my no-longer casted arm. He left with a folder full of resources and a rehab schedule. I'll start physical therapy for my arm tomorrow, and while I'm aware it isn't going to be rainbows and sunshine, this is part of the road to recovery.

"Do you think we could stop by Spark House on the way home? I'd love to surprise my sisters." I hold up my bony arm. I need to shower and wash away the dry, flaky skin, but I'm wearing a long-sleeved shirt so it covers the lizardy grossness for now. I'd forgotten how quickly a muscle loses its mass when it's rendered immobile for six weeks.

"Yeah, of course. I'm sure they'll be excited to see you're on the mend." He gives me another disconcerted smile as we head toward Spark House.

I clasp my hands in my lap to stop myself from picking at my nails. Declan, true to his word, filed and painted them for me a couple of days ago. It was probably the most hilarious and sweetest thing he's tried to do. He kept messing up, getting polish on my skin, complaining about how tiny the brush is, and how did anyone do this without getting polish everywhere? It's not the best job, but they sure look a lot better than they did, and now I'm not tempted to pick at hangnails. Instead, I want to pick the polish until it flakes off. "Maybe in a few days I could try driving, once my arm isn't so stiff." I roll my wrist. It aches, the muscles tight and weak from disuse.

"If you want to, sure. We can hit some back roads so you can get comfortable again behind the wheel."

I upgraded from a sedan to an SUV. We decided after the

accident to replace my car with something bigger that would make me feel safer.

For the first while, the anxiety over getting in a car was pretty intense. It's gotten much better since Declan's been taking me out on adventure dates. I picked up on the fact that he made each trip a little longer than the last and always finished it off with a stop at one of my favorite cafes or ice cream shops.

"The drive to Spark House would be a good start. I'm itching to get back to work full-time, and I think once I'm comfortable behind the wheel again, it'll be easier."

"I can drive you until you're ready to do it on your own, Ave."

"I know you can, or my sisters can pick me up, or I can call an Uber, but I have to be able to function on my own, and relying on everyone else to taxi me around defeats the purpose."

Declan reaches across the console and gives my hand a squeeze. "Let's take it one step at a time. I get that you want things to go back to normal, but there's really no rush."

"You can't take care of me forever."

He releases my hand so he can signal his turn down the Spark House drive. "I could, but I doubt you'd let me."

It only takes a couple of days for the stiffness in my wrist and elbow to dissipate and some of the strength in my arm to return. Sure, it fatigues easily, but I can deal with that. Having the use of both of my arms and hands is freaking magical. As is having a walking cast. I still have to rely on my crutches, but man, is it ever nice to be able to do mundane, normal things like wash my own hair. Although, I'm not opposed to letting Declan help me out in the shower should he feel like offering his assistance.

I can finally wear my nice panties again without destroying

the elastic in the left leg. I'm currently standing in my bedroom, naked, riffling through my underwear drawer in search of my favorite pretty panties.

This afternoon Declan is taking me to Spark House so I can put in a few hours of work on-site. And I'm going to drive part of the way. It's a first, and I'm excited yet still nervous.

"Hey, Ave, what time were you thinking you wanted to head over to Spark House? Maybe we can stop and grab lunch on the way. It's pretty nice out, we could sit on a patio, get some sun on that pasty, skinny arm of yours." Declan pushes my door open, eyes trained on the phone in his hand.

He's been ultra-attentive the past couple of days. Hovery even. "I just have to get dressed and maybe put on some makeup."

"Cool." His gaze lifts, and his device clatters to the floor. "Oh, hey." His eyes roam over my naked form in a hungry, feral sweep. "You want some help with that?"

I smirk. "I should be able to manage on my own."

"Right. Yeah." He leans against the doorjamb, not bothering to pick up his phone. "Maybe I'll just supervise then, in case you need my input on what to wear for your first day back."

I turn back to my dresser, a small smile tugging at the corner of my mouth. "Is 'supervising' the new term for staring at my ass?"

"It's a great ass. The whole package is pretty fucking awesome really." He pushes off the jamb and crosses the room.

I meet his hot, questioning gaze in the mirror. He pulls my hair over my shoulder and drops his head, lips brushing from my shoulder blade all the way up the side of my neck. He takes my lobe between his teeth, nipping gently, causing a wave of goose bumps to flash across my skin. "How much time do you have before you have to leave?" His free hand wraps around my waist, and he steps into me, his chest pressing against my back. He drops his gaze so I can't see the vulnerability lurking there, but I hear it in his voice.

"I didn't give a specific time." I tip my head farther to the side, giving him more access to my neck.

"Hmm." His hand glides up over my stomach, fingertips skimming the swell of my breast, over my clavicle, and along my throat until he cups my chin in his palm. "Interested in fooling around?"

His lips brush along the edge of my jaw, and I turn to meet his mouth. "I'm definitely interested," I whisper.

Something shifts between us, and it makes my stomach knot as his tongue slips past my lips. I lean into him, glad I still have the support of my crutches to keep me upright.

Declan keeps his arm wound around my waist and lifts me so my feet hover inches from the floor. My crutches slip out from under my arms and clatter. Lips still melded, he carries me to the bed. Our mouths disconnect long enough for him to spin me around and set me on the edge of mattress.

The bed is still unmade, sheets a tangled mess from my restless sleep. I brace most of my weight on my left arm, so much stronger after weeks of supporting my weight, and gingerly drop to my elbow with the right one. It aches, the muscles unaccustomed to bearing my weight, but I'm determined to pull myself up to the pillows on my own, and Declan knows that.

I lie back as he pulls his shirt over his head, tossing it on the floor. He makes quick work of his sweats, leaving him in a pair of boxer briefs, his erection straining against the black cotton.

He climbs up onto the bed and stretches out beside me. It's become automatic for him to lie on my right side, but now that

I have both arms again and my cast only comes up to my knee instead of all the way up my thigh, he doesn't have to be quite so careful.

Over the weeks since we started down this path, I find myself craving him more. I want the closeness being intimate like this brings. I love the way my heart pounds and my stomach flutters every time he looks at me with desire in his eyes.

It's not just the way he makes me feel—so revered, the center of his world—but the feelings he evokes in me. Being with Declan is easy, like breathing. He seems to be able to anticipate my every need, and I love that it's the same for me with him. I know what turns him on, which buttons to push, and how to make him lose control.

He shifts from his place beside me and carefully settles into the cradle of my hips as we kiss, and I push his boxer briefs down, wrapping my leg around his waist, luxuriating in the weight of his body pressing me into the mattress.

We both groan at the feel of his erection against me. In all the weeks since we've become intimate, we've never had sex. The awkwardness of my cast seemed to be a good enough reason for Declan to hold off. But I suspect there are other reasons at play. And now there are new lines being crossed, and stepping over this one will invariably change things even more. In some ways I've been okay with that invisible line because I'm scared too. Aware that me wanting to have sex with Declan means I have to acknowledge how deep our connection goes.

He pushes up on one arm, eyes flashing with heat and need. "Is this a good idea?"

I ease a hand down his back, settling my palm against the base of his spine, and roll my hips. "It feels like a great idea."

He drops his head, nuzzling into my neck on a low moan. His fingers flex, thumb brushing along the edge of my jaw. His back rises and falls with each labored breath, but he doesn't lift his hips or push off me. Instead, he grinds against me and makes a noise that sounds somewhere between desire and torment.

"Deck?" I turn my head and press my lips to his temple.

His pained, needy gaze meeting mine. "I don't know if you're ready for this. I don't want to hurt you."

"I am and you won't." I stroke his cheek, recognizing that it's him who needs the reassurance. "It's been weeks of you and me."

He nods, his tongue dragging across his bottom lip. "I just want to take care of you. I don't want to stop this, even if I should."

"What are we doing here, Deck?" It's a question I've been trying to find the answer to for a while now, and I've asked it once before but have been too afraid to broach it again.

"I want you. I want to be with you," he says quietly, uncertainty and fear swimming behind his eyes, emotions I understand only too well.

We've been safe in a bubble of us. Hiding from the world while I healed. Declan has always kept sex and feelings separate, but I'm not so sure he can do that with me. And I don't want him to.

"I want us to be together. I want to be an 'us.' We don't have to label it for everyone else, we can just be 'us' together for now." He strokes my cheek tenderly. "I think I can be good to you. I want to be good for you." There's so much weight in those words. It's so much more than a socially constructed label that tells the outside world who we are to each other. He's my best friend, he's been my rock for years, and in recent weeks he's become my everything.

I pull his mouth back down to mine and we kiss, soft and

slow as we grind against each other. Eventually, when we're both panting and desperate for more, Declan grabs a condom from the nightstand and rolls it down his length.

He doesn't stretch out over top of me, though. Instead, he rearranges me so I'm sitting in his lap, facing him, legs stretched out behind him. I brace my forearms on his shoulders as he lifts me with one arm, positions himself at my entrance, and lowers me slowly onto his erection.

My eyes roll up and I moan his name. It's been so long since I've been connected to anyone so wholly, physically or emotionally. And it's never been as intense as this.

"You feel so good, Ave. So fucking perfect." He rocks me over him, a slow and steady climb to the peak and a graceful swan dive into bliss. It's gentle and intimate and terrifyingly real.

I don't just love him. I'm *in* love with him.

22
STICKY LABELS
AVERY

Two weeks after the cast comes off my arm, I lose the one on my leg as well. My calf muscles have atrophied to the point where it looks like my left leg belongs to a preteen girl, complete with eight weeks of hair growth.

I don't get Declan to drive me to Spark House after the appointment. Instead, I ask him to take me straight home.

I lock myself in the bathroom, fill the tub with bubbles, and have myself a good solid cry. Sure, I'm relieved that the cast is off, but I'm also disturbed by how horrible my leg looks. Especially the much longer, uglier scar that runs up the outside of my ankle, on the opposite side of the original scar from the soccer injury I sustained as a teen.

The scars I can deal with. I'm already aware that heels are pretty much a no-go, at least for the foreseeable future. Even when I can wear them again, they'll only be for special occasions, and they certainly won't be London's borrowed stilettos.

I've never been huge on heels anyway, so it really shouldn't bother me as much as it does.

Maybe it's because I've seen the women that Declan used to bring home on a regular basis. Usually some random from a nightclub, always wearing clothes that showed off model-perfect bodies. Even the very few women he's kept around for more than a few weeks—but never more than a few months—have always been stunning and polished. At least in appearance.

Now I'm facing a long road of rehab, and eventually, depending on how my body adjusts, another surgery to have the pins and plates removed. But the thing that scares me the most is my ever-changing relationship with Declan.

In the days leading up to having my walking cast removed, he's been hyperattentive, fighting with me to take it easy when all I want to do is push harder. It's resulted in more than one argument. But in the past, one of us would find a reason to go out somewhere to take a breather from each other; now, we end up battling it out in bed.

It's exhilarating and exhausting.

It's terrifying.

I feel like even though I'm getting my body back, I'm more dependent than ever.

The only other relationship I can compare it to is the one I had with Sam, but even then, the connection is so much different this time. I'd been young, naïve, new to intense emotions, and painfully in love with him. It was the first time I'd loved someone so wholly.

But this is not the same at all. Declan and I have a decade of friendship as a foundation. He's seen me through so many tough times, and I've seen him through just as many. I love him.

He's my rock and my safe place and has been for years. And now there's a shift I don't know quite how to navigate. It's like he's my other half. But I've seen his patterns, witnessed them countless times. Declan's difficult family history and his trust issues mean there's a very good chance we're heading for disaster, and this time the collision isn't going to end in broken bones—it's my heart that could be the casualty.

Still, every night I invite him into my bed and my body, and invariably my heart. All I can hope is that I've managed to work my way into his as well.

I already know he loves me. I just don't know if he's in love with me.

I pull my knees to my chest. It makes the left one click and ache, and I rest my forehead on them, breathing through another round of tears. I'm not much of a crier, but I feel like now that I'm about to reclaim my self sufficiency, I'm also on the brink of losing something.

"Ave, babe? You all right?" Declan knocks softly on the door. "You've been in there a while."

I have to clear my throat, so it doesn't sound like I've been silently sobbing. "I'm fine. I'll be out in a bit."

"I have a glass of wine for you if you're interested." The doorknob rattles. "Ave? Did you lock the door?"

I take a deep breath, struggling to keep my composure. "Yeah, I'll be out soon. Just give me a few."

Heavy silence follows for a few long seconds. "Okay."

I exhale a relieved breath at the sound of his footsteps retreating down the hall. I go through two razors cutting down the forest that has taken over my leg. I drain the tub and have to use the chair to finish washing my hair and my body because my recovering ankle and knee can't take my weight for that long, and I don't want to end up slipping in the tub and breaking something else, or requiring more stitches.

I take my time toweling off and wrap myself in a big fluffy robe. I barely even have the bathroom door open and Declan is right there, blocking my way out.

"Babe? What's wrong?" He cups my face in his palms. "Have you been crying? Does something hurt? Should I call the doctor?"

I shake my head. Stupid emotions getting the better of me. "It's just a lot to handle. I'm afraid of the road ahead."

"It's gonna be okay." He wraps me up in a hug. "I promise."

I want to believe him, but we're about to leave our bubble, and I don't know what the world outside of it holds for us.

I feel bad for even having that thought because when I come out of my bedroom dressed in sweats and a crappy old T-shirt, I find Declan in the living room, an entire spread of food and a bottle of wine on the coffee table.

He's tried to replicate a charcuterie board like the ones my sisters bring over, but it's the man version with a lot of cheese, whatever crackers he could find, some chips, nuts, and a bunch of broken-up chocolate bars. And it's absolutely perfect.

A glass of white wine is sitting on the end table and the cushions are already set up for me, along with my quilt. A bottle of lavender body lotion rests against Declan's leg. He runs his hands down his thighs and stands when I move into his peripheral vision. "I thought maybe you could use some pampering and a little bit of a celebration maybe? I know how hard it's been on you not being able to manage everything yourself."

"This is really sweet, Declan, but you didn't have to go to all this trouble."

"It wasn't any trouble. I just took a bunch of stuff out of the cupboard and put it on the cheese board like I've seen Harley do before." He chews on his bottom lip. "And I picked up a couple of bottles of your favorite wine. I know most of the time all we have is beer, so I thought it would be nice." He takes my crutches and offers his hand.

"This is great, Deck, thank you."

As much as I want to dive right into doing everything on my own again, I'm aware that Declan also needs to feel needed, and I have to be careful about how hard I push. So I let him fuss over me while I continue to do what I can to keep the burden off him.

He settles my legs in his lap and holds up the bottle of lotion. "I thought I could massage your legs while we chill and watch TV."

"You don't have to do that."

He gives me that look, the one I used to get all the time when he forgot to unload the dishwasher, or left his gross sweaty gym clothes in the washing machine without turning it on. "Do you not want me to?"

I don't know why I'm so reluctant to have his hands on me when that's been my predominant craving over the last several weeks. "They don't look very nice at the moment, that's all."

He starts the movie and reaches over to turn off the lamp on the side table. It isn't until we're submerged in near darkness that he pushes my jogging pants up my calves to my knees. He runs his palms gently up my shins and back down. The left one, so bony and underdeveloped, is also hypersensitive, having been protected for the last eight weeks. His fingertips drag down, sending a shiver rushing up my spine.

When he gets to my ankle, my first instinct is to pull away, but he settles his palm on top of my foot. "Is it sensitive?"

"Yeah." I nod and take a sip of wine, working not to psych myself out.

"Does your ankle hurt?" He skims along the scars on both sides.

"More like a dull ache. It's stiff from being in the same position for so long. Bending is unnatural now, you know? It's going to take some work to get the range of motion back is all."

"I'm happy to help with that."

"Are you now?" I fight a smile.

"For sure." He presses his palm against the sole of my foot and pushes my knee up. "Working on your range of motion is definitely a boyfriend duty."

His gaze meets mine, wide and uncertain.

It's the first time he's ever said anything about this being an actual relationship, let alone referred to himself as my boyfriend. I don't want to upset the balance, especially not today. "Is there a list of duties I should know about?"

"I'm kind of making it up as I go along." He taps his temple. "Obviously orgasms are on the top of that list. Watching romcoms even when there's a basketball game on, helping with your range of motion, preferably in a multitasking kind of situation where I'm also giving you orgasms seems ideal. You know, two birds, one stone."

"Plus you get something out of it too."

"There is that." He kisses my ankle. "I don't want to mess this up, Ave. I don't want to mess *us* up."

"Why would you think you'd mess us up?" I ask carefully.

"I'm new to this. To the whole being in a relationship thing."

"We've been friends forever, Deck. I know we're taking it to a new level, and there are obviously differences between being just friends and what we are to each other, but you're too loyal to do anything that could mess what we have up."

"I don't know if Sam would agree with that."

Declan never talks about Sam. It's almost as if he never existed, so the fact that he's bringing him up now puts me on edge. "Sam doesn't really have the market cornered on loyalty, and I'm not sure what he has to do with us."

He bites the inside of his lip, thinking for a moment before he answers. "He doesn't. Not directly. I don't ever want to put our friend group at risk, not like it was when Sam screwed things up."

"That won't happen, Deck. Even if for some reason we don't work as a couple, I wouldn't want you to cut out the guys like you did Sam."

"If they made me choose sides like he did, I'd always choose you, no matter what, even if we aren't together like this," he says with conviction as he motions between us.

"Choose sides? What do you mean?" I sit up a little straighter.

"Shit." Declan sighs. "I forgot you didn't know about that part."

"What part? What are you talking about?"

"When you and Sam broke up, he told me I had to choose between him and you. You were so hurt by what he had done, and I was so angry at him for being unfaithful. It wasn't hard to make a choice at all. I chose you."

"I didn't realize." My heart squeezes. But now it all makes more sense, the way he cut Sam right out of his life and never looked back.

"I never want to see you hurt like that again, Ave. Just the thought scares the shit out of me."

"No relationship is perfect, Declan. They all have ups and

downs. We're going to have arguments, we'll fight like we always do and get over it, because that's how we are. We're still us, just a little different." I've been waiting for a conversation like this. Aware we've been circling it, almost like a wild animal, afraid of the bite should we get too close.

"It's a lot different, though. I've never done this before." He runs his fingertips up and down my shin. "I've never cared enough to do this before. Or let myself care. You're my best friend. I don't want to do anything that's going to jeopardize that, and I'm worried that I don't have the ability not to."

"Just because you haven't done it before doesn't mean you're going to mess it up, Declan. If anything, you'll be overly cautious. And that's okay. I think the good thing is that we know each other really well, and we're comfortable enough to talk to each other when we can see there's a problem."

"Yeah, I guess that's true."

"We'll take it one step at a time, okay? If you're worried, we can talk it through. You're better at this than you think, Declan."

He nods, then peeks up at me shyly. "Maybe when you're feeling up to it, I could take you out, you know, on an actual date with dinner and drinks at a nice restaurant. You can wear that dress of London's, but for me this time."

"That night feels like a million years ago. What a waste of time and effort that date was." I relax into the cushions, sighing as Declan kneads the back of my calf. "I wish I'd stayed home and watched the game with you and the guys."

"Yeah, me too," Declan says quietly. "Things might've turned out a lot different than they did."

"How do you mean?"

"I think I was kind of disappointed that you'd made a date

and never told me about it." His gaze shifts my way. "I guess it was unexpected."

"Is that why you went out?" I ask, trying to understand what fueled his decisions.

He lifts a shoulder. "Of all the mistakes I wish I could undo, that one is going to haunt me for the rest of my life."

23

BACK IN THE GAME

AVERY

"Do you want to drive this morning?" Declan spins the keys on his finger. He's dressed in a crisp black suit and looks ridiculously delicious.

I pull the curtains aside and peek out the window. It's overcast, but otherwise the weather is agreeable. My confidence behind the wheel is growing every day, but I still have trouble handling the rain. I'm hoping I get over it sooner rather than later.

"Sure. I can do that. Or I can take an Uber. That's probably easier for you."

"I don't have a meeting until nine, and you know I don't mind."

"Okay. Thanks, I really appreciate it." I sling my purse over my shoulder and follow Declan down the hall.

My travel coffee mug is already waiting for me by the door. As is a breakfast sandwich. Over the past two weeks since my cast came off, we've settled into a new routine as I ease back into full time at Spark House. We alternate making breakfast in the morning for each other.

We head down to the parking garage, and I get settled in the driver's seat, checking mirrors and adjusting the seat, since my legs are significantly shorter than Declan's, before I put it in gear and head for the exit.

"You're still good with the guys coming over tomorrow night?" Declan asks once I've pulled out onto the street.

"Absolutely. The more they see us together, the less awkward things will be, right?"

"Yeah. I think so anyway. Maybe if Mark ends up going out with that Sabrina girl again, we could have a couples' thing. Like a dinner date or something, if that's something you're interested in?"

"That might be good, but based on how things are going with Jerome and Stephanie, he might be hitting single town sooner rather than later." Jerome has been on the fence about this relationship for months, but they've been together for a year, and their families like each other and get along, so he's been trying to tough it out. The issue is that Jerome wants a family and Steph would rather have a dog or three.

"We can bring it up when they come over? See how they feel about it? Unless you want me to drop it in the group text?" Declan offers.

"Maybe do that instead? Just to sort of feel it out?"

The guys seem to be handling the new, changed dynamic in the group well, although it hasn't been seamless. Not much has changed in the way we interact with one another, but there's a new edge to our hangout nights, with Jerome and Mark a little uncertain as to where the new boundaries lie. I get it, because I'm just as uncertain, and I don't want to create tension when there doesn't need to be any.

"I'll send a message later this morning and put feelers out. Sound good?"

"Works for me if it works for you."

"Definitely works for me." Declan drums his fingers on the center console. "So it seems like London is good with working with me again. She scheduled a conference call to discuss the Spark House portfolio."

I smile, happy that things are settling with my sister. After I realized how much she was taking on, and how focused I'd been on myself and nothing else, I made a concerted effort to take the things off her plate that caused her the most stress, like client calls and follow-ups. I don't even ask her permission since I know she'd just tell me she'll handle it. They don't really faze me, but they took up a lot of her mental energy. And now, with me back at work, she's less of a stress ball. "It wasn't really you she was angry at, it was me, but I'm glad things are finally getting back to normal."

"Me too." He gives my leg a squeeze. "There's an event coming up and Go Green will be there. I'm going to name-drop Spark House and see if I can get them to reconsider sponsorship."

"Don't risk your account over it." I also don't want to get excited in case nothing comes of it. "Plus, I made some good headway with a couple of local wildlife preserves. They're using Spark House to host a charity dinner in the spring. And London made a new connection with an ecofriendly party supply company, so that's another great step."

"I'm glad to hear that, but if I can get them to reconsider, that would be awesome all the way around, right?"

"Of course. I really appreciate you trying." I won't hold my breath, but it's nice that he's willing to give it a shot since any attempt at communication on my part has been met with polite refusal to host a call.

I pull into the Spark House driveway and park in front of the main entrance. We both get out of the SUV, and Declan meets me at the center of the hood, pulling me in for a semi-chaste kiss before he gets back in the SUV to head to work.

Spark House is quiet this morning, the office empty, with only a couple of staff cleaning or prepping for the event this weekend. Today London has an off-site meeting and Harley is dealing with event setup, which I had been involved in until she noticed me limping around yesterday. It's been damp the past few days, and the weather seems to affect my ankle, so I'm managing paperwork today, which isn't my favorite part of the job, but still necessary.

I do a double take as a new email appears at the top of my Spark House inbox, the sender's name catching me off guard. I click on it, sure it has to be some kind of odd coincidence, or a strange error, but it's not. I haven't heard from Sam in a long time. Not directly anyway.

Back when he broke things off, I had been gutted and hadn't been able to handle any kind of communication. His cheating had been such a betrayal, and it wasn't something I was able to really recover from. With time, I saw that his ending the relationship was the right thing to do, even if the execution wasn't. The relationship lacked balance, and he had moved on, so I did too.

So much has changed since then. But it's still a shock to see an email from him. Last I heard—through social media—he was married. He'd ended up with the woman he'd left me for, and

I sincerely hoped he'd stayed faithful to her in a way he hadn't with me.

I click on the email and read through the content. At the bottom is a contact number. I close the email and manage a few more, trying to decide what I should do about Sam's email, if anything. The decision to meet with Sam is made for me, though, when I make a follow-up call to one of the potential sponsor leads and am told, for what seems to be the millionth time in a row that they don't think we're the right fit, and to try back in the spring.

Five minutes later I receive a message from London, her dour mood reflected in the sad face emojis because her meeting didn't go as planned either.

Two hours and a phone call later I find myself behind the wheel of the old van we keep at Spark House. It's mostly used to move stuff around the property, but it runs fine. It's still a little overcast, but the sun keeps peeking through the clouds, alleviating some of my anxiety over the hour-long drive.

I'm still nervous, though, partly because it's been a long time since I've seen Sam face-to-face, and it's also the first time I've driven this far on my own since the accident. I stop halfway for a bathroom break because I sucked back half a gallon of water due to a dry mouth.

I arrive at Beaver Woods, the adult adventure camp that Sam and his wife, Lisa, have been running for the past several years. I did some research after I read the email and went on a little social media creeping adventure. Sam and Lisa even had a little girl. Seeing them together didn't hurt. So much time has passed since our tumultuous ending, and I'm in a much better place now.

Beaver Woods is set in the midst of a valley surrounded by forest and peaceful walking trails. But the best part is the amazing lake with the sandy beach and the adult-style waterpark. At least that's what the videos on the website tout. It's far too cold for watersport activities now, but in the summer months it is probably amazing. I'm about to find out for myself if it's true. Knowing Sam, it's 100 percent accurate.

I check my reflection in the visor mirror, apply another layer of lip balm—I don't have gloss with me, and it's not really something I'd wear anyway, apart from an event night or a date. If I had it with me, I might consider dabbing a little concealer under my eyes. Last night Declan and I stayed up later than we should have, enjoying each other a bit too much, based on the ache in my quads and the tightness in my calves.

I exhale a calming breath and remind myself that the past is in the past. I'm independent and self-sufficient and no longer reliant on someone else for my happiness. Sam and I have both moved on. And hopefully, if all goes well, we can start fresh, as business associates.

He's married with a family, and I'm in a committed relationship. Declan and I are happy, even if we're avoiding the difficult discussion about the future and what that might hold.

I shake my head, not wanting to go down that path right before I see my ex and the only person to have owned my heart completely until Declan. Ironically, I'm too afraid of what telling Declan might do to our relationship should I be inclined to admit the truth—that I'm in love with him. I don't want to upset the fragile balance we have, and I'm very aware that in the past, any time he so much as had an inkling that one of his "girlfriends" was getting close to dropping the "*I love you*" bomb, it signaled the kiss of death for that relationship. I'd like to think we're different, because our relationship is built on a strong foundation of friendship, but I don't know for sure. So I've been holding on to those feelings, hoping that maybe he would come out and say it first.

I park in front of the main lodge. It's a gorgeous, massive, rough-hewn log cabin with thick posts and Adirondack chairs lining the front deck. I barely have the car in park when the front door swings open and Sam comes down to meet me.

He hasn't changed much over the years, same short hair covered in a ball cap, same blue eyes, and wide smile—although currently there's a little strain behind it. He's dressed in a pair of khaki cargo pants, a long-sleeved Henley, and a vest. Memories of our time together—nearly two years of love that ended in bitter regrets and my broken heart—clog my throat and make my palms damp.

"Hey. Hi." I wipe my hands on my pants and hold one out, feeling ridiculously awkward. Maybe this wasn't the best idea.

He regards my outstretched hand for a moment before he engulfs it in his. I'm relieved that the contact is met with benign curiosity on my part and nothing more. There aren't any lingering feelings of sadness, all I have left is the disappointment over the way he managed our ending.

He releases my hand and steps back, giving me personal space. "You look great, Ave. How are you? When I saw you were in an accident, I nearly called, but I wasn't sure you wanted to hear from me."

I don't comment on not wanting to hear from him. Honestly, the only reason I'm here at all is because I feel like I owe London. "I'm good, thanks."

He hooks his thumbs in his pockets. "That's good. I'm glad. I, uh . . . I reached out to Mark a while back, just to check in. He said you were tough and recovering well. It looks like that's true." He bites at the corner of his mouth.

This is so awkward. "Mark never mentioned that."

Sam rubs the back of his neck. "I'm not really surprised. He wasn't all that excited to hear from me. He, uh, mentioned that you and Declan were living together."

"We are. We have been for a couple of years, now."

"Oh. Wow. That's, uh . . . he didn't seem like he was ever going to settle down." He chuckles awkwardly.

"People change. He's invested in making it work." At least I hope he is.

"That's good. I'm glad. He always had a thing for you, even though he didn't want to acknowledge it." His smile is rueful. "And maybe neither did you, at the time."

"I was already in a committed relationship, at the time." I arch a brow.

Sam nods and looks away as he spins his wedding band around his finger. "I'm sorry about the way things ended. I could've handled things better. It was unfair and not at all a testament to what we had. I should have broken things off before I started anything with Lisa, but I had my head in the sand and I honestly didn't want to hurt you." When his gaze shifts back to me, it's full of sadness and regret. "I know I betrayed your trust, I betrayed *you*. I would go back and handle things differently if I could. I don't expect it to make any of how I dealt with our breakup better, but I didn't mean to fall in love with Lisa."

I feel the weight of those words in my heart. "You can't help who you fall in love with, Sam, or when it happens. Would it have been better for both of us to have parted ways before you moved? Of course, but I know why you didn't, and I recognize my own role in that decision. I was holding on to something that was never going to work. I was clingy and insecure for a reason, because even though I didn't want to face it, the truth was we weren't meant to be together the way you and Lisa are. You needed to be there, and that's where you met the love of your life. So I appreciate your apology and taking responsibility for your actions, but we were both young and figuring life out."

"It doesn't excuse my actions, though."

"I've moved on with my life, and so have you. The past is in the past. Let's leave it there."

"Okay. I can do that."

It's been years without real closure, so it's nice to finally have it, especially at this moment, where I'm trying to navigate my way through a new relationship with someone I already have a history with.

It feels like a weight I've been carrying with me has finally lifted. I switch gears, wanting to move the conversation in a new direction. "You mentioned wanting to collaborate on some winter adventure camps. Do you want to show me around? I've seen a few of your videos, but it would be good to see how things operate here so I can get a better feel for what you want and how we might be able to partner with you."

His email today took me by surprise, but it came at the perfect time, especially on the heels of London's financial review. Beaver Woods is well known and working with them could help broaden our scope and give us some new, valuable opportunities.

"Of course, let's take a tour of the grounds, and we can toss around some ideas for our winter program. We're trying to balance the hard-core outdoorsy vibe with some team building and some slightly less severe camping options."

As Sam shows me around the campground, I consider how our breakup all those years ago was inevitable. It takes seeing him again to realize I'd been in love with the idea of us, not the reality.

I'd been dependent on him in ways I hadn't realized until our relationship was over. I had been looking for someone to fill the holes in my heart after my parents' death, and unfortunately I learned the hard way that dependence wasn't a good way to achieve that.

We're both in much better places now than we were back then. At least it seems that way.

The campground is freaking amazing. There are platforms with massive tents that sleep six comfortably, and a handful of cabins for couples' retreats.

"As you can see, the one thing we struggle with is heating in the winter. We can keep things warm and we're looking at the possibility of yurts, but they're an expensive investment, and it'll be a couple of years before we have the capital to make those purchases. I don't mind that it slows down in the winter, but there have been some requests from campers and companies for winter retreats. I'm not sure how you would feel about pooling resources to develop a winter adventurer program."

"Are you thinking a couple of nights in tents? Then a bus trip out our way for a few days of snow adventure with the comfort of bedrooms and indoor plumbing that doesn't require snowshoes to get to?"

"Exactly. I think most people can handle a day or two in tents, but a weeklong team-building camp spent freezing your ass off is only something that really appeals to the hard-core campers."

"This glamper can totally relate." I point to myself and we both laugh. "I definitely think this could work. How many weeks are you thinking?"

"Maybe four to start? We could break them up depending on your schedule. I figure if we can reserve a few weeks during the coldest months of the year, then we can start planning the programs now. That way we'll have time to get the marketing up and running to pull in interested parties. As long as your sisters are okay with it, and Declan, of course."

"I think London and Harley are going to love this idea."

"Neither of them had a lot of love for me after the breakup." Sam rubs the back of his neck. "And the last words Declan and I had weren't all that pleasant. I don't want to rock the boat."

I don't know all the details, but from the little Mark and Jerome said, Declan had lost his shit on Sam when he found out he'd been cheating on me. There had been harsh words and some punches thrown.

"It's been the better part of a decade, I'm sure if I'm over it, they should be over it too." At least I hope so. "Let me pitch the idea to my sisters and talk to Declan."

"I think that's probably a good idea. Thank you for coming here. I know it's been years and that I should've reached out long ago, but I just . . . didn't know how."

"It's okay. I could've reached out too. It wasn't the right time."

24

ALL THE WAYS TO MAKE A MESS

DECLAN

"What's the balance owed on the wedding and bachelorette party combo?" I flip my pen between my fingers and scan the spreadsheets for Spark House.

"Forty thousand, but most of that has already been spent, so it'll have to go right into paying for the next event and hopefully I can put back what I had to use from the fountain fund." London's on speakerphone and her frustration bleeds through in her tone.

"And if you're able to do that, will we be within five grand of being able to make that happen?" I keep trying to find creative ways to make the fountain happen, but it's proving impossible without pulling from their slush fund. While that account seems flush with cash, it's fluid, money coming in and leaving just as quickly for the next event they're setting up.

Avery had hoped to be able to have the fountain restored before her grandmother returned from Italy, just before her seventy-fifth birthday. And London, being London, doesn't want to disappoint her sister. And I would like to move myself all the way back to London's good side by making it happen.

"If we don't have to pull from it again, yes. But we have two more weddings coming up this fall and we'll have to make deposits, so there's a good chance we'll have to dip back in."

I shift in my chair and flip through some spreadsheets, trying to find money that just isn't there. "So unless you can secure a sponsor or pull in a client who is going to spend a lot on multiple events, then I'm not sure you're going to be able to get the fountain restored before Gran gets back."

London sighs. "That's what I figured. I'm not looking forward to telling Avery we have to put it off."

I've had a few calls over the past several days with Go Green, and I'm making some headway, but I don't want to say anything to London or Avery about it until I have something concrete. It seems the CEO needs to sign off on the sponsorship and he hasn't had time to take a look at it. "Okay, let me go over the numbers again and see if there's any short-term investments we can get into. I'll get back to you in a couple of days."

"Okay. Sounds good. I appreciate you trying to help find a solution."

"It's the least I can do, London."

"Thank you." She ends the call. I run my hands through my hair and lean back in my chair, staring up at the ceiling.

My phone rings and I check the caller ID before I answer. "What's up, J?"

"Hey, man, are you still at work?"

"Yeah. Just wrapping up, what's up?" Things with the guys were tense at first after the whole me and Avery thing came out, but we talked it out over a game of squash—during which Mark and Jerome took cheap shots at my balls—and since then, things have been back to normal.

"Want to go for a beer? We're down the street at Phinn McCool's."

"What are you doing there?"

"I had a lunch meeting that turned into an all afternoon meeting and Mark stopped by on his way home from work."

I check my messages. I have one from Avery saying she's going to be late on account of work and not to worry about dinner for her. I haven't hung out with just the guys since our squash talk. "Yeah, sure, I should be there in, like, fifteen."

I finish up my emails and head down the street to the bar. Jerome and Mark are in a booth, game highlights playing on the wall of TVs across from them. I slide in beside Jerome and we exchange a round of props, and I order a beer from the server.

"How's it going?" Jerome asks.

"Good. It's an adjustment being back in the office every day. I was getting used to my sweats and T-shirt uniform."

"I bet. How's Avery dealing with full time back at Spark House?" Mark swirls his beer around in his pint glass.

"You know Ave, she likes to do everything at Mach 10, so by the time she gets home, she's beat." Lately she's been passing out in front of the TV by eight. "Otherwise she's doing well."

"And the two of you? How's that?"

"Good. We're good. It's uh . . ."

"Good?" Jerome supplies.

Mark and Jerome exchange a look and Mark chuckles, but it sounds a little tense.

"Is there something going on?"

"Nah, man. We're glad things are good." Jerome glances at the TV across the room.

"Sounds like there's a but in there."

"No *but*," Mark says. "It's more that this whole shift has to be kind of hard. Avery going back to work full-time, you doing the same. New stresses, new dynamic to the relationship, that's all."

"Everything's basically back to normal." I take another gulp of my beer.

"You mean in the sense that she's healing and you're both back to working five days a week, if not more for Avery. That can be hard on a relationship, any relationship, and we don't really know where the two of you stand. It seems pretty serious, and I guess we're just worried."

"About what?"

"How things are going to work out in the long run. This is the longest you've ever been with anyone." Mark gives me a small, worried smile. "Usually as soon as the feelings come into play, you're out the door, but you can't do that with Avery, because you live together."

I can feel my defenses going up, mostly because he's right. That's exactly what I usually do, and I don't want to admit that now that she's back at work and so am I, I'm worried about how things are going to play out too.

She's gone all day. Out of my sight for chunks of time. It's hard not to wonder what she's doing all the time and resist the urge to check up on her. It's not that I don't trust Avery; it's more that I don't think I've ever been around healthy relationships to even know what a good one looks like. My dad screwed around with his secretary, and my mom went behind his back and slept with his best friend as revenge. It was a messy, unhealthy way to grow up, filled with paranoia and vendettas.

Any attempt I've ever made to get into a real relationship has basically gone up in flames, usually because I start to worry and can't deal with all the paranoia that brings. No one wants to be with someone who smothers them. Until now, I haven't had to deal with all of my trust issues because Avery and I have been together basically twenty-four seven. But we're both back at work full-time now, and I recognize that we can't continue to be together that much.

I don't say any of that, though. Instead, I go with: "Everything is under control."

"Does she know you're in love with her?" Mark asks.

Jerome laughs. "Dude, that's a ridiculous question."

"Huh?" Those words feel like an electric shock.

Mark's eyebrow lifts. "Come on, man, you've been in love with her since college. I mean, we could see it." He motions between himself and Jerome. "We figured when you moved in together two years ago, you'd finally acknowledge it, but uh . . . you kept up with the extracurriculars." He rubs the back of his neck uncomfortably. "Anyway. We're here if you need to talk this stuff through. I mean, we're not relationship gurus or anything, but we know you, and we know Ave, and we've both done the long-term thing, so if you need to talk stuff out, let us know."

"Yeah. Right. I'm good for now." I don't think that I am actually good for now, though. Because what Mark is saying feels a lot like a slap across the back of the head. Have I been that oblivious?

The conversation rolls around in my head all the way home from the pub. Because I realize Mark is right. I've spent years burying my head in the sand when it comes to my feelings for my best friend. I've been in love with Avery this entire time, and I didn't want to own up to it. And how horrible does it make all the flings I've had while I've been living with her?

I'm in a crap frame of mind by the time I get home. The condo is empty, and it's closing in on seven. Maybe she's hanging with her sisters. Or still working. I know she's trying to pick up the slack after being out of commission for nearly two months.

My phone rings from the other end of the couch. I assume it's Avery letting me know she's on her way home. It's dark and she doesn't love driving at night if she can help it, but at least it's dry out there. There have been a few instances in which one of her sisters has driven her car home when it's been raining. It isn't the most convenient scenario because they live closer to Spark House than our condo, but no one makes a big deal out of it.

I scramble to answer the call before it goes to voicemail. "Hey, how's it going?"

"Oh, thank God you answered. Your father will be calling you any minute, I'm sure, and I wanted to get to you first."

I sink back against the pillow tucked behind my head. My mom doesn't usually call me to chitchat, so I'm reasonably wary. Especially when she brings up my dad in the first five seconds. "Why? What happened?"

"What do you think happened? He got caught cheating. Again. On wife number four. She's posted all over social media too. You should see the pictures she put up! It was bad enough that he married his secretary, but now apparently, he has a mistress who's a stripper. Can you believe it?"

"Unbelievable," I mutter.

It's actually not unbelievable at all. My father is the king of philandering. My parents' relationship was basically a dysfunctional joke, and I had the unfortunate experience of being subjected to their train wreck of a relationship until they finally divorced when I was eighteen. And the only reason that happened was because my father knocked his intern up and got caught taking her to a doctor when she had a miscarriage. And that isn't even the half of it. In between all their dalliances and marriages and relationships, they always end up back in each other's beds. It's like they can't quit each other, so it's a perpetual cycle of hurt and revenge. I don't even know if they're aware it's what they do.

This call from my mom feels like an omen, a bad one.

"I'm glad I was smart enough to leave him when I did. A leopard never changes its spots, and your father has proven that time and time again. I'm actually surprised it lasted as long as it did. This better not mess with what's left of my alimony payments. I can just see your father claiming bankruptcy over this because he has another ex-wife to pay off."

"At least he doesn't have any more kids to put through college." I rub my hand over my face.

"Such a mess your father has made of his life. I can't handle the drama. All of our mutual friends keep calling me, asking if I've heard and do I know what's going on. As if I keep tabs on my ex-husband!" I let her have her rant, because the alternative is her getting upset, saying I'm siding with my dad on this.

"You're not talking to him again, though, right?" I ask, hoping she'll get off the hamster wheel this time.

"Of course not. Although he did leave me a voicemail asking to have drinks. It may be a good time to make sure the money will still continue." And with that she's back on the wheel.

The reality is they're both assholes and they deserve whatever hellish relationships they end up in. It would honestly be better if they both wound up alone, but they're fiends for the drama, and they seem to derive an ungodly amount of joy from messing up other people's lives.

She finally lets me go so she can take another call. When my dad calls, not two minutes after I hang up with my mom, I let it go to voicemail. I can't handle a conversation with him after the one I had with my mother because I know exactly what he's going to say. All he ever does is give excuses and refuse to take ownership for his actions.

When shit like this happens, I second-guess what I'm doing with Avery. I love her, I'm in love with her, but I don't know if I'm capable of giving her what she needs long-term. Avery deserves the world and someone who is going to take care of her, probably better than I can. Especially since the relationship modeling I experienced as a child was far from healthy. And the conversation with Mark drives that point home in ways I don't want it to, especially now. It just proves how relationship inept I truly am.

I don't know how to navigate this new us. It was fine when she needed me for everything and depended on me, but this is different. Now that she's standing on her own two feet, I feel like I'm the one developing a dependency. I've never been that guy. I've always been determined never to be that guy. And now, here I am, sitting on the couch, waiting for her to come home. I don't like the way it feels.

It's seven thirty by the time Avery finally walks in the door. I hear her keys jingle and her shoes thud on the mat. The closet door opens and closes before she comes around the corner. "Hey, you." She glances at the TV, which is blank, and tips her head to the side. "What are you up to?"

"Just thinking. You're later than usual. Everything okay?"

"Yeah. I had a meeting off-site that I want to tell you about."

She shuffles over, drops her phone on the coffee table, and flops down on the couch, leaving a cushion of space between us.

"Oh? I thought you were on paperwork duty."

"I was. The meeting was unexpected."

"You wanna tell me about it?"

She twists her hair up off her neck and wrinkles her nose. Tucking her chin against her shoulder, she sniffs her armpit. "Oh, wow. I am ripe. Give me fifteen minutes to freshen up."

She hops back to her feet.

"Do you want some help?" I could really use the distraction from all the crap floating around in my head right now.

"Give me a five-minute head start."

"Okay. Sure."

"Perfect. Thanks." She braces her hand on my knee and bends to give me a quick peck on the lips before she wanders down the hall and into her bedroom.

Where I sleep with her every night.

I sit on the couch counting down the minutes while I try to reset my mental state, but the phone call from my mom weighs heavy on my mind, and so does that conversation with Mark at the bar. I don't want to think about the shitstorm that's coming my way with my parents.

Even though I'm an adult and I live in a completely different state than either of them, they love to bring me into the middle of their battles. Every single time I get to listen to them blame each other for their current circumstances, when the reality is they're the ones who continue to make bad decisions. And now I'm seeing that maybe I'm exactly like them, more than I wanted to be, because for the past couple of years, I've brought countless women home while I've been in love with my best friend. I was too stupid or emotionally stunted to see it until Mark pointed it out.

And what does that say about me? How the hell can I be a good boyfriend when it took almost losing her to recognize that I was in love with her?

Avery's phone buzzes with a message, pulling me out of my thoughts. A name flashes across the screen. I grab it off the coffee table when it lights up a second time and my throat tightens instantly.

I don't even think about what I'm doing, or how it's an invasion of privacy as I key in her passcode. I tap on the message feed. It's a new thread, started moments ago, but the content makes my stomach flip and drop.

Sam: Thanks again for agreeing to see me today. Let me know how things go with D, hope we can work this out.

I scan the message several times. There's only one, but that doesn't mean there weren't others. Those are easy enough to delete. I know because I used to watch my parents do it all the time with voicemails and texts back when they were still together and cheating on each other. I click over to recent calls and find one from the same number that came through earlier in the day. Much earlier. Like more than eight hours ago earlier.

I break out in a cold sweat and find it hard to swallow. I can't believe what I'm seeing. Sam and I were tight all through high school and most of college. But when he cheated on Avery, I dropped him like a bad habit. It was too close to home. And now that I'm truly acknowledging my stupid fucking feelings—it was an easy choice to make. He'd had what I wanted and screwed it up. I hadn't been in any state to step into the boyfriend shoes and Avery hadn't been in an emotional place to get into another relationship, but axing Sam as a friend was the clear choice. My loyalties would always lie with Avery.

Unfortunately, now I have to question hers.

I drop her phone and pull up the Life app on my own that allows me to track where she is and where she's been. We added it when she went back to work for peace of mind. Based on the tracker, she drove more than an hour out to some adventure camp place and stayed there most of the day before finally heading home around dinner.

Which means she basically spent the entire day with Sam. Her ex and my former best friend. And now she's in the shower washing away the evidence. Exactly like my parents used to do. My dad would come home in his tennis or squash gear, all sweaty like he'd been working out, but he reeked of women's perfume. Or my mother would come home from one of her friend's houses, stinking of wine and men's cologne that belonged to my dad's best friend.

I push up off the couch, anger and betrayal propelling me forward. Her bedroom door is open, the bathroom door ajar. It bangs against the wall as I stalk into the bathroom and yank the shower curtain back.

Her smile drops when I hold up her phone, not giving a shit that I'm getting it wet. "You're cheating on me."

25

I SAW THE FUTURE AND IT WASN'T BRIGHT

AVERY

I spent the entire drive home going over the conversation I needed to have with Declan in my head. It wasn't going to be easy. And in all honesty, the shower had been a stalling tactic. I'd been thinking a little connection would be a good idea, pre-conversation. And a good opportunity to tell him how I feel. That I'm in love with him.

So when Declan pulls back the curtain, I expect him to be naked and ready to join me for the back half of this shower. That usually entails some fun foreplay in the form of soaping each other up while paying special attention to our naughty bits.

However, Declan's face is a mask of rage. His lip pulls up in a sneer. "How fucking long, Ave? How long have you been talking with *Sam* behind my back?"

"What?" I glance at the phone he's thrust into my face. Water dots the screen, but I can see very clearly who the message is from. My stomach sinks, not because I've done anything wrong, but because Declan's first instinct is to jump to conclusions.

He jabs at the screen. "Thanks for agreeing to see me today? Let me know how things go with D? What the fuck?"

I cover my breasts with my forearm and turn off the water. "I think you need to take a breath and let me explain."

"Explain what exactly? That you've been seeing your ex, the one who trampled all over your heart, behind my back? How long? How many times? Are you fucking him?"

I grab a towel from the bar and wrap it around myself before I step out of the shower. "I get that it's a shock, but that's a pretty extreme conclusion to jump to over one message, Deck."

"You were with him all damn day! I checked that app, or did you forget I can see where you go? Or maybe you thought I was too fucking stupid to see what you were doing. I want some answers. How long has this been going on? When did you two start talking again?"

The only other time I've seen Declan this upset is when he found out Sam had been cheating on me. I don't know how to deal with this level of anger from him when it's directed at me.

I move around him, unable to have this conversation while I'm naked and feeling particularly vulnerable. Today was hard for a lot of reasons. I had to swallow my pride to go out there, aware that my screwup was the reason we were floundering and London was so stressed. I quickly slide my legs into a pair of panties and cover myself with an oversized nightshirt before I turn to face Declan. His face is a mask of betrayal.

"It just happened today, Declan. You can check my work emails. Sam contacted me this morning."

"Why the hell would you even entertain talking to him, let alone seeing him? He put you through hell. He *cheated* on you!"

"He reached out about a potential opportunity to set up a program with his camp and Spark House. That's the only reason I went out there."

"He was my best friend and I cut him out of my life for you and he sends you one goddamn email and you go running to him. What the fuck, Avery?"

I take a breath, aware one of us needs to remain calm, and that this is a sensitive topic. "You're jumping to conclusions, Declan. I get that you're upset, but give me a chance to explain."

"I watched you fall apart, and I was there to pick up all the damn pieces when you and Sam broke up. You've never gotten over him. You might say you have, but obviously you haven't if you're willing to drive a damn hour to spend the day with him!"

I hold a hand up, as much to get him to stop as to keep some space between us. "Declan, please listen, I understand how upset you are, but you're not being logical. I am very much over Sam. I wouldn't have gotten involved with you if I wasn't, and I certainly would not have considered speaking with Sam, let alone working on any kind of project with him."

"There's no way you're working on a project with him. Absolutely fucking not. I won't allow it."

I take a step back, not liking the version of Declan that I'm seeing. "You won't *allow it*?"

"You can't think I'm going to be okay with you talking to him again. How would you feel about me working on a project with one of my exes?"

"You don't even have any exes." I cringe, because that was

absolutely the wrong thing to say, but telling me what I can and can't do isn't going to make things better.

"How about Becky?" he sneers. "How would you feel about me hanging out with her for an entire day? Then me coming home and jumping right in the shower?"

I see all the ways this has gone wrong, but I don't know how to fix it, not with Declan going off the handle and me feeling overwhelmed and defensive. "First of all, Becky's conversation skills are on par with a drunk twenty-one-year-old's, so any hanging out the two of you have done in the past has involved nudity only, which isn't the same thing, or the definition of a relationship. Secondly, I jumped in the shower because I'd been running around an adventure camp all day, coming up with ideas to help Spark House because we happened to lose a major sponsor on account of a video featuring me acting like an asshole. And third, Sam is married, with a daughter."

Declan scoffs. "And being married is somehow supposed to put my mind at ease. He cheated on you!"

"I know. But that's not the point, Declan. He's happily married, and you and I are supposed to be in a relationship, one I thought was pretty solid until now. If you don't trust me, how is this supposed to work?"

"This isn't just about trusting you, Avery. I walked away from that friendship for *you*. I chose you, and the first contact he makes in damn well years, you go to *him*. And now you're telling me that you're going to be working with him? How the hell am I supposed to be okay with that? After everything he put you through, you're still willing to pick him over me."

I didn't realize he would see things like that. "I'm not choosing him over you."

"But you are. He called. You went. I think that speaks fucking volumes, don't you?" Declan's eyes are wild, his nostrils flared, jaw clenched in anger.

"Not for any of the reasons you think." He's approaching it as though it's cut-and-dry, and while technically what he's saying is true, the reasoning is all wrong.

I've known for a long time that Declan has trust and relationship issues. And in the back of my mind, I worried that this would happen, that something would trigger that insecurity. Declan is very good at self-sabotage, and I naïvely wanted to believe I would be the exception to this rule.

"That's not the fucking point! You think you're over him, but now you're telling me you're going to be spending time with him. What's this project you're working on? Is it a one-time thing?"

"No, probably not." While I didn't expect Declan to be happy, I definitely didn't expect this.

He paces the room, shaking his head. "I know how this works, Ave. You say you're over him and that he's happy, but then you'll have meetings that go late, and I'll be wondering if it's just a meeting or if you're screwing him while I'm sitting here like a chump, waiting for you to come home."

"And if it wasn't Sam, if it was Brock or some other guy I might have gone out with once or twice, would that make a difference?"

He runs his hand roughly through his hair. "I don't know, and it doesn't matter because it is Sam."

"Spark House needs this opportunity, Declan. You of all people *know* we need this. We lost a major opportunity when Go Green pulled their sponsorship, and this is my way of making a significant contribution and recouping some of our losses, and maybe, if we're lucky, getting back into the good graces of the company who dropped us."

"I know you lost the sponsor and it's partially my fault. Everything is my fucking fault! The fact that you ended up broken is my damn fault. I was pissed off that you went out with that stupid Brock guy, and I went out and got drunk and picked up the first random who looked even remotely like you. I have to live with that for the rest of my damn life. I don't need you throwing it in my fucking face in the form of your damn ex."

His words settle under my skin, turning my blood to sludge. I suspected there were other reasons for Declan going out that night, but to actually hear it, and to know that the reason I was alone that morning is because of Declan's jealousy, one he refused to acknowledge, and a monster he clearly can't get a handle on, breaks my heart. Because it means that the end I didn't want to see coming is here, even though I tried my hardest to keep it from happening.

"Are you saying you don't trust me?"

"How the hell can I after this?" he seethes.

"If there isn't any trust, Declan, there can't be any us."

His expression flattens. "I guess that's it, then."

He turns and walks out of the room. A few seconds later the front door slams shut, and I'm left wondering how so much could change in the span of one single day.

26

SHIFTING GEARS

AVERY

By the time I get up the next morning, Declan is already gone. I slept like garbage, a million unfortunate scenarios playing out in my head, along with the awareness that he'd gone somewhere, and that he wasn't with Jerome or Mark, kept me from experiencing any kind of peace.

In the hours between our fight and this morning, I've had plenty of time to really think about my actions yesterday. While I still don't believe I did anything wrong technically, I hadn't considered how Declan would react, or how he would see it as such a betrayal. He was right to be upset, but this isn't just about Sam. He was what sent Declan over the edge. If not this, it would have been something else eventually.

I'd planned to tell him about the meeting with Sam, and about how seeing him made me so very aware that what Declan and I had was so much better than what Sam and I ever did. That there wasn't a comparison. That I'd been in love with him longer than I realized and was afraid to admit it.

But I didn't get the chance and his reaction was painfully enlightening. I can't be with someone who doesn't trust me and who will actively sabotage our relationship the moment he feels threatened. And that's how Declan operates, not by any fault of his own, but that's just how he is. He has no idea what a stable relationship looks like.

Apart from ours.

But we complicated that with sex, and now I'm afraid our friendship has been completely obliterated.

I pack a bag, throwing in a few outfits, bed wear, and any other essentials. I need to figure things out, and I can't stay here while I do that. I leave for Spark House with a full suitcase and a heavy heart.

"I'm so sorry, Avery. Is there anything you can do to make it better? Anything we can do?" Harley gives my arm a squeeze.

"I don't know. I get that he's upset, but he's blowing this whole thing out of proportion. I don't know. I can't change his past, and we can't live in a bubble where there aren't any outside influences. He just . . . lost it. He was completely irrational, making demands and telling me what I can and can't do."

London sighs, looking sad. "I'm still trying to get my head around the fact that Sam reached out and contacted you."

"Yeah, well, half of me wishes he didn't, because then I wouldn't be dealing with this." I rub a hand over my face, exhausted emotionally, mentally, and physically.

"I wish one of us had been there when you got the email

so maybe we could have dealt with it as a team," Harley says softly.

"The only thing I was thinking about was the opportunity to make up some of the revenue I'd lost us. And I get why Declan is upset, I really do, but the way he handled it was way offsides. He didn't even try to give me the benefit of the doubt, and he sure wasn't willing to listen. And then he dropped the bomb on me about why he hadn't been able to drive with me to the damn event, and it all made sense."

"I thought it was because he picked up some random at a bar," London says, arms crossed over her chest.

"It was, but the reason he picked her up in the first place is because I went on the date with Brock the Rock and he was jealous."

"Oh my God." Harley slaps her hand over her mouth.

"It's the icing on the shit cake, you know? I don't even think he realized it was jealousy at the time, and what does that say about his ability to have a healthy relationship? We've been friends for years, he knows me better than anyone, and he still jumped to conclusions without giving me a chance to explain." I rub the bridge of my nose. "I knew there would be conflict. And I get that no relationship can survive without turbulence, but if there's anything I can count on, it's Declan's ability to sabotage relationships as soon as there's the slightest threat of it getting too serious or the possibility of getting hurt, and that's exactly what happened."

"Maybe he needs some time to think things through." Harley flips her pencil between her fingers, back and forth.

"Maybe." I don't want to believe that this is the end for us, but I also don't know how to navigate this new path, especially since now we seem to be traveling in different directions. "He was so angry, and so ready to accuse and believe the worst."

"Maybe it was just the shock of it all. When was the last time you actually spoke to Sam? It's been years," London offers.

I blow out a breath. "I haven't spoken to him since we broke up, so yeah, it's been a long time. Maybe I should have handled it differently. The timing was just . . bad. I would have ignored that email, but Go Green wasn't budging. Maybe we need a few days to cool down."

"Why don't you stay with us while you let the dust settle?" London suggests.

"I figured I could stay in one of the hotel rooms here. Besides, you don't have a spare room."

"Actually, we do now." London taps on the arm of her chair, gaze shifting away.

"Since when?"

"Since about two weeks after the accident. I wanted to have a space in case you needed it, so we converted the office. It's still partly an office, but it has a double bed and a dresser. And it's yours as long as you need it." She offers me a small, sad smile. "I know I haven't been very open to you and Declan being together, but know that I didn't want this to happen either. Maybe all you need is a little time and perspective."

"Maybe." I want to believe that she's right, but the ache in my heart is hard to ignore.

The opportunity to create a new business partnership is overshadowed by the upheaval in my life. I don't know if working with Sam is even worth it. Not when I'm facing this kind of heartbreak. And that's exactly what this is. Ironic that it happens to be connected to Sam once again. Declan has made no attempt at contact even though I've texted him and left him several voicemails. Mark and Jerome haven't heard from him either, which worries me.

On day four, I have to stop by the condo to grab some more of my things. I'm half hopeful, half scared that Declan will be there. I want to talk things through, but I worry that based on his silence, it's not going to go well. London and Harley offer to come with me, for moral support, but I decline.

I need to deal with Declan without an audience, which will only get his back up even more. I don't bother to message or call before I go, unsure if giving him a heads-up will make him run.

When I step inside the front door, I'm greeted by laughter and cheers, some of them coming from the TV, some of them not. For a moment my chest constricts, thinking that maybe the guys are here and hanging out, and that they lied to me.

Except it's not the guys who are over. It's some of Declan's friends from work, including two women. Declan's still wearing his dress shirt and dress pants, tie loosened, and the top button undone. He's seated in the middle of the couch. A guy I've met a couple of times before but whose name currently escapes me takes up the spot to his left, and on the right is a woman in a pencil skirt. Her makeup is perfectly applied, lipstick still in place, and she's drinking wine. Out of my favorite glass. She's probably also drinking *my* wine if I had to guess.

All of the throw pillows are gone and the quilt I love to curl up under is also missing.

His expression shifts and goes carefully blank. An awkward silence settles around us and the rest of the unfortunate witnesses in the room.

He takes a swig from his beer and the guy to his left glances between us. The woman on his right shifts, crossing her legs so her foot is no longer at risk of touching his leg.

I raise my hand in an awkward wave. "Hey, didn't mean to crash the party."

He spins the bottle between his palms. "I didn't realize you were coming back."

"I needed to pick up a few things."

He motions toward the hall. "Everything's where you left it."

I've never been subjected to this version of Declan, although I've witnessed it before, when he ran into one of the women he spent a few weeks entertaining in his bed and for whatever reason decided he was done with her. He's icy, cold, and remote.

"Do you have a minute?" I hate how unwelcome I feel in what used to be our space.

"I'm a little busy here." He motions to his group of friends, who all shift uncomfortably, apart from the woman on his right, who smirks a little before she schools her expression.

My stomach twists at the thought that the very polished woman beside him is going to end up in his bed tonight. Although I might take a little solace in the fact that he generally avoids sleeping with the women he works with.

Still, she's here, taking up the space beside him, and based on the way she's looking at me, with judgment and a lot of questions, she obviously has intentions that are less than pure. And I can't blame her, because Declan is gorgeous, charismatic, and loyal—until he's not, or he believes he has a reason to mistrust someone. He's also emotionally damaged, maybe more than I realized.

I don't bother to push because I realize it's pointless. He's posturing for his friends, and obviously made up his mind about what was or wasn't happening with Sam.

I cross the room on unsteady legs, and I have to focus twice as hard so I don't end up rolling my ankle. The throw pillows and my quilt have been tossed on my bed.

But that's not the worst part. My suitcase lies open on the bed, one side already filled with clothes. Which means that Declan already took the initiative to start packing for me. I yank open my dresser drawers; the top one is already empty, the contents presumably in my suitcase.

I move to my closet, but it appears nothing has been touched in here. I start throwing clothes in, hangers and all. I'm so hurt and angry, I can barely breathe. I hate that he's already started cutting me out of his life, exactly as he did with Sam all those years ago.

"Does this mean you're moving out?" Declan leans against the doorjamb, picking at the label on his craft beer.

I stop tossing things into my suitcase so I can face him. I want to throw something at him for being so blithe. "Well, I came here hoping that we could have an adult discussion, but based on the fact that you've been going through my things, I'm going to go ahead and say a conversation is actually pointless."

His stone-faced expression shifts for a moment. "I figured you'd need more than whatever you left with, so I wanted to make it easier for you, but then I realized you probably didn't want me going through your things, so I stopped."

"How thoughtful of you." I don't bother to hide my sarcasm, but there's relief in knowing that his intention wasn't meant to be sinister. I cross the room and get right in his space, flicking the bottle in his hand. "How many of these have you had?"

"What does it matter?"

"Because I'm hoping you're still sober and you'll remember

this tomorrow. I came here with the intention of trying to figure this out. I should have talked to you first, before I saw Sam, and that's on me. I know your view of relationships is skewed and that you don't have a lot of confidence in people's abilities to remain faithful or loyal. But you're not even willing to talk this through. And worse, that you would assume I would cheat on you, especially with someone who had hurt me so terribly before, and then start packing my stuff for me? It's beyond hurtful and tells me more than I'd like."

He pokes at his cheek with his tongue. His nonchalance is feigned. His heavy swallow gives him away. "Which is what?"

"I am in love with you, Declan, which is unfortunate for me, it seems. I believed once we left this little bubble you created for us that we'd be able to find a way to navigate life together. As a couple. I knew it wouldn't be easy, and I'm very sorry that I hurt you by talking to Sam without telling you first, but shutting me out like this isn't going to help." I motion to my drawers. "And this jealousy, it's a monster. We both know that it makes people do horrible things. I cannot walk on eggshells, or compromise who I am because you don't have control over your feelings, and you're unable to manage them in any kind of constructive way or talk them through with me, as your partner."

"You went to Sam within hours of him contacting you for the first time in years." That he's so fixated on this point is yet another knife in my heart.

"I can't undo it, Declan, and I would if I could. But it wasn't because I wanted to be with Sam or reconnect with him on a level that was anything other than business based. Whether we like it or not, he was a significant part of my life for several very pivotal years. Frankly, I needed closure and Spark House needs opportunities to grow. I knew you wouldn't be happy about it, and I was prepared for that, but I thought we could have a discussion that would be reasonable rather than accusatory. I know you don't want to hear this, Declan, but you need to talk to someone about this. Just like I did after my parents died, and then again after Sam."

I turn back to my suitcase, tossing in whatever else will fit. I need to get out of here before one of us says something we regret. I have a feeling it will be Declan who does that first, given that he's on the defensive and I'm too angry and hurt not to fight back. I zip my suitcase and heft it off the bed. It hits the floor with a heavy thud. "I sincerely hope that whatever choices you make tonight aren't fueled by a need for unnecessary retribution."

"What the hell is that supposed to mean?"

"I made a mistake. I own that." I sigh and look at the ceiling, holding back tears. "The hardest part, Declan, is knowing how capable you are of being loyal and faithful, but you seem to need to prove the opposite to yourself to keep you safe from being hurt. You self-sabotage. I've watched you do it countless times, and you're doing it again. Sleeping with one of your coworkers to get back at me for something I didn't do isn't going to make things better. Not for you, not for me, and certainly not for her or your job." I wheel my suitcase across the room and Declan steps aside to let me pass. His expression is no longer full of spiteful ire, it's just sad.

"If you want to talk this through, I'm willing, but I obviously can't stay here. It's not healthy for either of us. I'll be back for the rest of my things as soon as I can arrange to have them picked up. I'll email you to let you know when, so you can plan where you want to be when that happens." We'll have to talk about what's going to happen with the condo, since I own half of it, but I'm not ready to tackle that issue yet. I leave him standing there, so many things left unsaid, and wonder if I'm destined for a life full of unfinished relationships and love that can't ever be fully realized.

I hire movers, and as promised, I email Declan to let him know the time and date. I'm hopeful he'll reach out to talk, but all I get is a thumbs-up in response. Unwilling to put myself through any more unnecessary heartbreak, I get London to supervise the removal of the rest of my things from the condo, most of which goes into storage. I don't ask about Declan and she doesn't offer up any information, but she hasn't fired Declan when it comes to our financial portfolio, which says a lot.

I throw myself back into work and physical therapy, and piece by piece, I put together the site for London's Etsy store, asking her to make an extra centerpiece for every event and squirreling them away in one of the storage rooms I know she never goes in. I also put the opportunity to work with Sam on hold, which thankfully he understands. Even if Declan and I can't be fixed, I'm not sure it's worth it. London and Harley back me, telling me whatever I think is best. I'm not sure it's best for Spark House, but right now it's best for me to let things settle before I make any decisions.

Since Declan and I split up, I've messaged the guys, but I haven't seen them. It's not that I don't want to, but I have my sisters, and Declan needs their support now more than ever.

At three weeks post-breakup and move out, I finally cave and take Jerome up on an offer for a beer and wings night at his place, without Declan. He pulls me into a tight hug the second he opens the door. "We missed you, Ave. It hasn't been the same without you."

"I missed you guys too." I struggle not to give in to the emotion and go with a joke, instead. "It feels a lot like we're in a custody battle over the kids. Thank God we never gave in and got that dog Declan was always talking about."

"Yeah, well, I think Deck might seriously be considering the dog," Jerome mutters.

I follow him down the hall and into the living room, where Mark is setting up the coffee table with a huge spread of super unhealthy food.

As soon as he sees me, he abandons the bowl of chips to envelop me in a hug. This time I'm unsuccessful at keeping my emotions in check and end up in tears. I miss my friends, I miss hanging out, I miss the connection, and most of all, I miss Declan.

"How are you? Have you lost weight? Here, take a plate and load up." Mark motions to the snacks spread across the coffee table, all of them my favorites.

In the past few weeks I have most definitely lost weight, not a ton, but enough that it's noticeable. I'm starting to get my appetite back, but heartbreak takes its toll on me—mind, body, and heart. And Declan's silence eats at me. I want to know how he's doing. I want to force him to talk to me so I can tell him how important he is to me. That we're worth the fight.

"How are you guys? Tell me everything that's been going on. I want all the details." I sit back and listen as Mark relays another one of his terrible online dating stories. It's nice to hang out with them again, but there's a hole in the group now, one I created when I pushed Declan outside the boundaries of our friendship.

"We miss you at game night." Mark gives me a small, sad smile. "It's really not the same without you."

"Snacks have gone downhill. Last week Declan burned everything because he forgot to set the timer on the oven when he put the appetizers in," Jerome adds.

"Tell me he didn't set off the fire alarm." It's happened before, and if we can't get it to stop beeping fast enough, it triggers a call to the fire department and they end up evacuating the entire building. Winter in the middle of a snowstorm is not a great time to be standing outside in jammies and slippers.

"He managed to get it to stop before the alarm went off, but the smell was pretty rank. He said the couch still stinks like charred spring rolls."

I laugh, but my voice cracks, and I ask the question I've been avoiding: "How is he?"

The guys exchange a look, and Mark says, "He's pretty miserable, Ave."

"We had to stage an intervention because all he was doing was drinking beer and eating shit food. We got it, he was in the moping phase and stuff, but the place was literally a maze of empty take-out boxes." Jerome rolls his beer between his palms. "He knows he messed up, and not just because of the way he lost it on you, but with the whole thing, starting with picking up that random at the bar before you were supposed to go to that alumni meeting. He's had feelings for you for a long time, longer than he wanted to admit to himself or to us, but we could all see it. Even back in college when you were with Sam. He's trying to work through it. It's a lot for him to figure out."

"I wish he would reach out. He won't even message me back."

Jerome pushes his glasses up his nose. Usually he wears contacts, but not tonight. "He started seeing a therapist last week."

"He did?" That's a shocker. In the past, Declan blew off the idea of therapy as silly.

They nod in unison.

"Wow, that's . . . great." My heart clenches. Declan has always been good at keeping his feelings bottled up. He's a master at hiding his hurt, at least until he can't anymore. "How has that been going for him?"

"He doesn't love it." Jerome's smile is wry.

I laugh. "I can imagine."

"He knows he needs it, though, so he goes twice a week. He kind of lost his shit after you left. It was really a perfect storm for him. I guess the night he freaked out on you he got a call from his mother."

"What kind of call?" Usually he calls her on birthdays and always sends her gifts, but conversations are generally strained. Most of the time he'd go to the condo gym right after a call and take out his frustration on a punching bag. Or he'd hit the club and find other ways to expend that energy.

"I guess his dad got caught cheating by wife number three? Four?" Jerome looks to me for confirmation.

"Number four."

"Right, so I guess the wife went and posted all over social media, and Declan's mom called to warn him. You know what that looks like."

"She did what she always does and put him in the middle of it." I rub my temple. "And then he saw the message from Sam and freaked out."

"Yeah. He understands what happened, or didn't actually

happen. He knows he wasn't rational, and he doesn't want that to happen again, so he's working through it."

I flop back into the cushions and blow out a breath. I can see how wrong this went on both sides. "No wonder he lost it the way he did." It was never just about Sam; it was everything, all his fears rolled together and laid out before him.

"He loves you, Ave, more than any of us realized, to be honest. He's working on himself because he doesn't want to repeat his parents' history. Give him some time, he'll come around." Mark pulls me into a hug.

"Oh, and he left this here last week." Jerome picks up a slightly tattered newspaper crossword from the side table. The downs are all finished, the across waiting to be completed.

27

ACROSS CROSSROADS

AVERY

That night when I get home, London is sitting in the living room watching DIY craft videos, likely for one of her centerpiece creations.

"How was your visit with the guys?" she asks as she snips away at some fabric.

"Good, but not the same as it is when Declan is there."

She sets her scissors down and gives me her attention. "Have they heard from him?"

I drop down in the chair across from her. "Yeah, apparently he's going to therapy."

"Oh wow. That's serious."

"It is. He always brushed it off as pointless since he already knows his parents' relationship is the reason he's so messed up."

London pours bright blue sand into the bottom of a glass fishbowl. "Can I say something without you getting upset?"

"Probably. Why? What is it?"

"I think he sort of had a right to be upset with you, regardless of his reasons."

I open my mouth to protest, but she holds up her hand to stop me from interrupting. "I'm not saying the way he dealt with it was right, or good, but he walked away from his friendship with Sam when things went sour with your relationship in college. He took your side. And then with one email, you drove over an hour to see Sam? That had to hurt, regardless."

I take a moment to really think about what London is saying and realize that she has a point. "I think I knew he was going to be upset about it, and I thought it would be better to ask forgiveness than permission. It seemed like such a good opportunity for Spark House," I say meekly.

"I get it, Avery. But you can't always put Spark House before everything else."

"I was trying to right a wrong. I think that was all I could see, not what it could do to my relationship with Declan."

London's expression is empathetic. "We Spark women are independent, but this was one scenario where it would have been better to talk it out first instead of asking for forgiveness later. Can you imagine how betrayed you would feel if the roles had been reversed?"

I don't know how I'd feel if Declan suddenly decided he wanted to be friends with Sam again. Or to casually hang out with any of the women he's previously been involved with. "How are we going to ever make this relationship work if he can't trust me? He's never even really had a girlfriend before, not a serious one."

"No offense meant, Avery, but have you considered that maybe you're not a relationship guru either? I'm not saying I am, or that I have the answers, because I don't, but Sam was the only really serious relationship you'd been in. And since then, you haven't put a lot of effort into trying to make another one work. Until Declan."

She's right. And now that I'm seeing things more clearly, I realize that I'm as much to blame as Declan. I should have told him, and maybe I should have realized that there was more to it than his feeling betrayed. "What do I do? How do I fix this?"

"Take responsibility for your actions, or your inactions in this case. Neither of you are right, but you're also not wrong either. Relationships are about give and take, so give him something."

"He left a crossword puzzle at Jerome's place."

"Um, okay?"

"We do them together every week. Or we did when we were living together. I took across and he did the downs. All the downs on this one were done and the across ones were empty."

"Maybe he's trying to reach out in the only way he knows how. Give him a hand to hold on to." She pulls herself up from the floor and folds me into a hug. "You two have loved each other for so long, I can't even begin to imagine how much it hurts to be separated like this."

"It feels like half of my soul is missing."

"Then get the other half back."

The next morning I'm drinking my coffee, eating avocado toast, working on the crossword puzzle Declan left at Jerome's. Whether or not he left it there intentionally, I'm unsure, but it makes me miss Declan and our comfortable, easy friendship.

When I get to thirty-six across, I grin. It has something to do with the financial sector and there's a little smirky face drawn beside it, as if Declan knew I'd struggle with it. And that's all the confirmation I need that he left it behind on purpose.

I take a picture with my finger beside the smirky face and message it to him with the question: "Six letter word beginning with F?"

"You ready to go, Ave? We need to be out the door in five." Harley appears with her camera bag already slung over her shoulder and her to-go coffee cup that reads HELLO GORGEOUS. She has one for every day of the week, and she chooses them based on her mood.

"Yup. All set." I leave the crossword on the table, put my dishes in the dishwasher, and scan the cupboards for a travel mug so I can bring another coffee to go—I only have one and Declan gave it to me two years ago for my birthday. It's a Yeti, and there was no way I was going to leave it behind in the move. Although now it feels a lot more like another one of the threads that tie us together.

Instead of borrowing one of Harley's many travel mugs, I use the Yeti for the first time since I moved out of the condo. On our way to Spark House my phone buzzes with a message.

Declan: You're not even going to guess?
Avery: I figured the smirky face was your way of saying there's no way I'd be able to get the answer, but if you prefer I struggle for a while that's fine too.

The inchworm dots appear and disappear a couple of times before another message finally appears.

Declan: I miss you.

I stare at those three little words and feel them in my heart like a hug.

Declan: So ducking much.

A GIF appears with a guy shaking his fist and the words *"Damn you, autocorrect."*

I chuckle and fire off another message.

Avery: Autocorrect is a jerk. I miss U2.

Avery: and by U2 I mean you also, not the band.

We're pulling into the Spark House parking lot when the next message comes through.

Declan: Can I call you?

I wait until the car is parked before I tell Harley I need to take a call and message him back with *"I'd love that."* Instead of heading for the hotel, I walk toward the obstacle course that's been set up for the corporate team-building event we're hosting later this week.

I answer on the first ring. "Hey."

"Hey, yourself." Declan clears his throat. "How are you?"

"I'm okay. I'm really glad you called." During the first week I left voicemails and messages for him, hoping he'd respond, but it hurt too much to see them unanswered every time I opened my phone, so I had to stop. At least until now. I sit on one of the rope swings designed to be walked across. There are six spread at two-foot intervals. "How are you?"

"Okay most days, not so okay other days. It's good to hear your voice. I miss you so damn much." He exhales a long, slow breath, as if he's trying to get a handle on his emotions.

I've already lost that battle. Tears track down my cheeks and drop onto my pants, soaking into the black fabric. "I miss you too." I hate the heavy silence, and the compulsion to try and fill it with jokes, anything to lessen the ache in my chest.

"I'm sorry," he says quietly.

"Me too." I lean my head against the rope and close my eyes, wishing I could reach out and touch him, knowing it's a good thing I can't.

"I know I messed up, Ave. A lot. Maybe more than you can forgive me for."

"I should have talked to you first. Now that I've had time to really process it, I know what I did was wrong. I wasn't thinking, not about how seeing Sam would affect you. Affect us. You put me before your friendship with him at every turn. I should have realized it would be a huge betrayal. I'm so sorry."

"You don't need to apologize. I know I overreacted."

"I don't know that you did, though. Not considering the history, and his ultimatum, and the fact that your mom had called with news about your dad. I'm sorry about that too. I feel awful. I wish I could have been there for you instead of giving you something else to be upset about."

"I could have handled it a lot better than I did. I should have explained what happened with my parents and talked it out with you."

"We both could have. And I want you to know that I'm going to tell Sam we can't work with them. It's not worth the pain it causes."

"Don't do that. Not because of the way I reacted. I don't want you to give up the opportunity because I can't get a handle on my jealousy. I don't want to see you lose out on account of that. My jealousy is the reason you got hurt in the first place."

"That kid in the white truck is the reason I got hurt. I had other options, and I made a choice that morning."

"Because of me."

"I've forgiven you for that. I think you need to do the same so you can move forward."

"You're right. I know that. And I didn't call for your forgiveness, although it means a lot." He clears his throat again. "I'm working on becoming boyfriend-worthy. I don't know how long it's going to take, or if you'd even consider trying again with me by the time I get there, but I want you to know I'm under construction, and I'm hoping in the meantime I can also work on mending our friendship."

"The guys told me you're seeing a therapist."

"Yeah, Jerome sort of convinced me I needed to talk to someone."

"Funny, I remember someone else mentioning that."

"I wasn't ready to hear it then, but you moved out and well . . . I didn't take it all that well."

"I'm glad Jerome has excellent persuasive tactics."

"Especially when he has you in a headlock and is threatening to kick your ass."

I smile, because Jerome is tall and lanky and not the kind of guy to resort to bullying, except maybe for Declan's benefit. "He left out that part."

He chuckles. "Yeah, well, I would've deserved the ass-kicking, so I'm lucky he didn't follow through, and he was right. I want to let you know that I called Sam."

"Oh? And how did that go?" Sam never mentioned it to me, although we've only spoken once, and that was when I asked him for some time to figure things out.

"We had some words. He admitted he was a stupid asshole back when we were in college and deserved the black eye I gave him, and that he never should have asked me to choose between you and him in the first place. Then he told me I should get my head out of my ass and that he never would have reached out to you at all if he knew it was going to screw things up for us. He said you were on the fence about the camping partnership, but I told him he couldn't back out, just to give me a little time. This was my issue and I'd done enough screwing things up when it came to you, and I didn't want to screw anything else up." He exhales a long breath.

"I had no idea." I'm a little stunned. Or maybe a whole lot stunned.

"We agreed that it would be me who told you, and only when I was ready."

"Does that mean you two are talking again?" I don't know how to feel about that. On one hand, I know how hard that loss was. But I'm not sure I can handle Sam on more than a business associate basis.

"We're civil, and I think that's good. I was angry for a long time, and I needed to let that go. Anyway, my therapist suggested I reach out, and the crossword puzzle was my lame but apparently effective attempt."

"Not a lame attempt at all. I'm glad you did, reach out, I

mean, and I would really love it if we could work on mending our friendship." It's been grief on more than one level. I lost my boyfriend, my best friend, and my home all at once, and all the familiarity that came with it.

"Okay. Good. That's good. I'm glad to hear that. My therapist said it would be a bad idea for me to see you, not because he thinks you're bad for me, but because I'm most likely to defer to sex, which sort of defeats the purpose of fixing the friendship I broke in the first place. Not that you'd want to have sex with me at this point, but you know, fuck, I should probably shut up."

"I get what you mean, or what your therapist means, anyway, and I agree that it's probably best if we avoid the opportunity for such activities since they tend to complicate things. And getting upset and jealous doesn't mean you broke us, Declan."

"I've never been jealous before, or really understood what it felt like to have something so important to me threatened by someone else. It brought back a lot of bad memories. I didn't know how to deal with that, and my response was to accuse and cut and run, which I realize has a lot to do with how things went down in my house as a kid. It's not an excuse for how I behaved, but I wanted you to know that it wasn't about you."

"I knew it wasn't about me, but I appreciate that you wanted to explain, and I'm glad you're working on you. I realize that seeing that message from Sam would've been hard on a good day, let alone *that* day."

"It was, but it still doesn't excuse how I treated you. I never want to do that to you ever again. Anyway, um, I have to get ready to leave for work, but maybe if it works for you, we can talk later in the week?"

"I'd love that."

"Great. Me too."

"Have a good day."

"You too. And Ave?"

"Yeah?"

"Thirty-six across is fiscal, not fucked, since I know that was the first thing you thought of."

I end the call with a smile and a beautiful seed of hope that if nothing else, we'll be able to save our friendship.

Winter sets in, blanketing the world in white, and what started as a few weeks of separation soon becomes a couple of months. I message Declan nearly every day, just to say hi or send him a funny meme. Easy conversation meant to open the door should he want to walk through it. Little steps meant to help mend the fractures in our friendship, and hopefully little steps back to each other.

We talk on the phone regularly, often the day after he's been to therapy and had time to digest everything. I want to be there for him emotionally, even if he's not ready for me to be there in any other capacity.

We host our first week of Spark House Beaver Woods Adventure team-building event and it turns out to be an extraordinary success. We manage to get the attention of a few local news stations as well as some prominent social media influencers who are camping enthusiasts, which gives us an influx of new opportunities.

On top of that, I finally managed to finish setting up London's Etsy store. She cried when I showed her, and then proceeded to sell more than three thousand dollars in one-of-a-kind items in the first month. It's definitely her happy place.

I fill my time with work, physical therapy, the guys, and my sisters. And through it all, Declan and I manage to rebuild and repair our friendship, one crossword puzzle and phone conversation at a time.

We work on them over video chat and although the distance is sometimes hard to deal with, we're finding a new balance. Our chats often span over several hours. What starts as a crossword puzzle challenge often turns into movie night on separate couches. Or in my case—a separate bed, since I tend to watch them in my room, so Harley and London aren't witness to our awkward date nights. At least that's what I'm calling them in my head.

"What are we watching tonight?" Declan sets the phone on the counter and opens the fridge, his head disappearing as he grabs what I assume is going to be a beer.

"You can pick tonight."

His head reappears and he cocks a brow. "You don't mean that."

"Maybe I'm in the mood for action, gratuitous violence, car chases, and short skirts." I fluff the pillows behind me, find a good angle for the phone, and grab my glass of wine.

Declan snorts. "I highly doubt that."

"It happens on occasion."

He caps the beer. "No, it doesn't. Your version of gratuitous violence is Thor swinging his hammer."

"I love Thor's hammer."

"You love my hammer more." He cringes. "Shit. Sorry. I didn't mean to say that, it just came out."

"I sort of walked right into that." Also, he's not wrong. Which is part of the reason I'm in my bedroom and he's in what was once our shared living room, sitting on the couch we've had sex on.

And that's another reason why I'd rather watch an action movie over a romantic comedy. We're working so hard on rebuilding our relationship, starting at the friend level while he's learning what it means to put your trust in someone who makes you feel vulnerable. I don't want to make this harder on either of us, but it's nights like this that I miss him the most, when he's close, but still so far away.

The phone jostles while he carries me, a bag of chips, and his beer over to the couch. "I hope you don't mind, but we have company for the movie."

"Company?"

My heart feels like it's made my way into my throat and then drops into my stomach. He flops down on the couch and I spot an arm beside him. He leans over and holds the phone up so he can get whomever he's sitting inappropriately close to into the small screen.

For a few seconds I'm super confused because the shirt I'm looking at is very familiar, although it's stretched across a chest much larger than mine.

"Avery, meet Pseudo Avery."

"Oh my God! Is that a blow-up doll?"

"One of the guys from Jerome's work had a bachelor party, and this was a prize. He brought it over yesterday so I wouldn't be so lonely." He pouts and rests his cheek on Fake Avery's boob. "I found one of the shirts you must have left behind and put her in your spot on the couch. So far I've tried to get her to talk to me half a dozen times since Jerome brought her here. She's rather quiet, but it almost feels like you're here."

"The quiet part is probably welcome."

"Not even a little. I miss that sassy mouth of yours, but I'll be honest, I'll probably bring her to bed with me again tonight."

"Again? You're not serious."

"I might be, you never know." His smile turns serious. "I have this thing I want to try with you."

I'm taken aback by the abrupt change of topic, so I stumble over my response.

"It's okay if the answer is no. I'll understand if you're not ready," he says quickly. "Let's just forget it. Why don't you pick a movie?"

"Hold on a second, you went from sleeping with a blow-up doll to asking me if I want to do a thing with you, with zero transition. What kind of *thing* are you talking about?" I tip my head.

"I thought maybe it would be cool if we did something together. Like we both visited a familiar place at the same time. Actually, in truth, my therapist said it would be a good idea, and I agreed since we've done a lot of cool things together."

"We really have, haven't we? Where should we go?"

"They've put up the holiday decorations at that park where we used to play soccer with the guys. We could go there."

"Sure. That sounds great."

"Tomorrow morning work okay for you? Eightish?"

"That sounds perfect."

"Okay, great." He turns on the TV and pulls up the shared Netflix app. We settle on an action flick, because we agree that any movie with making out is probably off the list for the time being.

The next morning I get up early, throw on a pair of jeans, a long-sleeved shirt, sweater, add all my winter gear, and drive over to the park. I spot Declan's SUV. The snow is fresh from last night, so I send him a message and follow the footprints he's left leading to one of the paths where we'd sometimes go for jogs to warm up before a game.

I fire off a message, asking where he is since I still can't seem to see him.

Declan: Head for the bench with the best view.

I'm tempted to ask which one, because there are several benches with the best view around here and we always used to debate which one we loved the most. There are several that are popular and then a few benches that are hidden gems. I head for one of those.

When I get there, I'm disappointed to find it vacant, apart from someone's discarded travel mug. I hit the video call button and Declan's face pops up on the screen.

He's wearing a beanie I gave him for Christmas years ago and a scarf that I knitted for him when I briefly took up the hobby for one season and made literally everyone I loved a scarf because they were simple and hard to mess up.

"Hey. You're not here."

He smiles and my heart stutters. "You picked the bench with the view of the valley, the one that's perfect during sunset, right?"

"Yeah, where are you?" As soon as I ask, I already have the answer. "You're where the sunrise is the prettiest, aren't you?"

"Yup." He pans out, showing me the view from where he's standing.

"Should I head there?" It's on the other side of the trail. At least a good fifteen minutes away.

"It's okay. Why don't you stay there and I'll stay here, and we can have a coffee and talk."

"I don't have a coffee with me."

"Yes, you do. It's on the bench."

I touch the side of the travel mug and find that it's warm. "How long have you been here?"

"A while. Remember when we stumbled across that bench?"

I brush off the powdery snow and take a seat, thinking back to when we first started playing outdoor soccer together on the rec league in this area. "Oh my gosh, a couple was dry humping each other!"

"Yup. I had to cover your mouth and drag you out of there so we wouldn't interrupt them."

"I think short of a bear charging them, they wouldn't have stopped for much."

"Probably not," Declan agrees.

"I wonder if they're still together." I run my fingers along the smooth wood, passing over letters carved by another couple.

"I wonder how many benches they dry humped on in this park."

We sit there for a while, reminiscing on opposite sides of the park, close but still apart. It's pretty much a metaphor for our current relationship status.

After a while I notice that Declan is on the move. "Where are you going? Are you heading this way?"

He shakes his head. "Not yet. Give me a little more time, Avery."

My heart clenches, but I understand that he needs to work through this, and I'm willing to wait, because I think we're worth it.

Over the next two weeks we plan several more of these

outings where we meet, but on opposite sides of wherever it is we are. The distance between us shrinks until I can see him standing on the other side of the skating rink in the park close to our condo. But I know better than to try to get to him at this point. He has to come to me, not the other way around, in his time, when he's ready.

"Tomorrow can we go for coffee? Real coffee? Face-to-face?" he asks.

I have to shake off my surprise. "Yeah. Of course. Name the time and place and I'm there."

"Nine? Would that work for you? At Coffee Corner? The one near the indoor soccer park?"

"That's perfect. I can't wait."

"Me either. See you then."

The next morning I'm up ridiculously early. I spend a stupid amount of time getting ready, change my outfit six times, and end up settling on a pair of jeans, a Henley, and one of my favorite hoodies that Declan bought me for Christmas a couple of years back. It gets worn at least twice a week.

I'm aware the coffee shop location of choice is purposeful. It's far enough away from the condo to prevent us from making choices that might set us back before we're ready to move forward again, if we're ever ready to move forward.

I made a bad call when I went to see Sam without talking it through with Declan first. I should have put his feelings ahead of Spark House, especially since he always put me first where Sam was concerned. I would have handled it differently if I could. My biggest fear is that we won't be able to get past this, and that I won't be able to manage my own feelings for him and remain his friend. The hardest part of being in love with him is that I don't know how not to be that anymore. But for now, this is where we're at.

Despite my being fifteen minutes early, he's already sitting at a table in the corner, coffee in hand, fresh pastries sitting in front of him and the empty seat.

He pushes his chair back and stands, a shy, somewhat uncertain smile pulling at the corner of his mouth.

I cross over to him, tugging my gloves free. "Hey."

"Hey."

We both laugh and then look away. It's never been awkward like this with us. But everything is new and different, and our history has changed our story.

"Macadamia nut latte for Avery!" the barista calls out.

"I went ahead and ordered for you. I hope that's okay."

"Yeah, sure. Perfect timing, really."

I grab my coffee and Declan stands there, waiting until I return to the table with my latte and shrug out of my coat. He hangs it on the hook and waits for me to take my seat before he takes his.

"You look fantastic. I've missed you like crazy."

"I've missed you too. And you always look fantastic."

We both chuckle again.

"This is harder than I thought it would be. I want everything to be the way it was, but so much has changed," Declan says softly.

"It's a fresh start of sorts, but we already laid a strong foundation, Declan, and we're rebuilding slowly."

He nods. "There have been so many times over the past few months that I've wanted to say fuck it and come knocking on your door, but every time I had to ask myself if doing that was going to set me back, set us back, and if there was any doubt, I knew I wasn't ready."

I love him so much, my heart feels like it's breaking and sewing itself back together at the same time. "What changed?"

"Nothing? Everything? I needed to see if I can be a better version of me when I'm with you. I don't ever want to hurt you like I did again, Avery. That kind of guilt is too hard for either of us to carry around with us."

He reaches across the table, palm up, and lines my fingertips up with his, our hands curling together. It's the first time I've touched him in months. And despite the fact that it's very much innocent contact, it makes me hyperaware that the separation had been very necessary for both of us. We'd spent so much time together, immersed in each other's lives, that we'd almost become an extension of each other. We need to learn how to stand on our own before we learn how to stand together again.

It's so good to be with him, but bad at the same time, because I know now that I can never go back to being just friends. My heart can't handle it.

28

ONE HAUNT AT A TIME

AVERY

On Sunday evening my sisters and I arrive home after a weekend mascot event. It was three days of adults dressed in mascot costumes trying to participate in group activities. It reminded me suspiciously of furry conventions, which we've also hosted in the past. I would not want to shine a black light on any of the rooms, or the mascot costumes this morning when they were loading up on the bus.

London is lagging behind, likely checking her messages since Daniel, the photographer she's been dating, is coming back from one of his trips tomorrow and they're probably making plans. He seems nice enough, but I almost prefer it when he's away because that means fun London comes out to play. Harley's arms are full of tonight's dinner, which happen to be leftovers from last night's event.

I root around in my pockets for the key. I was holding it ten seconds ago. I finally find it and slide it in the lock, noting that there's something taped to the door. I pull it free as I turn the knob.

"What's that?" Harley asks as she brushes past me and drops the bags on the kitchen island.

"Dunno." I scan the flyer. It's for my favorite coffee shop. It's independently owned and they have the best lattes in the history of the universe. It's where Declan and I went for our first face-to-face coffee date since we broke up. There's a note attached requesting that I be there tomorrow morning at eight.

I snap a quick photo and send it to Declan, asking if he has anything to do with it. Mondays are generally Spark House work-from-home days. And sleep-in days since our weekends are typically full of events and Saturday nights often consist of some kind of dinner. We rotate so we each have a weekend off a month, but Mondays happen to be our catch-up-and-wind-down days.

I kick off my shoes, drop my phone, and give Harley a hand transferring the dinner leftovers into oven-safe dishes so we can heat them up.

"Holy crap!"

London startles me, and I almost drop an entire container of coconut milk soup on the floor. "What's going on?"

"I can't be reading this right."

"Can't be reading what right?" I ask.

"You remember Go Green?"

As if I could ever forget. "Of course, why?"

"The secretary of the CEO emailed me asking if we can schedule a call. It looks like they're interested in referring us for a potential sponsorship opportunity with one of their clients." London's eyes are wide with excitement.

"That's amazing!"

"Apparently Declan manages their accounts and put in a word for us with someone on their team. Did you know about this?"

I shake my head. "He said he was going to talk to them. I guess that means he called in a favor."

"It seems that way. They've been watching our social media and they really love what we're doing with the adventure camp collaboration. They're particularly impressed with the use of recycled products and the ecofriendly approach we've been using, according to the email." She sets her phone on the counter. "It's just a phone call, so we can't be sure of anything yet, but I'm crossing my fingers."

"Do you want to go over the notes from last time so you're ready?" London likes to be prepared for calls, which means reviewing notes and going over potential questions.

While we eat dinner, we review the mile-long list of ecofriendly practices we've adopted at Spark House, and hopefully, if all goes well, the call will turn into a meeting and we'll come out with a great sponsor for future events.

London is keyed up, so she pulls out her laptop and starts going through spreadsheets. I help Harley clean up, and then I head to my room to get ready for bed. It's only closing in on nine, but I'm beat.

I check my messages, noticing Declan has gotten back to me. He responds with a series of questioning emojis and "*I guess you'll have to wait until tomorrow to find out.*"

The next morning I get up early, throw on a pair of jeans and a warm sweater, pull on a beanie and my coat, and head out into the brisk morning. I park my car in the lot behind the coffee shop and head inside, but I don't see Declan anywhere. I check my phone. It's just eight now, so I get in line to order while I wait for him, firing a message to ask if he wants his usual.

"Avery, macadamia nut latte," the barista calls out. Her name is Ellie and she's worked here for a long time, so she knows my order by heart, but she's not fast enough, or psychic enough to know I'd be coming in at exactly this time today.

I look around the coffee shop, assuming there has to be another Avery who loves the same lattes I do, but no one steps up to claim it.

Ellie calls my name again and looks around the shop. When she spots me, she holds up the travel cup. I recognize it as Declan's. I leave the line to claim my coffee.

"Hey, Avery! It's good to see you again!"

"You too. Staying out of trouble?"

"Unfortunately." She pushes the cup across the counter.

There's a piece of paper under it. I assume it's a coupon or a promotion, but upon closer inspection, I discover it's a note. "What's this?"

She gives me a sly smile. "I'm not sure, but I was told to give it to you when you came in to pick up the coffee and that you're not supposed to order anything but the latte."

"Those are some very specific instructions."

"Yes, they certainly are." She's smirking now.

"Is that all you know?"

She shrugs. "I was supposed to give you the note and the coffee and nothing else."

"If I gave you a twenty, would you have more information?"

Her grin widens. "I was given a twenty to provide *only* that information."

I laugh. "Fair enough, have a great day, Ellie."

"You too, Avery."

The note has me stopping at a bakery two blocks down, where my absolute favorite muffin—which is usually only available seasonally—and another note wait for me.

Avery,

I hope you enjoyed the macadamia nut latte. I'm sure you've already finished it, and burnt the roof of your mouth because you tried to drink it too fast. I'll never forget the first time you had one, you were a little skeptical, but when the flavors hit your tongue, your eyes lit up. I remember thinking that it was my favorite of your expressions, surprise and pure joy. After that I tried my hardest to find ways to make your eyes light up like that as often as possible.

~xo Declan

With each stop, I get a set of directions to the next place and something else to take with me, along with a little note from Declan, explaining what each item represents.

After the muffin stop, I'm led down the street to a music store. When I was in college, I had a CD player. It was old-school, but my parents had a ridiculous number of CDs and I hadn't wanted to part with them, so I brought them with me to college. Declan loved the nostalgia of it, and we'd always listen to CDs when we studied together.

When I approach the counter, the barely awake teenager slides a CD and a note toward me. It's a copy of *Kiss Me, Kiss Me, Kiss Me* by The Cure. My mom had been a huge fan of their melancholic and angsty music, and I'd grown up hearing it all the time.

My copy had been scratched to the point that it skipped during all but two songs. I refused to get rid of it, though, because of the memories I associated with that CD. And now I'm holding a new copy of the same vintage CD with yet another note.

Avery,
We used to listen to this all the time back in college. It took me two years to realize you listened to it more when we were approaching the anniversary of your parents' death. And I struggled a lot with that—realizing you associated this album with someone you loved and lost, and I associated it with how much I loved you.
This one is skip-free.

Love,
Declan

I realize as I head to the next stop that he's set up a scavenger hunt that echoes one of the first events we ever took part in together. It was during frosh week. I'd been on the fence about doing it, thinking it was probably going to be silly. I hadn't really known anyone, living in a co-ed dorm on campus and only having moved in two days earlier.

So when I joined the rest of the students from my floor and they broke us up into groups, I was teamed up with a bunch of other students and Declan ended up in my group. We hit it off right away—both of us wearing shirts that displayed our love for the same soccer team and the same player. After that we became fast friends. I'd come to college with a boyfriend out of state, so the lines were already drawn in the sand.

I'd broken it off a couple of months in, and by then I'd had a chance to witness Declan's incredible ability to bed hop like it was a job. He was charismatic, gorgeous, and fun to be around, so I could totally see the allure. But at the time we'd established ourselves as friends. I'd become part of his core group and there was no way I was going to mess with that. And then I met Sam.

So it stayed that way for a lot of years, until circumstances and proximity changed us. I wanted it to be for the better, and for a while it had been. Losing him a few months ago and all the work we've had to do to get our friendship back has made me skittish to make any more changes.

But I know that we can't erase where we've been, so all we can do is move forward and see where this new path takes us.

Each stop brings with it more memories, all the reasons we've been so compatible over the years. Why living together was never a challenge for either of us, why it was so easy to call him my best friend.

There's an ornament waiting for me at the Christmas All Year store, my favorite shampoo and conditioner at the holistic store I love to visit and Declan swears always smells like someone just smoked a joint. I almost start crying when I stop at the sporting goods store we frequent and find a jersey waiting for me with my name and number on the back. I needed a new one after last season and hadn't bothered to place an order because I wasn't sure when I was going to be able to play again.

The last stop is my favorite restaurant. It's not fancy, but it serves the lobster-bacon mac and cheese I love so much. When I reach the host stand, I look around and spot Declan in the booth in the corner—the one we always sit in when we come here.

He slides out of the booth and runs his hands down the front of his pants. He's wearing jeans and a shirt I bought him for Christmas last year. I drop my bag of treasures on the bench seat and wrap my arms around his waist, absorbing his warmth. I feel the soft press of his cheek against the top of my head and the steady beat of his heart in my ear.

"That was so much fun. I haven't been on a scavenger hunt since—"

"Freshman year." He links his pinkie with mine. "Come on, I bet you're starving."

"Absolutely."

There's already a pint of my favorite beer sitting at the table, freshly poured. I slide into the booth and instead of sitting on the other side, Declan slides in beside me. We're barely in the booth when a server delivers a basket of fried pickles and a plate of nacho chips.

I prop my cheek on my fist and smile at him. "I can't even imagine how much planning went into this."

"Well, I can't take all the credit. I had a lot of help from the guys and your sisters." He pulls out a gift-wrapped box. "I have one last thing for you."

I move my pint and the plates out of the way.

"Your wrapping jobs are the best." I run my fingers along the edge of the blue ribbon. One year we volunteered with our soccer team to help wrap presents for the elderly. They loved Declan, and at least three of the women sat him down and gave him one-on-one lessons in gift-wrapping. They also brought him an endless supply of cookies so he could keep his energy up for all that grueling work and the risk of paper cuts.

I teased him relentlessly for it. But we went back in the years that followed, and during the holidays he would bring little wrapped gifts to those women. He didn't just drop the gifts off and leave, he'd stay for tea and cookies and basically make their entire month with that half-hour visit and pretty packaged gift.

He shrugs. "It's a valuable, underrated skill set."

I carefully unwrap the box, trying not to tear the paper, but my hands are shaking for whatever reason, so I'm unsuccessful. I lift the lid and find a photo book inside the box. The front cover is a picture of Declan and me together, my arm around his waist and his around my shoulder from that first day of college when we went on the scavenger hunt together and kicked everyone's asses.

I flip through the book, stopping to read the captions under each photo, when and where it was taken, and why it's a special memory. There are so many great moments cataloging our friendship and our history.

I stop when I reach a photo of me caught mid-laugh, sitting in this very booth, a pint in front of me, and a half-empty plate of lobster-bacon mac and cheese pushed off to the side.

"Do you know why I picked this place, apart from the food?"

I glance at the date before he can cover it with his palm and consider his question and the picture. "That was the day I agreed to buy the condo with you?"

Declan smiles. "It was."

"What was the guy's name that you'd been living with? Harvey? Harry?"

"Harvey. He moved out at the perfect time. Man, the guys were annoyed at me for asking you if you wanted to take the second bedroom."

"Annoyed? Why?"

"Because they already saw what I couldn't." He chews on the inside of his bottom lip.

"Which was what?"

"That I was in love with you, but I was too blind to realize it. Or too afraid is more like it." He traces the edge of the photo. "I've had a lot of time to reflect on the way I've handled things with you, or haven't, actually. I kept having meaningless flings because I was terrified of commitment, and I was convinced I could never be good enough for you."

"That's not true at all, though. You've been my best friend for years, Declan. And honestly you were the best roommate a girl could ask for."

"Minus all the extracurriculars." His ears go red with embarrassment, or maybe it's shame, which is something I don't want him to feel right now.

"I knew relationships were hard for you, and mostly I was sad that you were shortchanging yourself on finding something with meaning. But maybe if I'm one hundred percent honest about it, as much as I didn't love being a witness to your flings, part of me was happy that you weren't settling down, because if you had, we wouldn't be here." I sigh and hook my pinkie with his. "I think I've had feelings for you as long as you've had feelings for me. I didn't want to mess with our friendship."

He nods, as if he understands exactly what I mean. "When you went on that date with Brock, it really hit me that you might find someone and then what would happen to us? I kept thinking about the way Harvey had finally settled down with his girlfriend and moved out. How Mark was ready to find someone. College was long over, we were all on career paths, looking to take the next step. Things were going to change eventually. I either had to change with it or risk losing you altogether." He threads his fingers through mine. "I want us to be friends like before, Avery."

"I don't think I can do that, Declan."

He drops his head and his shoulders rise and fall on a long exhale, and when he peeks up at me, his eyes are full of sadness and panic. "But we've been doing so good, don't you think? Or maybe it's not enough?"

"That's not what I mean. I've realized something over the past few months. I love our friendship and what we've built over the years. I think just like you've been avoiding relationships because you're afraid of ending up like your parents, I've been avoiding them too. Not because I didn't want to experience the hurt I did with Sam, but because I didn't want to lose you. And I wasn't sure I could ever find a partner who would be half as amazing as you were as a friend." I squeeze his hand. "If you're ready to try again, to be together, so am I, and even if you're not, I'm okay to wait until you are, as long as that's what you want too."

"I'm ready. I want you. I want to be with you. I can't promise it's going to be easy and I'm probably going to make a lot of mistakes along the way, but if you're willing to be patient with me, I will try my best not to be a jealous asshole."

"It's okay to be a jealous asshole sometimes; it's just in the delivery."

"I've noticed that being an accusing dick doesn't win me a lot of points." He exhales a relieved breath. "So we're going to do this? Be a couple? Date?"

"I would love that."

He leans in and presses his lips to mine briefly. "I missed you so much, I can't even tell you. I missed the way you always leave your underwear hanging on that stupid line in the laundry room. I missed finding the empty milk carton in the fridge.

I missed leftovers and crossword puzzles and horrible romantic comedies."

"And Thor?"

"Not Thor."

"Not even a little bit?" I hold my fingers apart a fraction of an inch.

"Nope."

The server brings out our entrees.

"Do you want to pack these up and take them home? I mean, back to the condo? Or are we not at that point yet?"

Declan runs a hand through his hair. "Uh, well. We can do that, but I'll be honest, it's been a lot of months since I've been alone with you, and I'm not sure how amazing my self-control is going to be."

"I can deal with that if you can."

"I can. I would like to deal with that." He nods a couple of times, like he's reassuring himself. "Let's get out of here."

Declan pays the tab and they pack up our food. We speed walk the two blocks to the building that's always felt like home, not because of the condo we shared, but because I shared it with Declan. We manage to get into the condo and lock the door before our mouths are glued together.

"I missed this feeling," he groans into my mouth. "I'll do anything to keep you in my life like this, Avery."

"I think you should start by taking me to bed."

And he does.

For so long, we were magnets repelling. Facing the wrong way and orbiting each other, missing the connection until the world finally aligned and brought us together, only to tear us apart again.

But this time we're both whole and ready.

This time there's nothing holding us back, not our pasts or our fears.

This time I can fall in love completely and know my heart is safe with him.

EPILOGUE

RUN THE COURSE

DECLAN

SIX MONTHS LATER

"Why are they taking so long to get here?" I check my watch for what feels like the hundredth time and pat my pocket.

Harley raises her eyebrow. "You need to relax. She called fifteen minutes ago. She'll be here soon."

It's Avery's birthday and tonight Spark House is closed to the public because we're throwing her a party. Guests aren't scheduled to arrive for several hours, but Avery and London are on their way here so we can test out the obstacle course.

In the months since Avery gave me a second chance, I've continued with regular therapy, aware that now more than ever I need the support and the strategies to help me deal with relationship conflict in a healthy way. Once a month Avery and I go together, and I feel like it's made us stronger as a couple.

It's a way for us to talk about our fears and find constructive ways to cope. I couldn't ask for a better partner. She's my best friend and the person I want to spend the rest of my life with.

Our relationship isn't perfect, because nothing is, but we're working through the tricky parts. I've learned not to let my fears rule me, we talk things out, and she's patient with me. I'm learning how to allow myself to be vulnerable, and every day I fall more and more in love with her.

It's interesting how we'll bury our head in the sand and pretend not to see what's right in front of us until something threatens to take it away. Which is exactly what happened to me, more than once where Avery is concerned.

I still have guilt over not being in the car with her that day, and I don't know that it will ever go away, not completely. Especially on those days when her ankle aches, or she limps those first few steps after she's been sitting for a long time.

But she's strong and independent and forgiving. When those feelings crop up, I remind myself that she's moved past that, and I should too. I've also realized that just because my parents' relationship was messed up, it doesn't mean mine has to be too.

Avery's birthday is in the summer, which is perfect because it means the obstacle course is set up in the water. She joined a rec soccer league two months ago after getting the all clear from her doctor. This one isn't competitive, and she's probably the best player on the team, but she's not willing to put herself at risk or give up on her favorite sport, so this is a good compromise.

As with every challenge she confronts, Avery finds a way to adapt and she's developed a serious love for water sports and anything that involves swimming, so that's what today's course is based on. That and our mutual love of word puzzles.

She arrives ten minutes later. I'm thankful that it's a balmy day with only a few fluffy clouds in the sky.

"Hey, birthday girl, how was your morning?" I wrap her in a tight hug and kiss the top of her head.

"Fantastic! Thank you for pampering me."

On London's recommendation, I sent her to the spa for a massage and a manicure and pedicure. Avery isn't big on the girly stuff, but I figure if there's ever a time to go all out, today is the day.

When I release her, she smiles up at me. "The guys called and said they'd be here around four. Is there anything I can help with before our friends get here?"

"Actually, yes. We set up the obstacle course, and I figured you and I could run through it to make sure we've worked out all the bugs."

Avery claps her hands and bounces excitedly. "Oh definitely! I'm totally down for that!"

She rushes back to the hotel to change into a swimsuit and returns less than five minutes later, hair pulled up in a ponytail.

I explain how the course works. There are four buoys in the water, we swim out, free a bag of tiles, and bring them back to the tile board one at a time. Once we both have all four of our bags, we can empty out the tiles and start working on our word puzzle.

"Oh, man." Avery hops from foot to foot, her excitement uncontained. "I've been word puzzling it up lately. You're totally going down."

I give her a lingering once-over. She's in a bikini, all her athletic curves on display. "I definitely plan to do that later."

She smacks my arm. "Seriously, Deck."

"One hundred percent. It's your birthday, babe, you get all the full service you can handle."

"Sex talk distractions aren't going to work. Prepare to have your ass handed to you." She makes her way to the beginning of the course, and Harley counts us down, giving the signal to race to the water.

Since Avery has been spending a lot of time in the water, she's become an incredibly strong swimmer. It doesn't take her long to come back with the first bag, but each buoy is farther than the last, so she slows a little as she gets to the final bag, but still manages to keep up.

I'm always impressed with her tenacity and determination not to let her injury hold her back. She's careful with her body, and some days are more difficult than others, but she doesn't let it keep her down for long.

We make it back to the puzzle station around the same time, and she starts untying the bags and dumping out the letters to form her four-word clue that will unlock the box.

My puzzle pieces are different from hers and only contain three words. Since I created the obstacle course, I have a distinct advantage.

She shifts the letters around, her expression fierce with concentration. She looks over at me every once in a while and frowns when she glances at her own pieces, realizing our letters aren't the same.

And then it all clicks into place as she shifts the pieces one more time to spell out the phrase:

WILL YOU MARRY ME?

Mine reads:

PLEASE SAY YES

I know London and Harley are around somewhere, probably secretly recording this. I slip my hand in my pocket and pull out a Ziploc baggie containing the small, velvet box and drop to one knee in the sand.

Avery shakes her head, but her smile is wide as I slip it free from the bag and tuck that back in my pocket.

I flip the box open. "I've loved you since I met you, Avery, and I tried for a long time to push those feelings down, thinking I could never be what you need, but your patience and love taught me that I can. You're my best friend and my favorite person in the world. There's no one else who gets me the way you do, and I want to spend the rest of my life showing you how much you mean to me every single day. Will you marry me?"

She runs her fingers through my hair, eyes soft like her smile. "You've been my rock for so many years, Declan. I don't think that I realized exactly how integral you are to my life until those few months apart. And while I know we both needed it, I never want to be without you again. You're my best friend, of course I'll marry you."

I slip the ring on her finger and stand. "Thank you for teaching me how to love with my whole heart. I promise I'll take good care of yours." I take her face between my hands and dip down so I can seal my promise with a kiss.

Avery is my best friend, my soul mate, my everything.

ACKNOWLEDGMENTS

As always, Hubs and kidlet, you're my two favorite people in the world and I'm so lucky to have you in my corner. Mom, Dad, and Mel, thank you for always being on my team.

Pepper, you are my bestie for life. Thank you for being such an amazing friend.

Kimberly, you're always there to bounce ideas off of and to help me make each book the best it can be. I'm grateful for your friendship and your guidance.

To my SMP team, it's an honor and a pleasure to work with you, and I'm so excited for what's to come!

Sarah, you're a blessing. Hustlers, you're a fabulous group of women and I love you dearly.

Tijan, you're amazing. Thank you for being such a fantastic friend.

Sarah, Jenn, Hilary, Shan, Catherine, and my entire team at Social Butterfly, you're rock stars.

Gel and Sarah, your incredible talent never ceases to amaze me.

Beavers, I couldn't be more honored to have you as readers. Thank you for always being excited, regardless of what I throw at you next!

Deb, Tijan, Leigh, Kelly, Ruth, Kellie, Erika, Marty, Karen, Shalu, Melanie, Marnie, Julie, Krystin, Laurie, Angie, Jo, and Lou, you're the foundation of friendship, and I'm blessed to have you in my life.

Readers, bloggers, and bookstagrammers, you're the foundation of this amazing reading community and your love and passion for romance never cease to amaze me.

New York Times and *USA Today* bestselling author HELENA HUNTING lives outside of Toronto with her amazing family and her two awesome cats, who think the best place to sleep is on her keyboard. She writes all things romance—contemporary, romantic comedy, sports, and angsty new adult. Helena loves to bake cupcakes, has been known to listen to a song on repeat 1,512 times while writing a book, and if she has to be away from her family, prefers to be in warm weather with her friends.